THE MARIANNA VOYAGES I:

HOW TO FILL A BLACK HOLE

BY

BENJAMIN HENDY

Milliways
Books

www.milliwaysbooks.com

First published in Great Britain in 2011 by
Milliways Books

Copyright © 2011 Benjamin Hendy

Benjamin Hendy has asserted his moral rights
to be identified as the author

A CIP catalogue of this book is available at the British Library

ISBN 978-0-9569962-0-6

FIRST EDITION

0 4 0 9 /500

Typeset in Helvetica Neue and cover
design by Gary Frost Design
www.garyfrost.co.uk

Printed and bound in Great Britain
by MPG Biddles

Acknowledgements

There are a vast number of people without whom, to some extent or another, this book would not have been possible. They are, in no particular order, Rob Butcher, Liz & Mike Barnes, Paul & Cath Dixon, Melly & Trevie Williams, Chris Connaughton, Caroline Cross, Richard Cole, Ben & Caroline Lang, Robyn Leate, the late, great Natalie Bennett, Neil Depoix, Karen Johnson, Susan Shaw, Rob Tilley, Kimbo Meeking, Richard Jones, Karen Milner, Robbie Penn, Anna Gist, Jane Mornement, Alison Gray, James House, Janine Gladwell, Ian McGowan, Rob Smyth, Mike Murphy, Bal Gill, Sarah Scrase, Jane Mazur, Veryan Grant, Carrie Bolt, Kirsty & Darren Rigby, Rhiannon Wilmott and Janet McKenzie. Tim Blackwell and Meaghan Murta seamlessly take me from the English collective to the Canadians, who continue with Ryan Hewson, Joanne Deer, Mark Dury, Annette Bruley, Katie Wilson, Nelson Silva, Marisa Iacobuci, Dave Noviss and Dan Slivinski. Phew.

Thanks to Milliways Books, and a debt of gratitude to Stuart Dixon for so brilliantly plumbing the series of pipes and tubes that make up the interwebs to enable the book to be sold, and to Gary Frost for an absolutely excellent cover design.

Then there's my dad and Sue, and Eleanor and Neil, followed by a tangled web of blood and step relations, all of whom have played their part one way or another over the past however many years.

Beyond them, of course, there is one person who deserves a list all of her own. Thank you Nicola.

Dedication

As anyone who knows me even remotely well will know, I am not one who dishes out emotion with the greatest of ease so this is probably the hardest page of the book to write, even though it should be the easiest.

This book is for my mother. There are countless ways she has supported and sacrificed through the years and for that I am eternally grateful.

In addition, this book is dedicated to the memory of a wonderful man.

My Uncle Roy was a warm and wonderful, kind hearted and funny man who brought light into the lives of so many people and will be sorely missed. I know that I and the rest of his family feel so much better for having had him in our lives.

Royston Dyer (26 February 1926 — 2 June 2009)

HOW TO FiLL A BLACK HOLE

Contents

Part One
Shark-Infested Cosmos

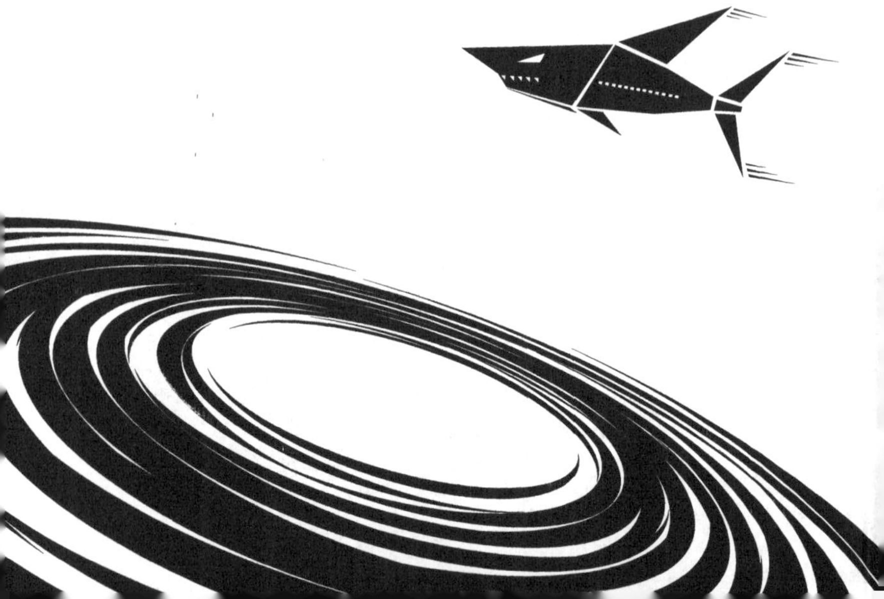

On July 1st, 2412, the 50th celebration of World Peace Day, five gigantic spacecraft set sail from the orbit of Earth to explore the universe. Each ship was identical, ten miles long, three miles high and four miles across. They were so large that if you stood next to one you couldn't see either end or the top. So big, in fact, that they had to be built in space because they couldn't launch from inside Earth's atmosphere.

Each ship had a crew of one-hundred-thousand people – the same as a small city on Earth. These brave men, women and children would be taking a trip into the unknown. Each ship was heading for a different solar system looking for other planets; planets like Earth, better than Earth, planets as yet unsoiled by human kind where man could make a new start.

Over the past five-hundred years, Earth had been ravaged by wars, famines and floods. Humans had finally worn the planet out, they just realised too late, nothing could be put right. When mankind finally understood the situation they were in, the wars ended and all the great brains on the planet started to work together for the first time, trying to devise a way to prevent the human race driving itself to extinction. The five huge ships of the Universal Colonisation Project were the result of their work.

The craft were named The Vespucci, The Janszoon, The Zheng He, The Ericson and The Magellan after five great explorers of the past. These were men who had risked everything to explore the globe, just as the crews of each ship would be risking everything to explore more distant lands.

The ships took 34 years to construct, so vast were they, and used up many of the natural resources available to them. Each was visible from Earth, casting a huge shadow across the land during the day, the blinking lights from the construction job twinkling every night like the stars they would soon be visiting. Anyone watching from the ground could monitor the progress of the building. Shuttles were launched daily to ferry materials, scientists, equipment and builders to the constructions until, one day, they were finally ready to set sail into great black yonder, their crews ready to fight for man's right to exist in the universe and prepared to learn the lessons of the past.

And so it was, cheered on by the world's entire population, that the five great vessels set off on their voyages, each in a different direction, each with their own route, but together they represented mankind's last hope for survival.

By 2576, The Magellan had a crew of 102,587, all of whom had been born aboard the ship over the course of the 164-year voyage. Life on board was the only life they knew, but in many ways life was just as it would have been on Earth. In fact, if anything, it was more normal than life on Earth. They had everything the population of the 'city in space' could ever need with none of the disadvantages of crime, poverty or starvation that were so prevalent on Earth. Amongst the many amenities available to the inhabitants of The Magellan were hospitals; shopping centres; farms; cinemas; parks; a golf course; and, of course, schools.

Chapter One
Flightus Interruptus

Grace Leung sat in the front row of her history lesson. Mr Telemachus, the rotund, balding, historian who taught the lesson stood at the front of the class, droning on and on in his dull, monotone voice, every-so-often firing out a question. Grace always knew the answer. She made sure she always read the chapters they were about to study before the lessons came around. Most of the children in the class had no interest in learning history, which annoyed Mr Telemachus no end, but Grace Leung annoyed him even more.

Grace was little miss perfect. Her uniform was always immaculate, her long, dark hair was always tied back with a different coloured perfect little bow, and her arm was always held up perfectly straight whenever he asked a question. While Mr Telemachus liked his students to be smart and keen to learn, he liked to be able to actually teach them himself. If they turned up in class knowing everything he was about to tell them, what was the point?

The lesson was on one of Grace's favourite periods of history, but Mr Telemachus had started it in a very dismissive manner that Grace didn't appreciate.

"Today we're going to start looking at the late twentieth century, a period laughably described as 'The Space Age' by mankind at the time," he had said with a little sneer in his voice.

Grace was far less involved in the lesson than usual. Mr Telemachus was making this exciting period of history seem dull and dry and rather than have it killed off for her, she was finding herself staring out of the window, day dreaming. If any other pupil had been daydreaming in his class, Mr Telemachus would have given them detention, but he was more than happy that Grace was ignoring him for once, keeping her interruptions to a minimum.

Grace was lucky, not just because she wouldn't be getting detention despite not paying attention, but because her classroom actually had windows. On a space ship as large as The Magellan there were very few units that actually looked out into space, and while almost all would have digital portholes projecting outside images, there was nothing to compare with a genuine view.

Dominating the view out of the window was the blood red planet Zulfura surrounded by the giant ring of rocks, meteors and space debris caught in its orbit. The ring, made up of many different minerals, glittered and sparkled as the sunlight glanced off it. The Magellan had just spent three months orbiting Zulfura while the scientific teams evaluated the possibility of it, one day, proving to be an inhabitable planet. Unfortunately the atmosphere had proved far too acidic and there was no way to produce a renosphere – a man-made atmosphere capable of supporting human life.

But that wasn't what Grace was thinking about; Grace was just admiring the beauty of the scene put before her. Once in a while she'd glance around the class to see if anyone else had noticed the spellbinding view available to them but no one had. It had become too commonplace to attract much of their attention. The view was always available but that didn't take anything away from its beauty or its majesty. She watched the ring glitter and dance as it moved slowly around the planet.

And then it all went dark.

Something was blocking the window in front of her. The other pupils, their heads only held up by their hands, bored, glazed expressions on their faces, looked up to see what was happening. Even Mr Telemachus stopped his droning to see what was taking the attention of his class.

Slowly, whatever it was moved back and turned to face the class, turned to face Grace. Two bright lights shone through the windows and everyone had to blink before they could focus on what lay behind them. Grace's eyes grew accustomed to the dazzling beams and she managed to recognise their source. It was an ITC – Ishiguro Training Craft – one of the small spacecraft the children are first taught to fly when they reach fifteen. Next year it would be Grace and her class' turn to get their wings. Once Grace had recognised the craft she tried to work out if she knew the pilot. The glass windscreen was causing a lot of reflections but finally she managed to spot the face. It was Connor Moran, one of the macho, show-off boys in the year ahead. Mr Telemachus recognised him too and was immediately talking to Cary, the ship's computer.

"Cary, give me radio contact with the boy in that ship and whoever his teacher is," he shouted at the top of his voice. It was completely unnecessary as Cary could see and hear practically everything that happened on the ship, but it made sure everyone knew the mood he was in.

Cary's handsome face appeared on Mr Telemachus' board at the head of the classroom.

"You're connected Mr Telemachus," Cary confirmed, "and his teacher is Mr Mizar."

Cary's job was to monitor everything on board the ship, ensure the safety of the crew, and do everything necessary to aid the Universal Colonisation Project. The computer had two identities to help in this task: the first was Cary, whose dark complexion currently adorned the board in Grace's classroom; the second was Carrie, a female face with long, brunette hair and hazel eyes. When called for, Cary would evaluate which identity would be better placed to deal with the situation. Some people respond better to a female voice and face, others to a male, and so it was up to Cary to choose the appropriate one.

"Mr Mizar, what do you think you are doing, letting pupils in your charge disrupt my lesson?" Mr Telemachus demanded, "And Moran! Or should I call you Moron? Get your craft away from my classroom!"

Connor Moran flashed one of the two headlights on his training craft off and on again, winking at the children trapped inside, before turning tail and flying back off into space.

"I'm sorry, Mr Telemachus," came the insincere response, "it's difficult to keep track of all 25 craft at once, and you know that Cary won't let anything untoward happen."

"It's not about something untoward happening, it's about distracting my class from studying something worthwhile," Mr Telemachus replied, putting the emphasis on 'worthwhile', making clear his disapproval of giving children lessons in such facile subjects.

"Good," thought Grace, "I may not be keen on the way he teaches, but at least he places the proper value on the subject."

"Right, now back to the lesson," he said. "As I was saying, this was centuries before Marco Moran's artificial gravity unit..."

As he droned on, Grace drifted off into her daydreams again. She watched out of the window as the craft moved off to join up with the rest of the fleet and she could return her gaze to the beautiful sight of Zulfura as it receded into the distance.

*   *   *   *   *

Connor Moran had been very excited that morning. It was the day of his first ITC driving lesson – a landmark day in any young crewmember's life, but for Connor it was the thing he'd been awaiting for what seemed like forever. He had woken early, done all his pre-school chores and even let his brother and sister off without any early morning teasing. He didn't want anything to stand in the way of him getting behind the controls of the ITC.

A small and light craft, the ITC was really only designed to train children in how to pilot ships outside of the confines of The Magellan. It was just a little larger than a car as it also needs to contain an artificial gravity unit (or AGU) and multi-directional thrusters. On the whole, it was a boxy craft; some even called it ugly, what with its bug eyes attached to the brow that overhangs the front windscreen and the three spindly legs which jut out whenever it comes in to land. But that didn't matter. What did matter was that you got to fly it outside, in real outer space, all on your own.

"Right then chaps and chappettes, welcome to flight school," Mr Mizar had boomed as they entered the docking bay. "I'm Mr Mizar and I'll be your flight instructor."

The docking bay was immense, two football pitches long by two football pitches wide, and it stretched over 300 feet up to the ceiling as well. This meant Mr Mizar's voice echoed around, bouncing off the walls and roof.

Mr Mizar was a tall man with a big, bushy moustache. He was always relaxed and friendly with the children and, above all, he was a man who really enjoyed his work. His enthusiasm was boundless and he always seemed to know how to deal with each and every student, no matter how nervous or excited they might be.

Walking onto what Mr Mizar called the Flight Deck ("Always wanted to be in the Space Force, don't you know"), the children looked around for the ITCs they would be learning to fly in. The deck was empty, desolate.

A voice came from the back of the class. "Where are our ships, sir?"

"Ah, that's what I like, a bit of respect and a bit of enthusiasm. Now, if we just had some observational skills, we'd have the lot," teased Mr Mizar. "Come on children, one of you has got to be able to spot 30 space craft somewhere in this giant room." His voice rose to a bellow for the last words of the sentence; "Giant room" repeated again and again as it bounced off the metallic surfaces.

The children started to spread out around the enormous hanger, trying to be the first to lay eyes on one of the craft. A hand belonging to a short boy named Spencer Spodding shot up straight in front of the teacher. Mr Mizar could spot a know-it-all when he saw one and immediately tried to dispel his smart-alek questions, "And before you ask, ITCs don't have cloaking devices."

Some of the children laughed at Spencer being taken down a peg or two, but Connor didn't, he just wanted to be the one to work out where the ITCs were hiding. He swept his eyes across the floor one more time before it came to him – they are spaceships after all. He looked up and sure enough, there they were.

He looked back down and over towards Mr Mizar. He was about to say something but the teacher had already made eye contact and put his finger to his lips indicating the boy should keep quiet and let the other children find them for themselves. The ITCs were like a swarm of bees, flying in and out of one another but never even getting close to touching. The big difference, of course, was that they were completely silent.

Gradually, the children realised where the machines were and each, in turn, would stop what they were doing and silently gesture. Somehow Mr Mizar always seemed to know who would be next to spot them and would silence them before they shouted out.

When most of the class had spotted the ships flying around at the top of the hanger, Mr Mizar put the rest out of their misery.

"It's OK, you can come down now!" he called out at the top of his voice, and the craft descended in one long line. The children walked back to him as they watched the ships float back down, the thin little legs popping out as they neared the ground.

The machines finally arranged themselves in a semi-circle behind Mr Mizar.

"Right, I think you'll find that's your first lesson. You have to remember that these ships can move in three dimensions, not just two like the cars out on the streets. That means they are that much harder to control and it is that much more important that you observe everything around you at all times."

"Now, if you'd all like to pick yourselves a ship, we can get on with the real lessons, the ones you've all been waiting for, eh?"

With that the children ran towards their craft of choice, each wanting to pick the best machine but not knowing how to evaluate them. Mostly they tried to get to the cleanest, brightest looking ship, but Connor didn't run towards them. Instead, he went jogging over to Mr Mizar.

"Sir, which ship's the best one?" he said. He figured he'd get the inside information before he made his choice.

"I admire your spirit, Connor, but they've all got limiters on them making their performance precisely identical," Mr Mizar said, before his voice dropped and he almost whispered to the boy, "But if you want the inside edge, that one over there, next to mine, might just be a little less limited than the others."

Connor beamed back at his instructor.

"Stellar! Thank you sir!" he exclaimed as he ran over to the chosen machine.

"You don't need to call me sir, Connor," Mr Mizar called after him, "You can just call me Flight Commander."

He chuckled at himself but the words were lost on Connor. As he reached the door of the craft his heart was pounding in his ears and the nervous, excited tension was building up inside of him. His palms were getting sweaty and he had to wipe them on his trousers before placing his right hand on the scanner to open up the craft. The door whooshed open and a set of steps appeared from the edge of the hull. Tentatively, Connor took his first step into the ITC.

The control deck of the ITC was quite simple. Once upon a time, spacecraft had been covered floor to ceiling with knobs and buttons and dials to control every last thing but over time it had all become quite simplified. Almost everything now was either voice activated or automatic; the only two controls that the pilot needed to be directly concerned with were speed and direction. Connor already knew all of this. He had been reading the manuals and practising in simulators for ages, waiting for this moment.

He clambered up into the cockpit. The seat felt a little awkward to Connor, not quite in the right position, lumps and bumps all over the place. In between his knees the control stick jutted up awkwardly; Connor rested his hands on it, getting used to the feel of being behind the controls of a spacecraft for the very first time.

"Welcome Connor Moran," a voice said from nowhere. It was Carrie's voice. "Adjusting cockpit."

Connor felt the seat shift underneath him. The lumps and bumps disappeared and soon it felt like the most comfortable seat he'd ever sat in. He relaxed, relieved he wouldn't have to put up with an uncomfortable journey.

The front windscreen was black, not allowing Connor to see outside. Suddenly Mr Mizar's face appeared on it. He was sat in the cockpit of his own ITC and was looking into all the children's ships. In his craft the windscreen had divided into 25 sections, giving him a view of each of the children he was in charge of, but the children only saw his face.

"Right then children, time to buckle up and get ready for the ride!" he said.

A seatbelt extended itself out of the sides of the seat and fastened Connor in. At first it was a little tight, pinching him but then it seemed to relax and Connor could barely tell it was there.

"There's one last thing you need to do before we can go anywhere. Who's going to tell me what it is?"

Connor put his hand up immediately but Mr Mizar picked one of the other pupils.

"Yes, Daisy Depoix."

Daisy's image replaced Mr Mizar on everyone's windscreens and she, being a timid girl, small and slight, almost shrank away to nothing when she realised everyone was watching her and waiting.

Daisy's selection annoyed Connor, not because he wanted to give the answer and show off but because she'd take ages to pluck up the courage to say anything, right or wrong, and he wanted to get on with flying. Mr Mizar, however, was intent on giving the girl an opportunity to gain some confidence.

After dithering for a moment, turning bright red and getting a little prompting from Mr Mizar, Daisy managed to squeak out the word "hood". That was enough for Mr Mizar, who praised her highly before telling everyone to put their hoods on.

"They're in the pocket on the right hand side of your seat along with your gloves and oxygen supplies. And make sure you put the hood on the right way round!"

Connor tapped the right hand side of his seat and sure enough, the pocket opened. Inside were 3 flimsy pieces of dark material and a small canister. Connor pulled them out. The gloves and hood were made of the same material as the flight suits that anyone who was going out into space had to wear. The children had got to try these on for the first time right before the lesson. The material was known as a polymorphic cutaneous layer, or second skin. It adjusted itself to fit the wearer perfectly and it modulated the temperature so the wearer didn't get too hot or too cold.

Connor pulled the gloves on and felt them adjust to his hands before finding the hole at the bottom of the hood and pulling it on just in time to hear Mr Mizar shout out "Spodding, I said the visor at the front!" followed by a ripple of laughter from the other children.

"You'll have felt the hood tighten and fit itself when you put it on. It is now capable of absorbing a fair degree of force that might come into contact with your head, protecting you, the same as your flight suits can," said Mr Mizar. "Now take the canister and attach it to the small clip just under your chin."

Connor did just that. It clipped into place, nice and easy.

"That is your emergency air supply. In the event of any accident that canister will give you 12 hours of breathable oxygen through your hood."

Connor silently nodded his approval but he was starting to get impatient. He wanted to be outside, flying, not inside getting fitted up with his kit.

"Now then, you should all have a reasonable idea of how these controls work. You all had some reading to do before you came along, but the one thing the reading doesn't give you is the skills to fly these things softly, smoothly and gently," Mr Mizar lectured. "That only comes with practice."

"All the best pilots, and I include myself in that," he said with a chuckle, "can convince a passenger they're not even moving."

"Brilliant," thought Connor, "Now the fun begins!" He rested his hands on the controls, waiting for the windscreen to become transparent so he could start to make his way out into space.

"There's one last thing," said Mr Mizar, "Earlier I told you that you have to be aware of everything in three dimensions in space, not just two. Well, that can be difficult with just a windscreen in front of you, and that is why we have these visors."

And with that, Connor's view changed entirely. Instead of seeing Mr Mizar sitting in his cockpit, he could see out into space. They were in space already! Not being able to see outside the ships, they hadn't noticed the smooth journey conducted by Carrie. Not only that, as Connor looked around he could no longer see anything of the craft he was in. Well, he could see the gloves on his hands and the controls, but otherwise, in every direction he looked, he could only see what was out in space. Looking left and right, he could see each of the ITCs nicely spaced out with 50 feet between each of them; behind him he could see the giant Magellan.

Then Connor looked down and gave himself a bit of a shock. He couldn't see anything. His arms weren't there, his body, his legs, all gone. It was the most disconcerting thing he'd ever seen. Or rather, hadn't seen. All that was left were his hands on the controls.

Mr Mizar's head reappeared in front of Connor, floating just to the side of his vision.

"As you will have noticed, you can now see everything in every direction. There are one or two other important things to note. Down the left hand side of your visor you'll see the dials and radar," and as he said this the dials and radar appeared; each of the other craft showing up as a blue dot. "These tell you your speed and the speed and location of anything else near you. You need to be aware of these at all times, but you must remember to concentrate on what you can see out there. It's difficult, but you'll get used to it. Try it now – glance at the dials and then back out in front of you."

Mr Mizar gave them all a moment to get used to using the dials before pronouncing "OK, let's get these babies moving, shall we?"

Connor was the star of the class, at least in his own eyes. Everyone else seemed to be stopping and starting and kept being over-ridden by Cary because they were almost hitting each other, but Connor was darting this way and that, weaving in and out of the other children. Eventually Mr Mizar had to stop him because he was disrupting the whole lesson.

"Connor," the teacher said.

"Yes, sir?" said the bemused Connor. He had no idea what

he could have possibly done wrong, he'd just been showing the class what they should have been doing.

"Connor, you're clearly very skilled with this machine and, at the moment, you don't need any help from me in piloting it."

"Thank you sir!"

"So, I think it's about time Cary provided you with a bit of an obstacle course to try. He'll set up a series of gates for you to fly through, in order, as fast as you can. When you're done you can see how you compare to my own records!"

A series of brightly lit rings appeared in the space around the Magellan, some distance from the other children, and Connor raced off to the start line. This was what he'd been waiting for.

After completing several laps of the course, Connor started to look for another challenge. He wanted to work out where he was in relation to the other people on the ship. Obviously he knew where the captain was, right up at the front, on the bridge, but what about some of the other people he knew? He wracked his brain, trying to think who would be in a room on the edge of the ship, looking out in to space. Then he remembered. The school! Of course! They had some classrooms with windows looking right outside. That was his new mission. And so it was that he came to fly his ITC up to the window of Grace Leung's class and wink one of his headlights in at them before being chased off by that miserable old walrus, Mr Telemachus.

As Connor was flying away from Grace's classroom everything stopped. All the systems. The computers. The visuals from the visor. Everything. Connor looked around. All of a sudden he could see his legs and his body again. He could see the walls of the ITC. The windscreen was clear so he could see out in front but he couldn't see in any other direction. He had no idea if there was anything coming at him from the side.

"Drek!" he exclaimed, "What's going on?" This was

something he wasn't prepared for. How could he be? "OK, don't panic," he told himself, "There's a rational explanation and a way out of this."

The ship was perfectly silent. There was no noise from anywhere. The radio had stopped working. Not even Cary could break the silence.

The silence signified something much greater though. Silence meant that the oxygen generators weren't working. Silence meant that Connor only had 12 hours of air supplies remaining. He started to breathe a little more heavily from the oxygen supply he'd been provided with at the beginning of his flight.

"It's OK," he said out loud, "The Magellan's right behind me, the class is in front of me, someone will come and rescue me."

And that was when he noticed that all the other ITCs in his class were looking as dark and helpless as his own. All of their systems had gone down too. Now he was starting to get very concerned. They were all just drifting in whichever direction and at whatever speed they were heading when the power went down. Connor could see one of the craft hurtling at quite some speed down the length of the Magellan. And then he looked dead ahead and realised that he was moving at quite some speed too, and not only that, he was moving straight at one of his classmates. He couldn't tell who, not from this distance, but they were pointing straight at one another and rapidly closing. The only result could be a collision. The ITCs were sturdy craft but they still weren't designed for a head on collision at speed. Now Connor really was starting to get scared. He breathed deeper and harder than before; than ever before.

"Cary!" he cried out, hoping beyond hope that the ship's computer could hear him and could do something for him, but Cary couldn't hear a thing. Not just because the computers had failed on the ITCs but because they had also failed all across the Magellan. All of the computers were out and the crew on board could do nothing about it. They were frantically working to get them all back online, but while they were down they could do nothing to help Connor or any of the other children drifting through space.

Connor's craft was getting closer and closer to his classmate's. He could now see it was Spencer Spodding he was on a collision course with. Spencer was cowering, trying to curl himself up into a ball, trying to pretend it wasn't happening, trying to block everything out. Connor, on the other hand, remained in his seat, his hands on the controls, constantly trying to do something. He wanted to make sure that if the ship came back online he had a chance to make a difference.

Connor and Spencer were homing in on one another. Connor's screen gradually filled with the ITC it was heading towards until it blocked out almost everything else. All he could see was Spencer Spodding curling up and hiding like a scared little boy, not trying to do something and save the situation like Connor was.

The metres turned to feet, the feet turned to inches between the ships. Connor shut his eyes and pulled back on the controls in the vain hope he could pull out of the collision course.

And then, as suddenly as it had gone, the power came back. The lights came on, the visors started to work again, the oxygen generators fired up and Cary's voice echoed through each and every ship.

"Emergency stop initiated. All systems online. Damage indicators zero."

Connor opened his eyes. His ship had stopped moving. So had Spencer's. And that was all he could see. The windscreens of the two craft were as close as they could be without touching. Spencer peeked between his fingers and saw that they were safe, that they had been saved at the last moment, and mouthed the words "Thank you Cary".

*   *   *   *   *

It was some kind of pulse that had knocked out all the computer systems across the Magellan and the individual computer systems on each of the ITCs. Every single computer crashed for forty-five seconds precisely. Fortunately, not everything electrical on The Magellan was operated by the computer systems, otherwise the pulse would have caused a lot more problems than it did. In fact, it could have had catastrophic consequences.

It was a terrifying moment for the 100,000 people on board the Magellan as well as for the children in their ITCs, especially because it seemed to happen for no reason whatsoever. So much of their lives relied on the computers on board the ship and for forty-five seconds they were without them for the first time in 164 years. In many areas this meant people were plunged into darkness, complete and total darkness. In a ship the size of the Magellan not many places have actual windows that might let some light in from the stars, suns and planets nearby.

Some people screamed, some ran in panic, others cowered in corners clinging on to their loved ones. Others stood stock still, waiting for things to return to normal.

And forty-five seconds later that's exactly what happened. All the systems came back on again without a single problem anywhere. People who had been screaming or running or in any way panicking were suddenly thrust back into the light. Now it was their turn to stop dead in their tracks, feeling foolish, feeling everyone's eyes on them, trying to pretend like it wasn't them.

Connor's ITC lesson had to be abandoned, much to his disappointment. Despite the absolute terror he'd felt when he was convinced he was going to crash into Spencer's ship, he'd enjoyed the lesson and wanted to continue. It had provided an adrenalin rush, terrifying but exhilarating. But the children weren't even allowed to guide their crafts back in themselves. Instead, the moment Cary was back online he took control of all the craft and guided them safely and slowly back to the Magellan.

Chapter Two
Lone Shark

It soon became clear that the pulse had not caused any damage and that everything was back to normal. In fact, most people had gotten on with their day-to-day lives. For the adults, there were jobs that had to be done to keep the ship running, but the children were given the rest of the day off school. The scientific team on board were investigating, of course, trying to get to the bottom of what had caused the astronomical phenomenon, but to most people it was just another strange thing that had happened.

Lots of strange things happened in space, things the crew had never known about before they left the earth and, in many cases, never came to understand. Once, the ship had flown through the site of a supernova and all the AGUs had failed. For a week everyone had to float around the ship and no one was able to explain why it had happened. Another time, after landing on a planet to investigate the possibility of creating a renosphere, the crew of the exploration craft swelled up to three times their normal size when they came back on board. They were put into quarantine and many tests were undertaken but nothing was ever found. There were no new germs, diseases or parasites. Then, three days later, the swelling went down and they returned to normal. No one ever knew why.

And that was why most people weren't as worried as they might have been about the pulse that had knocked out all of the ship's computer systems for forty-five seconds. As far as they

31

were concerned it was just one more weird space thing.

Adam Leung was different though. Adam was Grace's 12-year old brother and he was a certifiable genius. He had been putting the finishing touches to his robot, Isaac, when the pulse had wiped out all the computer systems. For those forty-five seconds he had been petrified that the months of work he had put in to building Isaac, programming his fully sentient robot brain, constructing his body, and articulating his limbs would all be for nothing, that the pulse would have rendered it all useless. He was as thankful as everyone else when the systems came back online, if not more so.

Adam was a child like no other on board the Magellan. He had most of his school lessons in his own lab room, separate from the other children, where he could build, test and experiment to his heart's content. He was too good at many of the subjects for it to make sense that he be taught with children his own age and besides, he found it very difficult to mix into larger groups. It made him very uncomfortable to be around a lot of people, even if he knew them all. He much preferred one on one company so most of his lessons were taught by Carrie – although she didn't have to do much teaching. Adam was always so keen to be learning that he would be reading up on whichever branch of astrophysics, advanced robotics, or quantum mechanics it was he was studying each week. He had essentially taught himself almost everything he knew.

Once Adam had checked all of Isaac's systems were functioning as they should be he set his mind to working out what had caused the pulse, studying all the data and visual evidence that Carrie could supply. He had been poring over it for 8 hours, examining every last detail time and again, and that was when he finally spotted something. Something that might begin to explain what had happened.

"Carrie," he called out.

The computer's female face appeared on a monitor on the wall of Adam's lab.

"Yes Adam?"

Carrie's face was a mix of concern and irritation. Her mind was on other matters. While most of the crew of The Magellan had accepted the pulse as an unusual event in the course of their journey and little more, the scientists on board were also trying to figure out what had happened, and that meant they were keeping Carrie very busy. She had a large capacity to do many things at once, but some of the calculations she was doing now were testing her to the limit. She didn't need Adam's interruptions.

"Can you call me up a map of the ship, please?"

The surface of the table in the centre of his lab suddenly changed from clean, crisp white to an image of the ship, seen from above, floating in black space.

"Can you survive with me working on V.A., Adam, only I'm very busy at the moment?"

"You go, Carrie. Just keep an ear open," said Adam. He only needed to shout out voice commands; he didn't need her to actually answer anything. At the moment.

"Plot the computer systems going offline on board and on external craft, please."

Thousands of tiny dots suddenly appeared over the map, one for each computer system that had ceased working when the pulse hit. There was a dot on each of the ITC in Connor's class at the exact points they were outside of the craft too.

"Now, I want you to turn on each of those lights in the order that the computers went down, but slow it down by a factor of one hundred," he commanded.

The lights all went out then came on in a slow wave from the front, left-hand corner of the ship all the way to the back, right corner.

"Now turn them off in the order the computers came back online."

The pattern was repeated, the lights disappearing from front left to back right.

Adam's suspicions were correct. The computers hadn't all crashed simultaneously; instead, one great wave of energy had passed through the ship, knocking them out. He now had the information at his fingertips to find the focal point of the pulse. That would tell him where the source of the pulse was when it was fired and from that he might just be able to work out where it was now.

"Plot the computers again please, but this time join together any dots where the computers went offline within 5 one-thousandths of a second of one another."

The image came back up on the table and virtually all the dots had been joined to at least one other. In some cases, chains of eight or ten dots were joined.

"Now plot those lines into curves and extend them beyond the extreme points."

The lines became concentric circles slicing their way through the ship and across the table, each one perfectly fitting inside the next.

"And zoom out to show me the centre point of the circles."

The ship shrank on the desktop, showing more and more of the black background and more and more of the concentric circles. Eventually the image stopped and a red dot was imposed at the far end of the desk. The dot represented the centre of the circles, the focal point of the pulse, the location of the source.

"Give me visuals of that spot right before and right after the pulse!" he called out triumphantly.

The screen on the wall split into two, each one relaying a separate image of the focal point earlier that day. There was nothing there. A complete blank. A few small chunks of rock flew across the screen, some space dust, but otherwise nothing.

Adam sat down, resting his face in his hands, dejected. He looked over at his incomplete robot.

"I was sure I was going to find something there, Isaac. That's definitely the epicentre of the pulse. Definitely."

The incomplete robot was yet to be given a power source by Adam and so sat impassively, propped against the wall, head tilted down towards his feet, looking almost as upset as Adam.

"I guess it's back to finishing you off then, Isaac."

Just as he got up to go back to working on Isaac, he spotted something out of the corner of his eye. Something which made him think again.

*   *   *   *   *

Evelyn Moran was making the most of her time out of school. She hated having to go in to the boring lessons and just sit there listening to her teachers drone on and on about things she neither cared about nor could ever imagine needing to use in her life. She'd much rather be out in the parks exploring, climbing and clambering, or trying to break her way into the engine rooms and other forbidden areas. Basically, anything that would get her adrenalin pumping – and nothing she did at school could do that for her.

Her parents were getting a little worried about her. True, she was only 11 and had a long time to grow out of what they hoped was "just a phase", but they longed for her to be a little more attentive in class and for her to worry just a tiny bit when she got bad grades. But Evelyn just wasn't like that. She was young and just wanted to enjoy herself. Worrying about grades and what to do with herself after school were things she could do when she was older.

And that is why she was so delighted not to be in school. Instead she was out on level 26, the level above the engine rooms, with Dex Franklin. Dex was Evelyn's best friend. They always went out exploring together, they looked out for each other and they covered for each other if one of them was going to get in trouble. Well, covered for each other as best you can when you have a computer acting as the all-seeing eye on board the ship.

Today, of course, was different. Cary was far too busy to be monitoring their every move and Dex and Evelyn thought that today might be their lucky day when it came to sneaking into the engine rooms. And so it was that they had travelled down the 137 levels from their homes, and walked the two miles along the ship to find the point they had identified months ago as the weak spot; the one place they might be able to squeeze through and into the engine rooms. It had taken them long enough to get there but it was worth it, they could feel it.

They had found the narrow alley after sneaking out of some dull cinegram set in the 22nd century. They had crept out when they realised it was a period drama, sliding out of the rear doors and finding themselves in the dark and dingy alleyway. Above their heads were tubes carrying the cinegram litter to the reclaimers where the raw materials could be recycled, as everything on board The Magellan had to be.

Dex had spotted the grill down near their feet first. It was hanging slightly loose in one corner and lead into the air vent system. He'd nudged Evelyn and nodded in its direction. They knew they had no hope of slipping inside the vent there and then without getting into a lot of trouble with Cary, and hence their parents; bitter experience had taught them that. Instead they would remember the location and make their way back at a suitable time, a time when they thought they might be able to get away with it. A time like now.

Back then, Cary had appeared moments after Dex had nudged Evelyn and had ushered them on their way. This time, however, they had hovered in the alley for five minutes to see if there was any imminent danger of being caught. When Cary had failed to appear they decided the time was right to make their move.

The vent was dark and narrow. Neither of them could see

further than about 5 feet along the metal tunnel. All they knew was that it was slanted downwards and the only thing below them was the engine rooms so it had to be leading there. Evelyn prised back the grill on the vent.

"Go on then Dex, in you go," said Evelyn, holding the grill open.

"Ladies first, Eve," was his reply. He'd never say it, but he was a little scared of the trip into the unknown. He and Evelyn had done some stupid and downright dangerous things in their time, but breaking into the engine rooms trumped them all. And the fact was they didn't even know for sure if this vent would lead them there. They didn't have a clue where it would lead them.

Evelyn could tell he wanted to chicken out. She knew that half the time Dex played adventurer because he wanted to impress her, not because he really wanted to, but she wasn't scared at all. She knew that if it really was that dangerous Cary wouldn't have left it as it was.

"Why? You scared Dex? Maybe I should just go on my own if you're not up for it." Evelyn knew he would never let her think he was a chicken and would rise to the challenge. She was right.

"No, I just thought you'd want to be the first one to take this giant leap." His voice quivered a little as he spoke, giving away his fear. He covered it up by diving forward into the vent at full speed. That was a mistake.

The metal tube was very slippery and the moment he was in there he lost grip and started to slide down.

"Drek!!" His voice echoed down the vent and disappeared with him into the darkness.

"What an idiot," she said to herself as she got into the vent. She got in feet first, putting the bulk of her weight onto her legs. She was relying on being able to stop herself sliding after Dex by sticking her elbows and knees into the walls of the vent and effectively wedging herself in. It was a good plan, and one that was working for the first ten feet, right up until the vent took a steep downward turn. She could no longer maintain her grip and started falling forward, into pitch black, straight after Dex. She let out a scream of her own, more in surprise than fear. She was still confident that no harm would come to either of them.

She changed her view fairly quickly though.

Evelyn couldn't see much in the metal tunnel. Every so often she'd feel a rush of air as she whizzed past an adjoining vent, but otherwise her senses could tell her next to nothing. Then the vent started to sweep round to the left and she became aware of a dim, flickering light coming from what she presumed to be the end of the tunnel. The further she slid, the stronger the wind felt in her face, blowing at her with greater and greater force, and not just because of the speed at which she was falling. Then the vent straightened out and Evelyn saw what was causing the blasting airflow.

In front of her was a giant fan, its blades spinning so fast she could barely make out that there was a fan there at all. It was only because of the blinding white light behind the blades and the noise of the engine turning them that she could tell. The blades caused the light to flicker and Evelyn had to shut her eyes and turn her face away, it was so bright. Now she truly was scared. She tried to force her hands and feet against the walls, the floor, the ceiling, trying to get a grip on anything, trying to stop herself from flying into the fan blades at such a velocity. She screamed, hoping to attract someone or something's attention but it was to no avail. No one and nothing could hear her. Even without the deafening noise coming from the fan's engine, nothing could have heard her screams.

Time slowed down. She was falling, out of control, towards certain doom, unable to do anything to stop it. She opened her eyes and looked around the vent for something, anything to grab on to, but there was nothing. She was now only a few feet from the fans blades. She tried to prepare herself for what must, certainly, be the end.

And then, all of a sudden, the blinding light was gone, the noise was slipping into the distance, and she wasn't sliding along the vent anymore. The floor of the vent had given way beneath her. Some kind of fail-safe trap door to prevent anything from crashing into the blades. But she was still falling.

Adam's eyes followed the chunks of dust and debris floating through space towards the point he had determined to be the epicentre of the pulse. There wasn't much of it and it only showed up as tiny specks on the screen but he could still see it, and right as it reached the supposed epicentre it either disappeared or its path was deflected. This was the proof that Adam was looking for, proof that something was there, something had actually caused the pulse, and he had found it.

"Carrie, I need you to track all particles of space dust flying towards this point in the four hours before the pulse. If a particle is deflected or disappears, mark the point on the screen."

The image on the screen fast-forwarded, though the only way you could tell was from the clock in the corner advancing through the minutes like they were fractions of a second. The pulse had struck at 9:39 in the morning so the clock had started at 5:39 and it wasn't until the clock had reached 8:53 that any marks registered on the screen. Carrie was capable of tracking individual particles which meant that in the 46 minutes that there was anything to track, thousands of points could be marked. When Carrie had finished, Adam could see an outline. It was by no means complete and offered no texture, but there, quite clearly, was the outline of some kind of spacecraft. It was almost shark-like in shape, with a fin jutting up from the top, a prominent nose at the front and a long tail at the back.

"Carrie, can you give me a scale to this, please?"

The craft was mammoth. When the scale appeared Adam could see it was far bigger than The Magellan, nearly 18 miles long and 7 miles high. The image that Adam had built up couldn't show any detail, but if The Shark-ship had a mouth it could open, he felt sure it could have swallowed The Magellan whole.

"Carrie, I think you need to see this," he called out.

Carrie appeared on the wall, beside the outline of the ship.

"What is it Adam?"

"I've found what caused the pulse. Well, I know where it was and if we just use my technique I'm sure we could work out where…"

But Carrie interrupted him.

"That's brilliant work, Adam, it really is, but we already know where it is now."

"What? How? I mean, where is it?" he exclaimed. He thought he'd solved the problem all by himself and now it turned out he was behind everyone else.

Carrie replaced the outline image that Adam had created with a picture from the other side of the ship. It was the ship that Adam had outlined. The Shark shape was even clearer.

"It appeared out of nowhere 5 minutes ago. If it makes you feel any better, if it hadn't appeared, you'd have been the first to find it," Carrie told him.

Adam flushed a little before he remembered how little it mattered at the end of the day. The bigger problem now was what did the ship want and was it going to shut down The Magellan again? It was something that every scientist on board would be working on but it was something that Adam wanted to help with.

"Have they communicated with us, Carrie?" he asked.

"We've not heard a thing, Adam, not a thing."

"No signals that could be a code or language we don't know or understand?"

"Nothing, Adam. It's been totally silent since it appeared."

Adam walked up to the screen, inspecting the image of the ship closely. At the front were rows of triangular windows looking like teeth, reflecting back the blood red glow of Zulfura. The image looked eerie, like blood dripping from the fangs of this ship-creature. It was like death, stalking them.

There were some markings on the side of the ship. They could be a code or another language but it was impossible to tell. They had been rubbed away or left incomplete. Aside from those windows at the front there appeared to be no portholes at all along the sides of the ship, something that was very unusual for a ship of that size, within the human world at least. But all of that just made its appearance even more intimidating. There was no way to get any kind of understanding about what the occupants of the ship wanted.

Adam was still studying The Shark, as he had decided to call it when, without warning, The Magellan shook. Not violently, but enough to cause Adam to fall over, enough to rattle everything on his shelves, and enough to throw Isaac onto the floor as well.

Evelyn hit the ground with a bump. She looked back up at the vent she had fallen from. It was about 12 feet above her; she hadn't fallen too far but she'd certainly have a bruised backside in the morning. She looked around. She was alone in a narrow passageway. On either side of her were two large dark machines – part of the engine, she assumed – covered in grease, dirt and slime and making a very low, deep, humming sound. She couldn't see Dex anywhere and she hoped that he hadn't managed to pass over the trap door and slide on into the fan's blades.

"Dex, where are you?" she hissed along the corridor. She didn't want to shout too loud in case someone caught her but she wanted to make sure her friend could hear her. There was no reply and she was now faced with a choice. She could stay where she was and hope that Dex came back this way, or she could start to search for him in one of two directions, and there were no clues as to which would be the correct one.

She stood stock still for a minute or more, listening for any clues, any signs of life. Once she was satisfied that there was no one close enough to hear her she decided to call out for Dex properly. It was most likely that he'd have tried to find a hidey-hole somewhere and wait for her; he was such a scaredy-cat.

"Dex, where are you hiding? Come out, come out wherever you are!"

Along the passageway behind her she thought she heard something, a couple of short sharp bangs, and went to investigate. Fifteen feet along on the right she found a large, heavy metal door. It seemed to be to some kind of closet or cupboard. It was the only place the noise could have come from. She tried to pull it open. It creaked and gave way a little but wouldn't acquiesce.

"Dex, is that you in there?"

Again, she heard some clanging and banging, still a bit muffled. The door was obviously quite thick. She thought she heard him trying to shout out but it was too stifled.

"Listen Dex, I can't make out anything you're saying so knock once on the door for yes, twice for no, OK?"

Clang!

Now she knew it was definitely him.

"I'm going to try pulling on the door. I need you to push as hard as you can at the same time. OK?"

Clang!

"Three, two, one."

Evelyn pulled on the door handle with all her might. Dex was pushing as hard as he could from inside too, but it wasn't helping. However, Evelyn could see that it wasn't stuck all the way down.

"Dex, wait a minute, I just need to find something to help."

She ran down the corridor looking for something she could use to lever the door open. If she could just wedge something into a gap between the door and the frame she should be able to separate the two. She ran up and down the corridor, her footsteps echoing around her, but she couldn't see anything remotely useful. She ran back to the door and called through to Dex, "I can't find anything to help. Is there anything in there you could use as a lever? Something you could wedge into a gap in the door?"

Evelyn could just about hear Dex rummaging around him. She knew it would be difficult because of the lack of light in the cupboard, but hopefully it was some kind of workman's tool cupboard and would be packed with hammers and spanners and things, any of which might help them in their current predicament.

After a minute, Evelyn heard a "Clang!" from inside the cupboard.

"OK, I'm going to pull on handle. You push your knee into the bottom half of the door. Then, when it starts to give, shove whatever it is you've found into the gap and start to use it to lever the door open. Right, go!"

Evelyn started to pull and Dex started to push, gradually forcing the bottom half of the door free of the frame. As soon as it was he shoved in what looked, to Evelyn, to be the head of a spanner into the gap. Together they worked hard, pulling on the handle and the lever, slowly inching the door wider and wider until finally it gave way.

It caught them both by surprise. Dex came tumbling out of the dark closet, bringing half the contents with him. Evelyn fell backwards and the edge of the door caught her in the middle of the forehead. She stumbled back against the other side of the corridor, hitting the back of her head on the machinery behind her. She sat in the middle of the corridor, more than a little dazed and confused. Dex immediately went to her aid but he could see that she wasn't cut and, aside from a nasty bruise, she'd be fine. Unfortunately, he knew that their parents would want to know where the bruise had come from.

Evelyn blinked as her eyes re-focused. "What happened to you? Why on earth were you stuck in there?" she asked him.

"It was open when I fell through the trap door. I heard a man coming towards me and I didn't want to get into trouble so I thought I'd hide in the only place I could see. It's not my fault he saw the open door and decided it was better off shut!"

"Yeah, well, we'd have been in serious trouble if I'd had to go to Carrie to get you out."

Dex felt affronted. He had been trying to save both of them when he hid in there, not just himself. He offered his hand to Evelyn to help her get back up. She took it and put all her weight on him, half trying to stand, half trying to pull him to the floor too. She got to her feet and looked around, trying to decide which direction to explore first, when the tremor came through the engine room. She and Dex both fell over, taken by surprise and caught off balance.

"What was that?!?" shouted a shocked Dex.

"Shhhh, keep your voice down. I don't know what it was. Probably just the engines calibrating or something, come on, we should get going."

Evelyn led the way down the corridor. Dex followed her, looking very nervous and wishing he could have stayed in school today, this was all a bit too scary.

Chapter Three
Light Saver

After his ITC lesson had been aborted, Connor had gone to Armstrong Park, the massive area of public parkland at the centre of the ship. He and 4 friends had gone to ride their hover bikes, jumping them off hills, hurling them around corners and generally having fun. Connor particularly liked taking his off-road, diving in and out of the trees at high speed, but he had been over-ruled and the boys had been daring and double-daring each other to make bigger and bigger jumps.

The hover bikes – normally known as vikes – tend to zip around a foot above the ground with the rider being able to give a short additional boost via a button on the steering column if an obstacle demands a little more clearance. However, the limited nature of the reverse polarity device meant that when the rider attempted a leap from too high a point, the vike would be unable to cushion the landing and the underside of the machine would crash into the ground. That was exactly what had happened to Connor, and it may have ended up saving his life.

Each boy had been challenged to out-jump the boy before and Connor wanted to win outright straight away so they could go out on a woodland trail. He'd tried to take his vike off a sheer 20-foot drop, a distance he was convinced he could manage but was equally convinced the others would chicken out of beating. He revved the engine and kicked it into gear. The air sucked in the front was forced out the back, pulling the vike along and spraying dirt and leaves up off the ground behind him. He was really travelling when he started up the hill. He stood up on the footboards, bending his knees ready for the moment of truth. As he went over the edge he jumped off the footboards, kicking his feet out to the side and taking one of his hands off the handlebars, really showing off for his friends. They whooped and cheered as he went.

Connor braced himself for the landing, feet back on board, arms and knees bent, ready to absorb the shock. While the air underneath the vike normally provided most of the cushioning, Connor knew he still needed to be prepared. However, the machine couldn't provide enough resistance and instead of a cushion of air, the vike crunched into the ground. The back end shook and twisted round, sending Connor sideways. He kept a firm grip on the handlebars, clutching at the side of the vehicle with his knees to make sure he didn't come off. It tried to get out of his control, twisting this way and that, bouncing up and down, but Connor gripped tightly onto the brakes and gradually the vike came to a halt.

Connor was a little shaken from the experience but he certainly wasn't going to show it to his friends. When they saw the jump had gone wrong they started to come over but, due to the speed Connor had been travelling, they had a fair distance to cover. In the mean time, Connor had tried to get the vike started but it just didn't want to. The propulsion system was caput but it would still hover; at least that made it a little easier for him to walk it home.

He walked over and met his friends before excusing himself. He didn't want to hang around with a broken machine while the others all had their fun. He wanted to get it back home and get it fixed as soon as possible.

Having pulled the grass, dirt and stones from the air vents, straightened out the few bent components and replaced the gearing mechanism he had managed to mangle beyond recognition, Connor was ready to get himself back out to Armstrong Park. It was then that the tremor came rumbling through the ship, causing Connor to stumble and drop the vike on its side.

Ornaments and books shook and fell from the shelves and he heard Max, his little brother, cry out in the living room. Connor ignored him, instead concentrating on picking up his vike and getting back to the park. A moment later a voice called him through to the kitchen.

"Connor, I need you to get Max…"

"Aw, Dad, don't lumber me with him, I'm going up to Armstrong Park in a moment," Connor protested. At eight years old, Max was too young to be any fun and Connor certainly didn't want to have to play at being babysitter.

"This isn't an option, Connor. You've got to get Max and Evelyn and take them to…"

"Evelyn's not here, she's gone off with Dex somewhere," said Connor. He looked up at his father, Laurie, for the first time and, seeing the concerned look on his face, realised that this was something serious. "What is it, Dad? What's going on?"

"I've just been speaking to your mother up on the control deck. Whatever it was that caused the computers to offline earlier seems to be," he paused, barely able to comprehend it himself, "It seems to be attacking us."

Connor was shocked.

"Attacking us?!?"

"Keep your voice down, Connor, you'll panic your brother. It's very important that you remain calm and look after him. You've got to be strong for him. I'm going to go and search for your sister. You get Max down to the Pod."

"Dad, I can't…"

"Yes, son, you can. Look, this is just a precautionary measure. Your mother says they'll handle it fine, we just don't want to take any chances."

Laurie placed his hands on his son's shoulders and looked him straight in the eye.

"Connor. Your brother looks up to you, but he's fragile. You're a strong young man. This could be a very scary situation for him but you can help him through it, I know you can."

Connor had never been spoken to like this before. The tone of his father's voice and the look in his eyes told him that things were far from fine. His father was asking him to grow up, to take responsibility. He was passing on a role to him. That scared Connor. He had never had any responsibility. He had always just done as he pleased, entertained himself, got by at school. Deep down in the pit of his stomach he got a horrible knowing feeling, a worry that he couldn't do it, that he wouldn't be good enough.

"Connor, I've got to go. Take Max, get on your vike, and get down to the Pod. I'll meet you there with Evelyn."

And with that his father dashed out of the flat, calling out to Cary as he went.

"Cary, get Maria on the line, and please, find my daughter…"

*   *   *   *   *

Anna Leung had been in bed when she got the call from her husband suggesting that they start moving the children down to their Pod. Anna had been working a night shift in the navigation suite, though calling it a night shift was a bit of a misnomer. Because they were travelling through space, the dark and light of day and night didn't occur – instead, the ship ran an Earth based 24-hour clock with simulated light keeping everyone's body clock in check.

Since Anna had got the call she had been frantically organising her children. Grace was not a problem. She understood the situation and was quickly packing up the few vital objects not already stored or that couldn't be replicated down in the Pod. Adam, on the other hand, was much more difficult. He had never been good with change, and moving him down to the Pod was a big one. Anna had to stand over him as he packed up Isaac and various other items he deemed essential. Still, it wasn't long before Anna, Grace and Adam were walking out the door, bags in hand, in search of a car to whisk them off to the Pod.

The streets were packed with people desperately trying to organise their families or find a vehicle to take them to their own Pod, so cars were in high demand. No one on board actually owned a car; instead, every vehicle on the road operated like a taxi. On a normal day you just had to tell Cary you needed a ride and a car would pull up, but there weren't enough for everyone to use them at once. Anna knew this would be the case and anticipated a long wait so she was as surprised as anyone when a car pulled up not thirty seconds after they stepped outside. She quickly bundled the children into the car and sat opposite them. As they got in a family from further down the street, the Eastwoods, came rushing towards them. They had their luggage in hand and Mr Eastwood was shouting, mixing obscenities with pleas to share the space in the car with his family. They'd been waiting for 20 minutes for a car and he was very upset to see the Leungs getting one the moment they stepped outside. Once the door had been closed, though, the car was off and running through the streets.

The vehicles were lightweight hovering machines, bulbous but not unattractive and, because Cary controlled the car, the seats were placed facing each other, allowing face-to-face conversations between the passengers.

As the children sat facing their mother, no one said a word. Grace could see the concern creeping across her mother's face and knew that she had to do all she could to help them get through this attack. Adam was a bit more detached, tending to Isaac, ensuring he didn't get bumped around or damaged while they travelled.

The car moved swiftly and smoothly along the roads

towards the Podzone. The fact that the roads were made of lumi-firma made travel very easy. Lumi-firma was a solid form of light projected across the decks. It allowed cars and pedestrians to move up and down decks very easily. The light could simply form a ramp where necessary for people or vehicles to seamlessly move up or down between levels, and with Cary controlling all the cars, there was no chance of an accident.

As the vehicle made the first shift down a level on its journey to floor 42 and the Pods, Adam looked up and broke the silence.

"Mum, is this the end?"

Anna's nervous laugh betrayed her own fear but she quickly tried to cover it.

"No, of course not dear. This is all just a precaution. We're just going get you settled in the Pod in case something goes wrong, and if it does, you'll be launched gently and safely away from the ship. You'll be fine."

"What about you? Aren't you staying with us?" protested Grace.

"I can't, Grace. I'm needed up in the Navi-suite to make sure that nothing goes wrong. But really, don't worry, it's a precaution."

Calling it a precaution had become a mantra to Anna. She had to convince herself that it was true because she didn't want to consider the alternative. She didn't want to think about the possibility that her life could be nearly over, and that her children were in severe danger of suffering the same fate. And so that was what she kept saying to herself, "It's just a precaution", again and again, as they made the remainder of the journey to the Podzone in silence.

Connor had Max sitting on the back of his vike, hanging onto his waist. Their bags were safely stashed in the storage box underneath their seats and they were now well on their way towards the Podzone. Connor was getting as much speed as he dared from the machine and had made sure Cary was well aware of his final destination so the lumi-firma ramps would suddenly take them down a level whenever a suitable gap in the pedestrians allowed it. This was harder than Connor had imagined because it seemed that everyone was out on the streets at that moment, something that only confirmed to the boy exactly how serious the situation really was. In fact, the pavements were so chocker-block with people, he constantly had to slam on the brakes and weave in and out. That was when he made the decision.

The roads on board the Magellan were for cars only. If people needed to cross over a lumi-firma bridge or underpass would appear for them, allowing the cars to go as fast as possible to get to their destination. Connor, however, had other ideas. He had no intention of slowing down to dodge so many people on foot and instead made a beeline for the road. He was half-expecting Cary to automatically put a bridge in front of him to carry him over the traffic so he was nearly as surprised as Max when he actually managed to veer into the middle of the speeding cars.

Max gripped him even tighter, making it hard for Connor to breathe.

"What are you doing? You're scaring me!" the poor boy shouted but it was lost on Connor. For one, the wind whistling in his ears rendered most of the words inaudible, but also he was concentrating so hard on making sure they stayed alive as the cars zipped by them in both directions that he wouldn't have heard anything his brother had said if he shouted it at the top of his voice straight into Connor's ear.

Connor darted to make a quick right-hand turn and was suddenly faced with the prospect of running head-first into a car travelling at full-speed. Knowing he didn't have time to brake or veer out of the way, he shut his eyes for a second, expecting the worst. Just in the nick of time Cary came to his rescue, forming a lumi-firma underpass to take Connor and Max directly underneath their oncoming fate. Connor opened his eyes, a little surprised he still could, to look above him and see the underside of the vehicle that had, moments ago, threatened to be the end of him.

A second later and the underpass brought him back up onto the road where he needed to have his wits about him again. The adrenalin was really pumping and he promised himself that he wouldn't leave his and Max's fate up to Cary again.

A swift left and then down a couple of lumi-ramps and they were on a minor road where the traffic had thinned out, letting Connor breathe a little easier. He slowed down for a moment, regaining his composure.

"You OK back there, buddy?" he shouted to his brother, looking behind him.

Max opened his eyes for the first time since they had first swerved onto the road, looked around, taking in that they were no longer on a busy main street, and he nodded back at his brother and even let out a little smile.

"See, piece of cake, this road riding," he said, still looking back at Max. Then he caught a different look in the boy's eyes. He quickly brought his gaze back onto the road and realised they were rapidly approaching a very solid looking wall. Connor hit the brakes, stuck his foot down and spun the vike left.

"Nothing to it!" he shouted back, though he didn't dare take his eyes off the road this time. Or show his brother the look of relief that he felt plastered across his face.

*   *   *   *   *

Laurie Moran was standing outside the giant, gun-barrel grey doors that separated the engine rooms from the general public onboard The Magellan. To move a ship the size of The Magellan required a massive, complex and dangerous engine and so Laurie wasn't going to be able to just walk straight in and find Evelyn. Instead he was waiting outside for one of the engineers to take him in. His attention was so focused on the colossal doors in front of him that he didn't notice a small man come out of a door over to the left-hand side to greet him.

The man strode purposefully across the engine room forecourt. He held his hand out and confidently introduced himself.

"Mr Moran, I'm Lucas Leung, chief engineer."

Laurie was taken by surprise but quickly returned the greeting before anxiously following Lucas into the control room. He was equally surprised to find the control room was not filled with manic staff desperately trying to deal with all the problems going on. Instead, the room was deserted.

"So, your daughter's gone missing and you believe she's got into my engine rooms?" said Lucas, before spotting Laurie looking around the control room quizzically. "Ah yes, all the engines and computer systems shut down 8 minutes ago. There's nothing my men could do in here so I've sent them all into the engine itself to try to fix things. They're all aware that – Evelyn and Dexter is it? – are out there and will report and return them, should they find them."

"So what are we going to do? We can't just sit here and wait for them to turn up while all this is going on," said the exasperated Laurie.

"I appreciate your concern, Mr Moran, I really do," began Lucas, "but given the number of floors that we have in the engine rooms, there's over 100 square miles of floor space to search and we don't know where to begin. Unless they call out for Carrie's help, we won't be able to get a reading on their location. Really, it's best left to men who know the engine rooms."

Laurie dejectedly sat himself in a chair at one of the consoles, leaning forwards and putting his head in his hands. He couldn't let this happen to one of his children.

"Damn that Dexter," he thought to himself, "He's always getting Evelyn into trouble."

It had been 15 minutes since everything went quiet. There hadn't been any more jolts or shocks to catch Evelyn and Dex unawares but there had been a couple of close calls when engineers came along their way. Fortunately they had been able to find darkened corners to hide in and had held their breath as the men and women walked or, more often, ran by.

"Come on Evelyn," whispered Dex, "We should just give ourselves up. We're totally lost, we're never going to get out of here undetected."

"Don't be such a pessimist, Dex. We found a secret way in, I'm sure we can find a secret way out."

She didn't really believe herself, but she wasn't prepared to give up just yet. It had been a couple of minutes since the last engineer came by and she decided it was time to continue the search. She grabbed hold of Dex's hand and pulled him out. Looking each way along the corridor, she made a snap decision to go left. She couldn't remember which way they had come from but couldn't show any signs of indecision or uncertainty that might get to Dex.

"Eve!" Dex called in a harsh, hard whisper.

"What is it?"

They were jogging along now and Evelyn didn't want to slow down and argue about what they were doing yet again.

"Wasn't it lighter than this before?"

"No, of course it wasn't…" but her voice trailed off and she slowed her pace. She looked around – both along the corridor and up and down through the lumi-firma paths above and below them. It definitely had been lighter before. Not bright exactly, but now she could only see maybe 20 or 25 feet in front of her, and only up and down to the adjacent levels.

"I really think we should just stop and call for…"

"No Dex, it's fine, it probably just means that…"

But before she could finish whatever convincing lie she was going to force Dex to believe she was knocked off her feet by what felt and sounded like a big explosion.

She and Dex toppled into the dark and greasy engine blocks that surrounded them. They both stayed down on their hands and knees, not because of any injury but because they were scared. That was far worse than any of the jolts that had occurred before. They looked around and couldn't see any evidence of an explosion but that didn't stop them from being convinced that that was what it had been.

Slowly, ever so slowly, they returned to their feet, keeping their knees bent and their feet wide apart so as to ensure they stood a chance of staying on their feet should it happen again.

Evelyn looked up and down the corridor and grabbed Dex's hand again, pulling him further along, but Dex wasn't having any of it. He stood firm – this was no longer an exciting adventure. In fact, it had ceased to be one some time ago. Now this was serious and he just wanted to get out of here.

"Come on, Dex," hissed Evelyn through gritted teeth.

"No. I don't want to go," he said resolutely, "Cary – help us!"

"Drek," Evelyn sighed and she visibly deflated. Dex had just blown the whistle on them and she wasn't pleased. "You donut. What did you do that for? We're going to get in so much trouble."

"I'm sorry Evie, but I'm scared," he admitted. She knew he was telling the truth, he must have been petrified if he was actually owning up to it.

Carrie's voice rang out from a nearby speaker, "There you two are. Do you know how much danger you're in right now?"

And at that moment the ship vibrated with another violent shock. While the noise accompanying it was much quieter, further away, it still caused the two children to lose their balance again. However, this time as they got to their feet they noticed a much more worrying effect on their immediate surroundings. More than half of the lumi-firma panels had stopped working. From above their heads, Dex and Evelyn could hear a voice calling out, pleading.

"Help!! Help me, please!"

The voice was getting closer and suddenly the two children realised why. One of the engineers was falling from one of the higher floors. They looked up and saw the shape of a body coming towards them. He was perhaps 10 feet further along the corridor and the children could see that the lumi-firma floor underneath him had gone from their level too. They watched him tumble through space, rapidly closing in on them and then passing them in the blink of an eye. They watched him fall down and down before he disappeared into the darkness. At the same time his screaming stopped and they were left with an eerie silence. Both of them knew what that signified.

The message came through to Lucas and Laurie immediately. Suddenly the screens showed the two children and Cary called up a map showing their location. Neither of them had time to do anything before they were thrown from their feet by the second shockwave, and they watched on helplessly as the engineer fell past the children. They both knew what it meant, not only for the children but also for the hundreds of engineers out there.

Lucas led Laurie through to the transport room. A hundred small metal cages were moving themselves out. They each had a solid, 4-foot square hovering base, with waist-high wire mesh on each side. Cary was sending these out to rescue the staff in the engine rooms. Lucas jumped into one and beckoned Laurie to follow suit. Lucas stood at the console. One screen showed him the children, who were now both huddled up against the engine, holding on in case the floor was to disappear from under them. Another showed the map of the engine rooms and the final screen had the controls on it. Lucas adeptly manoeuvred the small craft speedily out into the engine rooms and through the corridors.

Connor and Max had arrived safely in the Podzone without

Connor getting them into any more near-accidents. Connor got off his vike and pressed his palm up against the scanner. Nothing happened. It didn't reject him – that would require it at least reading his palm first. No, literally nothing happened. No scan, no whirring, no noises, nothing. He tried again. Still nothing.

"Drek," he said.

"Umm. You said a naughty word. I'm telling dad." said Max, still perched on the back of the vike.

"Oh, be quiet Max, he won't care. Now, we've just got a little technical problem. I'm calling Dad to sort it. Wait there."

Max pulled a face at his brother as he walked away from him. Connor walked out of Max's earshot and called for Cary, whose face immediately appeared on the wall beside him.

"I need to speak to my father."

Laurie intently watched how Lucas controlled the cage. As a lead explorer for the ship's expeditions to other planets he regularly used lots of different craft and this one seemed fairly simplistic to use. He was looking at the control panel at the moment the call came through from Connor.

Connor immediately recognised the concern on his father's face. In fact, he thought it looked like it might almost be panic. He was determined to make this as easy as possible for his dad.

"What's the problem Connor? I'm right in the middle of something here," he shouted, the speed of the cage necessitating his raised voice.

Connor could see the engine room background whizzing past at great speed and tried to be just as fast himself.

"Dad – the entrance to the Pod's broken. It won't let us in."

Laurie wasn't really paying attention. He was more concerned about Evelyn and Dex. He could see they were closing in on them, according to the map, and he could see them still huddled against the engine block.

"Sorry, what did you say, son?"

"The Pod – we can't get in. What should we do?"

Laurie didn't have a clue what they should do. If he couldn't get his family into a Pod then saving Evelyn now was a pointless task. He was stumbling, not exuding the confidence he wanted to, to reassure his son.

"Umm… Well… I don't know right now, Connor, I'll have to…"

Lucas interrupted him. "You can use mine."

"What?" shouted Laurie.

"Tell your boy to go to my Pod – Cary can direct him."

Laurie relayed the message on to Connor, hugely relieved that there was a solution.

"Lucas, I can't thank you enough, really, that's…"

"Hey, those Pods are meant for more than just two. My wife and I won't make it there, no sense the space should go to waste."

Laurie agreed. He knew that neither he nor Maria would be joining their children on the Pod either. There was too much else to do to try to save everyone.

But Laurie's train of thought was interrupted because at that moment another shockwave hit the ship. It wasn't a big shockwave and it didn't slow down their rescue mission, but it did appear to short-circuit a lot more of the lumi-firma floors.

Laurie and Lucas watched on as the floor beneath Evelyn and Dex flickered out of view. Evelyn had held on firmly to the engine but Dex was taken by surprise and his grip loosened, slowly slipping away from him.

Lucas reacted immediately, dropping the nose of the cage, taking it down a level, and increasing the speed.

Laurie watched the picture with bated breath. Dex's fingers, one by one, lost their grip on the engine, finally letting go. As he started to fall he tried to grab onto anything, first the engine block, then Evelyn's arm or hand and finally he just managed to catch hold of her ankle. Laurie could see that this was making things much harder for his daughter. She was now trying to carry twice the weight and it seemed obvious she wouldn't be able to manage it for much longer.

Laurie didn't want to watch but couldn't take his eyes away. Lucas, in the mean time, was doing all he could to get them there in time. His eyes were darting between the map, the pictures of the children, the controls and the corridors in front of them, always keeping track of the status of everything.

Laurie could see the strain on his daughter's face. He could see how every sinew of her body was trying to keep hold of the grip she had but even as he watched he could see it start to slip. He could see the same signs that he had seen in Dex when he lost his battle to hang on and Laurie knew that Evelyn wouldn't be there for much longer.

It seemed like slow-motion. First her left hand went. She desperately tried to get it back onto the engine but Dex was pulling her lopsided – she didn't have the strength to return her hand.

Then one finger at a time, Laurie saw her right hand give out.

Her little finger was first.

Then her ring finger.

And then, as her middle finger went, her whole hand came off and she and Dex both started to fall.

Laurie's heart was in his mouth. He couldn't believe what he was witnessing. He saw the children falling away from the camera and then suddenly, out of nowhere, something entered the screen.

From the bottom of the screen came a blurred object catching the children. At the same moment the cage shook and the back end was rocked downwards.

It was at that moment that Laurie managed to work out what had happened. He turned around, picked up Evelyn and gave her a hug, holding her against him for what seemed like forever. Just moments before he thought he'd seen her dropping to her death and now here she was. Her and Dex. They had done it.

Laurie couldn't help but cheer and once he'd put Evelyn down he had to give Lucas a hug too. After all, he was the man who had just saved his daughter's life.

Chapter Four
Finito Ergo Sum

Anna Leung left as soon as she had seen her children safely enter the Pod. En route she had received a summons to the navigation suite – in this time of crisis she was needed for emergency planning. It didn't matter that her sleep had been interrupted; she was more alert than perhaps she had ever been before in her life. She worried about her children, especially Adam as he seemed so disconnected from everything, but she had a responsibility to everyone on board, not just her family. And, ultimately, if she could help save The Magellan, she would be saving her children as well. So despite not wanting to leave them, she did.

Grace led Adam into the Pod through the winding maze of air locks and security that ensured that the inhabitants were as protected as possible. He didn't like the upheaval and so was dragging his feet on the way in, resolutely refusing to take in his new surroundings. He would have been much happier to stay in his lab back at home but at least he understood the necessity of the move; that was why he wasn't kicking up more of a fuss.

Finally Grace and Adam reached the living quarters of their temporary new home. Bearing in mind they were in an escape pod, the children were comforted by its size. They were first thrust into a large open plan reception area. At the front of the room was the bridge with the control panels and monitors. Much like the ITCs, the controls were minimal as everything was now voice activated or automatic, but there was still an impressive array of flashing buttons and dials. Above the controls was the viewing gantry – a giant projection screen that would, should they ever leave The Magellan, provide them with views out into space. Over to the left side of the room were a large dining table and several chairs. The final third of the room was dedicated to a lounge area with soft, comfortable couches, a table and some entertainment screens. Everything was decorated in plain white but, as with everything onboard The Magellan, the systems allowed easy, voice-activated changes to the colour scheme of everything on offer.

Adam immediately installed himself at the console. He picked up Isaac and sat him down on the edge of the work surface before trying to figure out what everything did and how it all worked. Meanwhile Grace decided to look around what she feared would become their permanent new home.

There were four bedrooms in the Pod. None were small, but there was certainly a difference in size between them. Each one had built-in storage hidden away, sliding out at the touch of a button or a simple word. The Magellan had been specifically designed to use space as efficiently as possible and the Pods were no exception. Each room also contained one large bed, though with one voice command the bed could split into two or disappear completely in one seamless move under the floor. Each bedroom had its own en suite bathroom and standard entertainment systems allowing the residents to watch, read, play or listen to whatever they chose.

Grace instantly chose the largest of these rooms to be hers, bringing her bags in. She hadn't brought much with her as anything that was already neatly stored away was transported down by Carrie. Though she didn't need to unpack, there were plenty of other important things to do with her time. If she was going to have to live here for the foreseeable future she wanted the place to at least feel like hers so, using VA rather than bothering Carrie directly, she re-coloured the walls a pale, warm yellow and had some of her favourite pictures 'hung' on the walls. She chose three pictures from Monet's 'Water Lilies' – looking at the beautiful rendering of the water always made her feel calm and that was exactly what she needed right now.

Once she was happy with what she had done with the room she went back to see how Adam was getting on.

Adam had barely moved at the console. He was still engrossed in all the things he had power over. He had just discovered that he could divide the room up using lumi-firma walls and was trying to work out his preferred layout. And so it was that as Grace walked out of what was now her bedroom and over to check on her brother, she walked straight into a wall he was busy putting in place.

Grace fell back onto her bottom and rubbed her forehead where she had hit it. When she realised what had happened she shouted at her brother.

"Adam! What do you think you're doing? You could have really hurt me!"

Adam didn't look up, he couldn't hear Grace as she was behind a sound-proofed wall; instead he continued moving the walls elsewhere in the room, still not sure of the perfect layout but never looking up to check his final results. Finally Grace and Adam were in the same room as each other and Grace, having stood up, dusted herself off and calmed down, spoke to her brother in a much calmer manner than before.

"Adam – you've got to look at what you're doing. I could have been really hurt."

Now he stopped and looked up.

"Sorry Grace," he said, though he hardly sounded like he meant it, "I thought I should figure out how we're going to divide up the room so we can get used to the layout."

Grace was used to Adam's unusual way of thinking and had grown to accept it. While she was very intelligent, she knew he was way smarter than she would ever be, but that he was eccentric with it. You just had to know the right way to speak to him. Shouting never worked, it was more important to be clear and concise. She also knew that he needed the Pod to feel more like a home else he'd feel uncomfortable, but she wanted him to do that without causing her any more harm!

"Why don't you pick out a bedroom? Then you can make it feel like it's all yours. We can then maybe start planning the rest of the space together afterwards."

Sure enough, that encouraged him and he duly trotted off to the room next to Grace's. She knew exactly how to handle him, but that's what comes from living with the boy-genius for the last 12 years, and now she could sit down, relax and clear her mind.

Adam took Isaac with him into the bedroom. He had nearly completed the robot and he was desperate to put the finishing touches to him. He didn't want to decorate the bedroom, instead he had the walls covered with his complex diagrams and formulas that governed the way that Isaac was programmed and put together. He put Isaac on his bed before going to the corner of the room and asking for a desk. Sure enough, a lumi-firma shelf came out of the wall for him to rest on and a chair came out of storage for him. He grabbed a Slice from his bag and sat down.

A Slice is as thin and flexible as paper but the tiny micro-chips built in turn it into a computer. It can call up any book or information you'd like to read and when you write and draw on it, it saves everything you inscribe. Adam had used it to write all of the calculations and draw all the plans that now adorned his walls, and intended to continue doing so. For Adam, this is what constituted making his room his own.

He had initially been a little annoyed with Grace for stopping his work on planning out the living rooms – after all, it was important that the Pod was designed right and he was doing it for both of them – but now he realised he could get on with some far more important work and Grace could have no cause for complaint.

Grace had always been really good to him and given him the space he needed. He often tried to do nice things for her but he never really knew what she would like him to do. Regardless, he knew he could trust her and rely on her.

He had found it difficult when he first went to school. He didn't really know how to talk to the other children. He couldn't relate to their desire to play games and mess around. He was always so focused on learning and it didn't make sense to him that they weren't the same.

At first Carrie had tried moving him up a few years in school as it was clear he was learning far too fast to make it worthwhile staying with children his own age, but he felt even more out of place, had even less in common with his classmates and, ultimately, was even less happy. In the end it was clear that what he really needed was to be left to read whatever he wanted and let him get on with his own projects. Carrie was always around to make sure he didn't cause any harm or do anything too dangerous – though some of his experiments could be pretty risky. But being taken out of school meant it was even harder for him to talk to other people, and that's why he appreciated Grace so much; she always made the effort with him.

And so, after working on Isaac for another half an hour, he went back out to see what he could do for Grace.

Grace was dozing on the sofa when Adam came out of his bedroom shouting something about helping her to feel better about being stuck in the Pod. Before she had time to take in Adam's offer, though, the main door into the living room opened and there at the entrance were Connor and Max Moran.

Adam stopped dead in his tracks, not knowing what to say. He didn't have a clue who these people were or what they were doing here. Grace was almost in the same boat. However, she at least recognised Connor and she wasn't at all pleased to see him.

"What are you doing here?" she demanded.

"Your dad told our dad we could share your Pod when we couldn't get into ours," replied Connor.

"Well Dad obviously didn't know who he was letting in when he said that," she said dismissively.

Adam slowly walked over to sit behind Grace, keeping quiet. He didn't like the animosity in Grace's voice and wanted her to deal with these two invaders.

"Yeah, well he still invited us, and our sister will be here soon too, so you'd better get used to it," said Connor defiantly.

"Yeah, Evie's coming so get used to it," said Max, looking up at his brother for approval. Connor smiled down at him, silently telling him he had done well.

"Well, I suppose you ought to come in," Grace said reluctantly, causing Adam to flinch behind her, "But don't get too comfy." He didn't like that Grace was giving in to someone she obviously had such a great distaste for.

Connor strode in, surveying the room and trying to give off an aura of authority. He was the oldest of the four of them and so needed to demonstrate the fact that, if things went wrong, he would be the one in charge. Max walked in behind him before standing, hands on his hips, and looking round the room, trying to copy his older brother.

Adam whispered to his sister, "Who are they? What are they doing here?"

Connor heard him and took it upon himself to introduce the pair of them.

"I'm Connor Moran and this little munchkin here is my brother Max. We're here to share this Pod until the whole situation has been dealt with."

"And what if it doesn't all get dealt with? What then?" demanded Grace.

"Then I guess we're ship-mates. Isn't that right, Maxxie?"

Connor ruffled his brother's hair and smiled smugly back at Grace and Adam.

"Yeah," said Max, "This is our ship now." It was most definitely not the right thing to say. Connor could see that Grace was about to explode, so before she got the chance he crouched down on one knee to talk to Max at his own level.

"Hey, listen buddy," he said gently, "This is still their ship, we're just going to share it until this is all over."

"But…" started Adam, but Grace shushed him up. She was at least mildly impressed with the way in which Connor was dealing with his brother, even if she still didn't want either one of them onboard – they were a recipe for disaster and she knew it.

Max was starting to get more nervous. The constant reassurance that everything was going to be OK only made it feel more like everything wasn't. He just wished it would hurry up and be over so he could get back to his own house.

An uneasy truce developed between the children, each pair splitting off and talking quietly amongst themselves. Adam divided the room in two using the lumi-firma walls, half for each group. Connor and Max sat at the dining table talking while Grace looked disdainfully in their direction, tutting when Connor put his feet up on the table. Connor tried to take his mind off things by playing some games but Max wasn't really interested; he spent his time fidgeting, still desperate to leave and get back home. Grace explained to Adam who Connor and Max were and why she wasn't happy about them coming aboard, but she also explained why it was necessary and that they should at least be cordial to their new companions.

When Evelyn came through the door, that's how she found them, the two pairings muttering to each other and excluding the others.

After the rescue by her father and Mr Leung, Evelyn rapidly regained her composure. Dex didn't deal with things nearly so well and was still shaking when he was met by his parents outside the engine rooms. Evelyn could still hear his parents scolding him as the car they'd arrived in drove away. Laurie, on the other hand, was just relieved to have his daughter back safe and sound and when he finally managed to stop hugging her, he put her in a car and sent her down to the Pod, before returning to the engine rooms with Lucas Leung to help rescue the engineers who were in ever increasing danger.

Her father had given her scant detail of the crisis going on but she had managed to coax a little more information out of Carrie. She knew that something big was happening from events in the engine room and she had taken the news of the attack pretty well, all things considered. She was scared, naturally, but she felt she had escaped the greater threat to her life when her father had caught her after her grip gave way.

On the way to the Pod, she was a little bemused as to why there appeared to be so little traffic on the roads and so few pedestrians on the pavement. Carrie told her that most people had already made their way to their Pods or were busy trying to save The Magellan from the attack, but Evelyn wasn't sure if she believed that or not. It was certainly eerie on the streets. Evelyn had never seen the roads so quiet and the effect was quite spooky. She had put all those thoughts to one side by the time she reached the Pod. The thought of being reunited with her brothers took over. She wondered just how much of her story she should tell them.

She felt guilty for making her father come and rescue her, something which had now led to him staying in the engine rooms rather than coming to the Pod with them, and she didn't want Connor and Max blaming her for his absence. Especially Max. He could be a sensitive boy on occasion. Connor could look after himself and could think what he liked but she didn't want her younger brother turning against her.

By the time she walked through the door of the Pod she had resolved to give as little detail as possible, whilst not actually lying. She didn't want to be caught out in the event that everything turned out OK, but she didn't want to admit to everything.

"Where's Dad?" was the first thing Connor said to her.

"He's in the engine rooms," she replied, knowing full well that it would only prompt more questions but not knowing what else to say.

"Why? What's he doing there?"

"The attack's doing some serious damage in there. A lot of the engineers are in trouble, he's trying to save them." It was all true, but she could feel her voice quivering, she felt like she was giving away that it was all her fault. "You know Dad, always got to be a hero." That much was true. Barely an exploratory mission went by without him risking his life to save one of his crew from something.

The thought of his Dad being a hero made Connor feel very proud, but at the same time he felt inadequate, like he should be out there doing something too. But then he remembered that his Dad had placed him in charge of both Max and now Evelyn and that it was his job to make sure that they were OK. For the time being he didn't need to know anything else about what had happened to Evelyn. He walked over to her and gave her a hug.

It was while she was being hugged that she looked over Connor's shoulder and noticed Grace and Adam sitting on one of the couches, whispering to each other.

"Why are they in our Pod, Connor?" she whispered.

"They're not – we're in theirs," he whispered back.

She broke the embrace and walked over, presenting her hand to the Grace.

"Hi. I'm Evelyn, pleased to meet you."

Grace took her hand and offered a slight smile but it was clear that she wasn't that pleased to meet Evelyn.

"Grace," was all she offered in return.

"And you're Adam aren't you?"

She recognised the shy boy trying to hide. They had briefly been in the same class at one point. They'd never got to know each other but she certainly knew his reputation.

"Yes," he replied meekly, trying to hide himself further behind Grace's shoulder. He wasn't comfortable with someone as outgoing and direct as Evelyn.

"Well, it looks like we're going to be Pod-mates for a little while. We should do something to get to know each other a bit better."

"Maybe," was the extent of the response she got from Grace before she was dragged away by Connor to give Max a hug.

Once the three of them had regrouped and were behind the soundproof wall, Connor laid it out straight for Evelyn.

"Evie, don't get too friendly with them. They clearly don't want us here and don't like us. We'll just get through this, the three of us. Stick together. OK?"

"Why? Why shouldn't we be nice to them? Who knows how long we could be stuck here with them? We should be as friendly as possible."

"Connor said we're going home soon," said Max, a little alarmed that Evelyn thought they'd be there longer. She shot Connor a look, telling him she disapproved of the false hope she was giving their brother.

"I hope so, Max," was all she could say to reassure him. It didn't work and his eyes began to well up. The brash exterior he'd presented to the strangers began to crumble as the realisation that this was more than just a precaution hit home.

Connor rolled his eyes at her, as if to say "Now look what you've done." Instead he said "We'll let them make the first move then, OK? Now, let's get unpacked."

Connor made his way to the bedrooms. When he found the two bigger bedrooms were already taken he went storming over to Grace.

"We need to sort out the sleeping quarters."

"What's to sort out?" Grace asked, a sweet, sarcastic smile on her face, "We've got two, you've got two."

"Yeah, but you've got the biggest two. That's not fair."

"Well, it's our Pod. You're the guests, you get the guest bedrooms."

"Yeah, but two of us will have to share so we need more space."

"Well that's just tough, isn't it? You should have thought of that before you came barging into our Pod."

Connor was getting more and more frustrated. Adam and Max were both getting upset by the shouting but Connor wasn't going to be calming down any time soon.

"Look, I'm the oldest here, I'm in charge so I'll have the biggest room. Evelyn and Max will share the next one, you two have the other rooms."

"It's not happening Connor. And you are definitely not in charge!"

Grace turned her back on him, making it clear the argument was over. Max let out a whimper and tears began to stream from his eyes. It was a traumatic enough time without all the shouting. Evelyn gave him a hug and stroked the back of his head. She glared at Connor, telling him to give it up, at least for the moment. Adam was nearly as upset by the commotion as Max and went running into his bedroom to get away from it. Connor was left standing in the middle of the room, angry and frustrated.

Just then Carrie appeared on the viewing gantry at the front of the Pod.

"Connor, Grace, I need to speak to you both," she said calmly.

Everyone looked round at Carrie but no one made a move in her direction.

"Now, please," she said a little firmer. Connor and Grace

both walked over, Grace with a little more enthusiasm than Connor, but neither of them was particularly happy about it.

When they reached the console at the front of the bridge Carrie closed the area off with a lumi-firma wall, making sure the other children couldn't see or hear any part of the conversation that was about to take place.

"Right, you two, you need to start getting along," said Carrie sternly.

Grace just stood there, arms folded, staring back at Carrie. Connor was still angry and Carrie wasn't helping. He had been done an injustice as far as he was concerned, and he was pretty certain that Carrie wasn't about to rectify it.

"Listen, those kids out there need you two to be strong for them. They look up to you and if they see you getting along, maybe they'll stand a chance of doing the same. I don't care whether you like each other or not, when you're with them, you're best friends, OK?"

Still the pair refused to speak.

Carrie's face morphed into the much harsher Cary who clearly wasn't happy with either of them.

"If it's going to be like that," he barked in their direction, "Then it's going to be like this. Connor – you get the large bedroom."

Connor's expression changed. Suddenly it was all going his way. He beamed in Grace's direction, she just scowled back.

"And you're going to share it with Max."

And the frown returned to Connor's forehead, but he didn't dare object. It was clear that Cary meant business.

"When you head back out there, Grace, you're going to amicably agree with Evelyn and Adam which bedrooms the three of you will have."

"Yes sir," she muttered, nodding to Cary that she understood.

"And once you've done that, you will prepare yourselves and the others for the fact that this Pod is going to launch in 10 minutes time."

Connor and Grace were both shocked. While both thought that this would probably happen, they still couldn't quite believe it. The Magellan had been their home all their lives and now they were going to leave it, possibly forever. Neither of them knew what to do or say.

"Now, if you've both understood that, I want you to shake hands and go out there and prepare those poor, scared children."

They each reluctantly stuck out their hands and went through the motions of a handshake before turning to leave. Before they got the chance to make their exit, Cary had one last thing to add.

"Oh, and Connor. You're not in charge here. I am."

Connor didn't look back, he was too embarrassed to meet the steely glare he felt Cary giving him from behind.

Grace and Connor stood together as a united front and told Evelyn, Adam and Max what was happening. Connor took Max into what was now their bedroom and tried to get him settled while Grace talked with Evelyn and Adam about the remaining sleeping arrangements.

All five of them were in shock and merely going through the motions, doing what had to be done while they waited for the inevitable. Assuming it was going to be fine with Evelyn, Grace had already decided to let Adam stay in his current room. Evelyn surprised Grace by immediately offering to take the smallest room to make the minimum of fuss before Grace could say anything. Once they had all moved in to their rooms – which took all of two minutes as everyone was too tense to do the job properly – they met on the gantry awaiting ignition.

Max stood on the bridge flanked by his brother and sister who each had an arm around him. Grace mimicked the pose with Adam. No one had anything to say. They all silently counted down.

Then they heard it. The ignition. They could feel the Pod

vibrate and the noise became all they could hear. Their ears was filled with a piercing sound, it was painful. Adam covered up his ears, trying to block it. Soon they all followed suit. It was almost more than they could take.

Connor began to suspect that this wasn't the ignition sequence, this was the end. The Pod was about to be destroyed. And then they felt it shift forward. The acceleration was immense. They were almost knocked off their feet. The moment they were no longer a fixed part of The Magellan, the moment they became a ship in their own right, was the moment that it became bearable once more. The sound died down and the vibration almost stopped as the momentum of the Pod grew and grew. And then, after what seemed like an age but was, in fact, only a few seconds, the sound and vibration went entirely. Everything was eerily silent.

Somehow they all knew what it meant. They had now left The Magellan entirely. Before, they were being forced out of the ship down a chute or tunnel, now they were alone, adrift in space.

But the screen in front of them stayed blank and black. They had all been expecting to see outside, to see where they were going, but Cary had decided that it wasn't going to be.

They stood there in silence. No one knew what to say. There was one thing they all wanted to say, deep down inside, but no one dared. Until Adam took the lead.

"Carrie, can I see what's happening please? I want to see outside."

"I don't think that's a good idea, Adam. Not now," she replied, "Now could the rest of you leave please, I need to speak to Connor and Grace alone again."

Adam was the first to leave the gantry, followed by Evelyn who kept her arm around Max.

Carrie again put up a wall to block the others from seeing or hearing what was going on.

"I'm going to show you two because you need to know, but I

don't think the others could deal with it. Especially Max."

Adam, Evelyn and Max perched themselves awkwardly on the sofas. Max pressed his face into his sister's chest, leaving damp spots on her tee-shirt. Adam was staring into space. He didn't look troubled, but his mind was definitely somewhere else.

"Wow, this is pretty strange, right?" Evelyn said, trying to break the tension in the room, but Adam didn't hear her. Evelyn felt awkward, trying to console her brother, sat in a strange place with a strange boy who was acting, well, strangely.

"I want Mummy," pleaded Max, "When's Mummy getting here?"

Evelyn was about to try to answer the boy when Adam snapped out of his trance.

"She's not coming. She's probably dead by now. They all are," said Adam.

Evelyn was aghast, her jaw dropped and she just stared at Adam. Max started crying, pleading to go home.

"This is your home now," said Adam, answering Max's cries again.

Evelyn snapped. "What?!? What are you saying? He's eight, what on earth do you think you're doing? Do you think that's helping? Just shut up!"

"He needs to know..."

"I can't believe you're so insensitive. He may need to know at some point, but do you really think that's the way to break it to him?"

Max was bawling his eyes out, screaming for his parents. Adam opened his mouth to defend himself but Evelyn cut him off.

"Just go away Adam, go to your bedroom or something, leave us alone."

Adam did as he was told, muttering under his breath about how he was just answering the boy's questions.

Evelyn hugged her brother, protecting him, her left hand over his ear so as to shut out any more nonsense he might overhear. She kissed the top of his head and whispered soothing nothings. There was nothing she could say to undo Adam's work, all she could hope was that she was providing some comfort to her brother when he most needed it.

Connor and Grace stood in silence, watching the big screen. At first it showed them the view ahead of them, the view out into the galaxy, across the solar system, away from The Magellan. But then Carrie changed the angle and showed them their home.

The Shark had moved in for the kill, its massive body dwarfing The Magellan. They could see the outside of The Magellan was severely damaged. They could make out fires in some of the windows. There were other segments where the hull had been ripped apart. There was no fire there because there was no oxygen. Connor and Grace both knew then that anyone that didn't make it into a Pod wasn't going to survive.

They saw beams being fired out by The Shark. They seemed to be indiscriminate, hitting The Magellan anywhere it felt like. There was no pattern to it.

They could see other Pods being fired out from The Magellan too. Occasionally one of the beams coming from The Shark would hit a Pod or piece of debris. It seemed to take at least two blasts with the beam to destroy these. Grace and Connor feared for their own safety. They were definitely further from The Magellan and The Shark than any other Pod they could see, but they had no idea of the range of The Shark's beams. There were still one or two Pods managing to make it away, seemingly catching up with their own, but the majority were just fish food for The Shark.

The random beams seemed to slow before stopping altogether. Neither Connor nor Grace understood what was happening. The Shark seemed to back off, moving away from The Magellan's carcass as though it had finished feasting.

Connor saw the glow first. On top of The Shark's snout

something was shining brightly. Grace saw it too. She instinctively reached for Connor's hand. He jolted in surprise when he felt her but took it nonetheless. And so they watched.

The glow became an intense beam of light, one which hurt their eyes. It was a cold, icy colour, neither blue nor white. It seemed to encompass the entire body of The Magellan.

The light dimmed and the entire ship seemed to have crystallised. They could see the light bending, bouncing and refracting off it in all sorts of directions. In a strange way it was beautiful. Beautiful but terrifying.

It appeared to be frozen. Frozen in time. In suspended animation. One final beam shot out from The Shark for a fraction of a second and with that the entire body of the craft shattered into billions and billions of tiny fragments. They drifted silently outwards in every direction from the centre of the craft.

For a moment Grace thought that it was one of the most beautiful sights she had ever seen. A full kaleidoscope of ever-changing colours floated before her eyes. It was a stupendous sight to behold, but it wasn't only a visual experience. It meant a lot more to Connor and Grace. That was their home, their lives. Their families, their friends, everything they had ever experienced was on that ship and now it was gone.

It was beautiful, but it was hideous. It was shocking, it was horrifying but neither of them could look away. They were transfixed, hypnotised by what had occurred before them.

Slowly, as the particles drifted apart, it seemed to melt away into the blackness of space until it was all gone.

Part Two
Intergalactic Rescue

Chapter Five
Black Holes

Connor felt his stomach collapse in on itself. He was crushed. He visibly shrank in his seat, folding up and shutting down.

"I'm going to talk to Adam." Her voice shocked him, woke him up, reminded him of his role and his responsibility. He gestured at her to go without him. He needed a moment to pull himself together.

Grace was numb. She walked slowly from the gantry back to the lounge but only found Evelyn and Max.

"Where's my brother?" she asked, almost demanding.

Not liking Grace's tone, Evelyn snapped back "I sent him to his room."

"You did...?" Grace's voice rose and she started to feel very uncomfortable. She lowered her voice and spat out "You did what?"

"He was upsetting Max," hissed Evelyn, "So I asked him to leave us alone."

Grace gave her a derisive look and turned on her heel. "Your brother wants to see you on the bridge," she called over her shoulder.

"What am I supposed to do?"

The question disarmed her. It was a question to which there was no answer and Grace had no idea what to tell Adam. She hadn't realised he even knew she was there. He had his back to her, perched at his desk, tinkering with some gadget or other, taking it apart and putting it back together. She stood and watched him while she pondered her answer.

"You're not 'supposed' to do anything, Adam," she eventually replied. "There's no right or wrong, no..." Her voice trailed off.

"But how should I feel? How do you feel?"

"I feel empty. I feel like there's a black hole inside me, pulling everything in."

"I don't feel like that, Grace. I feel bad, because I don't feel like that."

She moved to him and hugged him tight. Tears sprung from her eyes. "Whatever you feel inside is the right thing to feel." She sobbed into his ear as she spoke to comfort him. "Don't be silly and feel guilty."

Adam was uncomfortable hugging his sister but he knew it was what she needed. He was also confused. He understood everything that had happened, perhaps better than anyone on board, but he didn't know what to do. He felt anxious and awkward. He didn't like the others on board. He didn't know them and they were in his space, but at least he still had Grace. He gave her a squeeze and felt comforted. Perhaps hugging Grace wasn't so bad after all.

"So how do you feel then?" asked Grace, breaking the embrace. She let out a little laugh when she saw the damp patch on Adam's shoulder caused by her tears. She wiped her nose and face free of tears with the back of her hand.

"I don't know," said Adam dismissively. "It's strange. It's all so senseless. I want to know why."

"Sometimes things just happen, there is no why."

"I know."

"But if you figure it out..."

Connor lifted his head out of his hands to see his sister and brother staring back at him expectantly. They immediately noticed his eyes were red from the tears. He had been pushing his palms into his eye sockets as though trying to push the tears back in. He wanted to turn back time, to undo events, and failing that he wanted get his revenge, to destroy that shark, to destroy it all. But first he had to deal with his siblings.

He didn't say anything. He couldn't. Not right then. He had wanted to gather himself before he spoke to them. Looking at each other, they just knew and his words weren't necessary. They ran to him, he opened his arms and embraced them both. They all cried, and cried loudly.

Half an hour later, Connor was lying on his back on the floor, cradling a sibling with each arm. Max had gone to sleep, but his bottom lip trembled every now and then. Evelyn was sucking on her thumb, something she hadn't done since she was 5 but it felt comforting.

She pulled it out with a 'Pop'.

"Will Max be OK?" She looked up at him with hopeful eyes.

He didn't know. He didn't know if any of them would be. How could they be with all this going on? He looked down at her, seeing the softness of his sister's eyes, something he'd never noticed before, seeing the fear they held, and the compassion. He couldn't tell her what he really thought.

"We'll all be fine, Evie," he said, without much conviction. He repeated himself, with more confidence, telling himself more than her. "We'll all be fine."

She sat up, thinking. "Will we though? We might be the only ones left." She hadn't really thought about what she was saying but as the words came out they hit home. They hit home for Connor too. He hadn't thought about the other Pods. Maybe there were other survivors. He'd talk to Cary about it later. He needed to answer his sister now.

"We'll take it one step at a time. We'll get safe, get away from them." He was struck with the realisation that he didn't even know who he was talking about. Who were they fleeing? "We'll get safe and work out what to do next." He paused. He wanted to say they'd work out how to get them, how to get their revenge. "We'll be fine," he said.

Evelyn accepted him at his word. He was her big brother and he'd know best. She lay back down on his chest and gave him a hug. She could feel her eyes welling up again.

Grace didn't believe in destiny. The idea that everything was laid out before them made no sense to her, but she wanted to believe that this had happened for a reason. She had told her brother that sometimes things just happen, and no matter how often she told herself this she didn't want to accept it. Something so senseless, so tragic, causing so much destruction, had to have happened for a reason. It was the only thing she could accept. After all, it wasn't just a random event. It wasn't nature or the universe that had destroyed their home. The Shark had appeared from nowhere and had targeted them, hadn't it?

Adam had said that The Shark had appeared, cloaked, 46 minutes before the pulse struck. That hadn't left them much time to plan the attack, and yet it seemed so precise. The Shark had known exactly what it was doing. It must have been a premeditated attack, and that meant there was a reason.

She lay back on her bed and pushed her fingers back through her hair before returning them to cover her eyes. She could feel tears coming again and the thought that they had been targeted was making her head hurt. Why would someone do that? Who would have a grudge against them? They hadn't encountered any alien intelligence since they'd left Earth 164 years earlier, they hadn't made any enemies.

She gave up. What else could she do? She couldn't talk to them. If she tried they'd probably blow up the Pod. And anyway, knowing there was a reason, no matter how facile, was enough for now. It meant that her parents hadn't died in vain.

She thought back to her parents and smiled. She felt lucky to have had such good parents. They had encouraged and supported her in whatever she'd wanted to pursue. Yes, they had tried to point her towards being more active and sociable, but they had quickly realised their daughter was an academic, enthused by the pursuit for knowledge, not the pursuit of friends or a ball. They had supported that and indulged her with whatever she needed. She silently thanked them and promised to try to be more active and try to get on with the Morans, no matter how moronic they might be.

She asked Carrie for some music, and dimmed the lights as the gentle sounds of Dusty Springfield washed over her. She closed her eyes and slowly drifted off, smiling at memories of her parents as tears rolled down the side of her face.

Max slowly blinked awake, raised his head from Connor's chest, and sleepily said "Mummy?"

Connor didn't know what to say. He had been lying silently, dreaming of revenge against The Shark and its people, letting his anger slowly build. He was struggling to find the compassion he needed to help his brother.

"Mummy's not here right now Maxxie." Evelyn's voice rang out and Connor breathed a sigh of relief. She had sensed he wasn't prepared for the question and leapt to his aid. "Why don't we go to your bedroom and talk?"

She took her brother's hand and led him away from the bridge, leaving Connor with the space she knew he needed.

When he was sure he was alone, Connor stood up and sat at the console. "Carrie, I've got some questions."

"I know you do Connor," the computer replied.

"First of all, where are we?" He looked at the monitors and all he could see were rocks and boulders, from tiny to impossibly huge, flying past the Pod. It could have terrified him, but he trusted the computer to be doing its job.

"I took us into the ring around Zulfura. It's the only place we could hide from The Shark."

"Are there any other Pods hiding here with us?" He was hoping beyond hope that there were.

"I don't know, Connor. The radiation from these meteors is interfering with the radio signals," said the computer, as gently as she could.

"But did you see..."

The computer interrupted him. "Most of the Pods that launched were destroyed by The Shark as well. Some were damaged. I couldn't control them and..." The computer had difficulty telling the boy. "I couldn't control them and they crashed. There might be one or two, but it's highly..."

"But there might be, right?"

"Y-yes." The computer was hesitant in encouraging Connor with false hope.

"Well, we need to find them and we need to attack The Shark." He looked at the monitor Carrie had fixed on their attacker. It was motionless, doing nothing.

"With what, Connor? The Pod doesn't have any weapons. This is an escape vessel, not a fighter."

"We must have something."

"We've got a water cannon. That's it."

"Maybe we can sneak up on it, board it..."

"It's got technology way beyond ours, Connor, we wouldn't stand a chance."

He planted his hands firmly on the console, staring at The Shark, trying to come up with some way they could get their revenge. His face was red with anger, he needed to do something. He stared hard, looking for a weakness or a blind spot.

And then it disappeared.

"Carrie, put the camera back on The Shark."

"I've not switched cameras, Connor. It's gone."

"Gone?" he demanded, as though Carrie could correct this.

"Yes, Connor, gone."

"But how could it just... just go?"

"It arrived the same way. Like I said, it's got technology well in advance of ours." The computer was relieved to be able to put a stop to thoughts of revenge at the earliest opportunity. It made her nervous to hear Connor talking so bullishly, but that wouldn't be a problem now.

Connor was seething. How dare it disappear like that, without giving him his chance at vengeance. He wanted to spit something venomous in Carrie's direction, but it was futile. He turned on his heel and marched from the bridge to the kitchen. He poured a glass of water and drank it down in one go. Leaning against the counter, holding the glass in his hand, he felt his anger cool a little as the water flowed through him, and he decided that this was not what he wanted.

"Drek!" He shouted it at the top of his voice, a scream of anguish, and as he screamed he threw the glass at the floor, shattering it into tiny pieces. It felt good, hearing the smash, seeing the shards flying in all directions. At least he got to destroy something. He opened the cupboard and pulled out another glass, and another, and threw them both down before starting on the crockery. He was determined to break it all, but Carrie stopped him, shutting and locking the cupboards before he could do too much.

Connor stood and looked down at the chaos he'd caused and he felt a wave of satisfaction sweep over him.

Evelyn had taken Max back to his bedroom where they had curled up on the bed, holding each other. Max needed to feel safe and secure, he needed someone wrapped around him to protect him. Evelyn realised this. It was something she needed herself. As she held him she imagined that it was not her brother drawn close, but her father.

She repeated over and over words of comfort to her brother. It became a mantra. She stopped listening to herself, caught up in her own thoughts and memories of The Magellan and her parents.

She worried that her antics with Dex that morning had put the ship at risk, that her father might have been able to save the ship if she hadn't been exploring. The fear ate away inside of her and she longed for her father to tell her it wasn't true.

Max had stopped listening to his sister as well. All that mattered was the soft tone in her voice, not the words. She calmed him down. He wasn't stupid. He knew things weren't OK. He knew they were in danger, and he knew his parents were gone, but right now he felt safe. For these moments on the bed, huddled up to his sister, the universe wasn't the massive lonely space he was drifting through; his universe shrank until it was just him surrounded by Evelyn's soothing voice and his eyes closed again.

Evelyn's eyes wouldn't close though. She felt guilty like she never had before, and she worried the other's would find out. She didn't know what would be worse. She just kept repeating her gentle mantra as the black hole opened up inside her.

*   *   *   *   *

Several hours later, Connor found himself standing at the console on the bridge. He had cleaned up after his outburst, never regretting it for a second, and he had tried to sleep, but to no avail. His mind was buzzing, his blood was pumping, and there didn't seem to be any prospect of sleep any time soon.

He stood staring at the monitors, desperately hoping The Shark might return. The others were all terrified of it and glad it had disappeared, but Connor wanted it back. He wanted a target for his rage. However, it appeared that no matter how much he wished it, The Shark wasn't coming back. Still he stared.

The console in front of Connor bleeped and some text flashed up on the screen.

"INCOMING MESSAGE"

Chapter Six
Isaacstein

As Grace had left her brother, she had reached out and touched his arm, giving him a gentle smile that told him she was there if he needed her. She didn't expect him to need her; she knew her brother too well; she just needed him to know the offer was there.

As soon as Adam was alone he made his way over to Isaac, the robot he had spent the past eight months designing and building. Finally, after all that work, he was ready to put the finishing touches to him and to give him life. It was the ideal distraction; he was confused by the emotions churning around inside of him, not knowing how to interpret them, and he wanted to push them to one side, just until he worked out how to deal with them. And besides, somewhere deep inside, he believed that somehow Isaac might help them with their survival.

Isaac's metre tall body had been complete for over a month now. It was built of zirgenesium, an incredibly strong metal alloy which becomes soft and flexible when electrical currents are passed through it. By creating the correct strengths and pulses of current it is possible to control the strength and direction of the movements, and to do this Adam had woven thousands upon thousands of tiny electrical fibres, even thinner than hairs, into the metal. Each of these fibres made its way up Isaac's spine and into his head where Adam was connecting the last few into position. Before completing his task, he tested his work by passing a small current through some of the wires, making sure he had done his job properly. Each short zap of current made the metal jerk, moving Isaac's arms and legs, twitching his hands and feet.

Of course, if Isaac was to have full control of his body, he'd need a highly intelligent brain, and Adam had been working on just that. The chips were so small that he had to construct the circuit boards under a microscope using a robotic arm to place everything just so. Once he'd built the brain, he wrote the code to run it. It was an intense job but a challenge that Adam had relished. Many nights, his parents would have to take the circuit boards away from him to get him to go to sleep.

Thinking of his parents, Adam stopped what he was doing and froze. He looked out of the window and let his mind drift. He thought about his home, The Magellan, his parents and everything that had happened, everything he had lost. He saw the blood red Zulfura with the sun peeking out from behind it and then looked into the distance at the star formations twinkling so many light years away. He wondered if they'd ever get to visit any of them and where exactly this journey might take them.

*   *   *   *   *

Try as she might, Grace couldn't rest. Her mind was constantly moving, replaying the events of the past day. Whenever she closed her eyes she saw images of The Magellan splintering into a billion pieces, over and over, and every time she could feel the pull of the black hole growing inside her, ready to suck her in. She needed something to distract her, something logical, she needed to look forwards, not back.

"So what's the plan, Carrie?"

"What plan?" the computer replied, an air of distraction in her voice. Negotiating the hundreds of thousands of giant chunks of rock they were currently flying between was her main concern at that precise moment.

"Well, we can't orbit Zulfura forever, can we?"

"So what do you think we should do?" Carrie asked the girl.

Grace pondered the options for a while. They clearly couldn't head down to Zulfura. The Magellan's exploration crew – including Laurie Moran – had only recently finished their analysis and the acid planet was completely uninhabitable. And they couldn't stay onboard The Pod, if for no other reason than the fact that Connor would drive her absolutely mad. There was only one place they could realistically head to.

"We should head to Baldr, to Speropolis," she said.

Baldr, Zulfura's sister planet, was habitable. It had a breathable atmosphere, plentiful vegetation, and had been the subject of a successful colonisation attempt by The Magellan that had started 20 years ago. Speropolis – The City of Hope – was the result of the colonisation. When The Magellan left Baldr's orbit five years ago they had left behind over ten-thousand crew members to populate it. And right now that meant it was the only place within reach to host human life.

Carrie agreed. It was the only place they could head for. It was a conclusion the computer had reached some time ago but she realised that Grace needed something constructive to do to distract her, so she asked Grace to help plot a course to Speropolis. Deep down Grace knew that Carrie already had it all worked out but she was grateful to have something to do and the challenge of space navigation would certainly keep her occupied.

Adam picked up the hub and ever so gently placed it into the top of Isaac's head. It was a perfect fit, the connectors lined up just as he had planned and the moment that he turned the power supply on Isaac came to life. As Adam removed his fingers from the top of Isaac's head, the zirgenesium melted away from the sides, swallowing up the hub and becoming perfectly smooth.

One by one, Isaac's limbs twitched. When the power was

not connected, Isaac's hands and feet were just blobs at the end of his arms and legs but as the electricity pulsed through him they took on their normal form. Adam had designed Isaac's hands to be similar to human hands, except they had the ability to bend in either direction. They had also been built to enable them to change form – sharp or blunt edges, longer or shorter fingers, whatever the situation deemed necessary. Isaac's feet were less talented than his hands but still had plenty more going for them than Adam's own feet. They could be soft and flat for running on normal ground or they could take on many dimpled and grooved patterns to provide extra grip on wet, soft or dusty terrain. They were also capable of gripping, in the same way that a monkey's feet can grip, making Isaac a brilliant climber.

Isaac didn't have eyes in the animal sense. Instead he had one lens that wrapped all the way around his head. From inside this lens, sensors looked out in all directions giving Isaac what Adam called omnivision. Below the lens was a series of tiny holes, invisible to the naked eye, which allowed Isaac to hear and smell. When these holes became clogged by the tiny particles in the air, or when the lens became dirty, a thin layer of zirgenesium would sweep down from his brow and clean them in a blinking motion. It was Adam's design and he was very pleased with it, although he still wasn't sure if it would truly work. But as the power surged through Isaac, Adam saw it all worked perfectly. He watched with pride as his creation came to life.

Isaac sat on the edge of the desk looking up at Adam. He had been programmed with some residual knowledge – he knew who Adam was, as well as Grace, Carrie and a few other people that Adam had thought would be useful. Of course, they were all gone now and Isaac would require some education regarding his new surroundings, but he had been built to learn so it didn't concern Adam too much.

Adam walked over to his bed, sat down, and called Isaac over, patting the bed beside him as he did so. He had programmed

Isaac to walk, but he would still need to teach himself the finer details. Isaac watched Adam, taking in every detail of what he was seeing. At first he needed to focus. It was the first time he could truly see so he needed a few moments to understand, and then interpret, everything that surrounded him.

"Come and sit by me, Isaac," Adam said again.

He watched as Isaac studied the room. He covered every angle, recognising surfaces, judging distances, deciding on a best course of action. A hole slowly appeared on the front of the robot's head. It closed again. Then opened and closed, like a goldfish. Then, finally, some sound.

"Yes Adam," the robot said back, his voice soft and quiet, lacking confidence.

His legs were dangling over the edge of the workbench. He slowly swung them backwards and forwards. Adam watched as the thought processes went on; he was very excited to finally see his creation come to life. Isaac looked down at his legs, learning what tools he had to help him in his quest. All of a sudden, he lifted himself up with his arms and almost threw himself off the workbench and onto the floor.

He landed with a thud and stuck rigidly in place, computing what he'd just done. Again, he looked around, taking it all in much quicker this time. He evaluated what was needed and made his first effort. He put one foot in front of the other and tried to run. It was a good attempt but it made Adam laugh. He was all over the place, staggering from side to side across the floor.

Hearing the laugh, Isaac stopped in his tracks, trying to understand what the noise meant. The robot peered up at Adam. He looked like he was going to blink, but instead his brow furrowed over his eye, questioning Adam, objecting to the laughter at his first attempt at walking.

"Sorry," said Adam, "That was very good, very impressive. Try again, come here."

Satisfied with the apology and encouragement, the frown

disappeared and Isaac set his mind on the path he needed to take. He allowed himself a controlled wobble or two to get the hang of balancing and then he was off again, this time in a much straighter line, one foot in front of the other and gradually gaining speed. When he reached Adam he was travelling at a rate of knots. And then he stopped very abruptly. Adam looked down at him. Isaac looked back up. It was like a staring competition.

Adam wondered what was going through Isaac's brain. And then he realised – the robot was trying to work out the best way to climb up onto the bed.

The top of the bed was level with Isaac's chin and climbing up on to it might have been a bit of a challenge for the young robot. Isaac had no intention of climbing though. He looked up at the bed, judging the height and distance. Then he flexed his knees and sprung up into the air, twisting around mid-jump and landing perfectly on the bed beside Adam.

"Well, I am impressed, Isaac, well done."

"Thank you, Adam," the machine said back, looking up at the boy, his face developing a smile which mirrored his creator's.

Adam was about to have some fun with his new creation when Grace's face appeared on the wall out of nowhere.

"Adam – I need to borrow that big brain of yours," she said.

Adam sighed. He wanted to stay and train Isaac but he knew that Grace wouldn't ask if it was nothing. After telling her he'd be there in a second he turned to Isaac.

"Do what you like, but stay in this room and don't damage anything, OK?"

"Understood," the robot said, remaining sat stock still on the bed while Adam left the room.

Grace's astrophysics wasn't quite up to the standard of her brother's and she knew that this was a problem that he would quite like to wrap his brain around so she had asked for his help. Together they managed to create a comprehensive plan, factoring in the planets' rotational orbit around the star, Tau Ceti, the heat the star would be generating and the effect of gravitational pull on their velocity.

It would not be an easy journey. They didn't know what threats they might meet on the way and once they left the relative safety of the Zulfuran ring they would be sitting ducks for anyone who wanted to try and take them on. They knew The Shark had vanished but, as it could seemingly disappear and reappear at will, that was no guarantee they wouldn't meet it again on their voyage. With that in mind, they wanted the shortest possible route.

Unfortunately, that still meant spending nearly five months in open space.

Chapter Seven
Leap Of Space

The Comms Monitor had been dark and silent ever since The Magellan had been destroyed. As far as Connor knew they were the only survivors of the attack so when the monitor suddenly lit up, notifying Connor of the incoming message, it was only natural that he was more than a little surprised. Unfortunately, due to all the interference generated by the asteroids and meteors, Cary's reception was poor and the message was taking a long time to come through. Connor was bolt upright in his seat, staring at the screen, willing it to start.

As soon as Carrie realised Connor wasn't going to contact his Podmates she called Grace and invited her to come to the console. Adam sensed the urgent nature of the request and wasn't going to be left out either. He followed suit, marching to the front of the Pod to find out what all the fuss was about. They joined Connor in staring at the blinking light on the screen notifying them of someone's – or something's – attempt to contact them.

While they waited for the message to fully download the children speculated about the source. Were there some other survivors out there trying to rendezvous with them? Or could it be the mysterious crew of The Shark letting them know that they were next? It was now nearly a day since the attack had taken place. Indeed, it was several hours since The Shark itself had disappeared, so neither option seemed realistic.

Suddenly the screen flickered to life. The children were

greeted with snow on the screen and white noise filling the air.

"What is this, a joke? What kind of message is that?" said Connor, "All that build up and nothing."

"It could just be random electrical interference," said Adam, "When the universe was created it sent out radio waves that still fill space."

"Oh, and that would register as an incoming message would it, egghead?" said Connor, his voice filled with disdain for the young boy.

"Leave him alone Connor, he's smarter than you'll ever be..." interjected Grace, her voice trailing off as she looked at the screen.

An image slowly appeared through the snow, no sound at first. Two children, a girl and a boy, sat in front of a camera in what looked like one of the Pod bedrooms. Fear was written across their faces, their eyes darted around the room, their mouths moved and as the white noise gently faded, their voices became clear.

"...ashed into an asteroid in the belt around Zulfura..." said the girl, the elder of the two.

"Help us, please help us. If you can hear us, please help us," pleaded the boy, his voice soaked in fear.

"Is it working yet, Carrie?" the girl, looking to the right of the camera, asked of the computer.

"One more time," the computer replied.

"May day, may day. We're from The Magellan. Our Pod has crashed into an asteroid in the belt arou..."

A short, sharp screeching sound cut through the air, chilling the children to the bone. The screen turned blue, electric blue, just for a moment, and then the message was over. The sound and vision cut out abruptly.

Connor, Grace and Adam sat in silence for a moment, digesting what they had just seen and trying to interpret the way in which it ended. Grace thought it was the sound of The Shark attack and that the kids they'd seen and the pod itself would be destroyed by now. Connor thought the excruciating sound was metal, bending, buckling and breaking under pressure from the rock and debris they were currently flying through.

"Well, either way they're dead," said Grace, resigned.

"No, no, not necessarily," said Connor, "It might just have been the transmitters that got destroyed, they could be fine."

Adam could sense that the conversation could rapidly escalate into another argument and decided it would be best to defuse it if he could, so he asked what he thought was the most important question that needed to be asked at that time.

"Does anyone know who they are?" Grace and Connor stopped their bickering and looked back at the screen. Carrie had frozen the message with the two children's faces staring back out at them. Grace was immediately uncomfortable and looked away. She didn't want to consider what might have happened to those two children; after all, the fate that befell them might also have been hers, all of theirs. It might still be. She didn't want to give them names, make them real, turn them into people. It would only feed her fear.

Connor couldn't look away, staring deep into the girl's eyes. The image was far from clear but he felt pangs of recognition.

"She was a swimmer, wasn't she Carrie?" He was trying to find her name somewhere deep inside. Six months ago his friend Oliver had dragged him along to the ship's junior swimming championships to watch his latest girlfriend defend the title she won the year before. The girl had won again but she and Oliver had split up within weeks. Connor was convinced the girl in the video was her, and her name was on the tip of his tongue. "Free... it's Free-something. Freamon. Renee Freamon, swimming freestyle. That's her, isn't it, Carrie?"

"Yes, and her brother, Isaiah, Connor," replied the computer mournfully.

The children were silent. Now they weren't just images on a

screen, they were people. Children who, like them, had lived their lives on the Magellan and who, like them, were now in fear for their lives. They were Renee and Isaiah Freamon.

Grace didn't want to be a part of this. Whatever conclusions they came to, whatever decisions they made about what to do next, she knew she would never fully believe they were right.

"Well, I think we should investigate," said Connor. Deep down he wanted to salvage as much as he could from the disaster that had befallen them. If those children had been left alive then they had a duty to try to save them.

What Grace said next took her a little by surprise but equally she knew that it was what she truly believed. "I think we should ignore it," she said. Connor and Adam each shot her a look, surprised that she could sound so callous.

"Think about it. Firstly, it could be a trap. The Shark could be setting us up so it can take us out too. Secondly, wherever they are, and we don't even know that yet, could be too dangerous for us to get to. It already seems to have ended badly for them and we don't want that to be us as well. Thirdly, if we can make it there safely, we have no evidence that they are alive anyway. We have to make sure we survive. We don't want to kill ourselves trying to save people we don't know can be saved."

Connor and Adam both had to admit she had made some good points but their guts told them she was wrong.

"That's ridiculous," said Connor. He refused to let her know that he secretly agreed with some of what she had said. "Reverse the situations, you'd want to be rescued, or someone to at least attempt to."

"I wouldn't want them to die trying. We could all be dead if it goes wrong instead of just the two of them."

"There's one other thing," said Adam. Connor and Grace turned to face the young boy. "We've only just got enough food for the five of us to make the trip to Speropolis. If we rescue two more people we'll all end up starving."

"Well that decides it then," said Grace, "We can't do it now." She felt smug. The point had been made now and there was no way they could launch a rescue mission if they couldn't support the people they were rescuing. Her elation was short lived though.

"Unless," replied Connor, "If we can get two children off that Pod then we can get some of their food supplies too."

There had been heated debate between the children. Evelyn had got involved too and had sided with the boys, even volunteering to go herself. She wanted to make amends, to somehow satiate her guilt, but they had all quickly shouted her down on that point. This was no mission for an 11-year-old girl. Grace was fighting her corner on her own, but she fought it hard and she fought it well. She had managed to get each of them to reconsider their point of view but each time they came back to the same conclusion, they had a moral duty to try and rescue the others. It came down to one detail. Carrie had to track down the source of the signal and evaluate the safety of any mission they might launch. If the crash site was too dangerous they wouldn't go and in the face of the three children and the computer, Grace gave way. On one condition.

*   *   *   *   *

Grace buckled herself into the ISC – the big brother to the ITC – and wondered why exactly she had insisted upon going on this mission. She'd had four hours to change her mind while they navigated the Pod in the direction of the crash site, but she couldn't face what she saw as the humiliation that would come from backing out. The ball of fear inside her had been growing ever larger and so her layer of denial grew thinner, and now she was strapping herself into the lumpy, uncomfortable seat and trying to think of anything other than what she was about to do.

The crash site was in a densely packed area of the ring,

with rocks and debris blocking a clear path through for the Pod. Instead Connor and Grace would be flying in the 4-seater Scouting Craft. It was much more agile than the Pod and would easily be able to weave a path through to the crashed Pod of the Freamon children.

Grace and Connor had changed into their flight suits, secured their hoods and breathing apparatus and were ready to go. Cary had Adam, Evelyn and Max leave the small flight deck before the ISC set off. It was just a precaution. There shouldn't be any danger as the flight deck had a twin set of doors designed to act as an air lock. The inner doors would open, the ISC would move past and they would close behind them before the outer doors would open, but given everything else that happened, Cary wasn't prepared to take any chances. Max wasn't happy; he didn't want Connor to leave, he was scared enough as it was; but Evelyn had helped to calm him down. Now he just wanted to wave them off but instead they had to go back to the bridge to follow the progress.

The inner doors opened and the ISC slowly left the deck and inched forward. Cary took control of the vehicle and under no circumstances was he going to let Connor or Grace take over. Connor had weakly protested his case for flying the craft himself but he was quickly overruled, despite his stunning showing in the ITC class.

As the inner doors closed behind them, briefly sealing them into the blackened airlock, Grace and Connor each took a deep breath. They held it in until the large external doors slowly blinked open in front of them. The view that gradually revealed itself was truly spectacular. They immediately got a true feeling for the enormity of the universe and their own insignificance. When Connor had taken the ITC out previously, he had had the Magellan for reference. It was his home and it was never far away. Now, as they left the Pod, he realised just how alone they were. There were no classmates to fly alongside, no teacher to keep an eye on them, just the vastness of space in every direction. Added to which, he was soon reminded of the perilous position they were in as a giant rock five times the size of the Pod tumbled past less than ten metres away, and suddenly he was glad it was Cary in charge of the ship and not him.

The rock terrified Grace. Its size and continual motion made her realise how little the universe cared about their existence. If it had hit them it wouldn't have slowed, it would just have continued on its path. They'd have merely been a bug getting squashed under foot; insignificant; a minor annoyance. She wished she'd had the courage to speak up when she had the chance but it was too late now. They were on course for the crash site and she had to accept that.

Cary expertly navigated them through the mass of debris that made up the Zulfuran ring that Grace had admired from the window of the Magellan. Back then it had seemed thin, delicate, fragile, but now they were in the midst of it she could see how wrong she had been. It had to measure at least twenty miles across and was probably two miles deep. Using the hood she was wearing as part of her flight suit, she looked around, admiring the scale of it all and gradually allowing herself to relax into the journey. It was going to take them the best part of an hour to travel to the crash site so she might as well admire the view.

As if reading her mind, Adam spoke to her on the radio. "What does it look like, Grace?"

"Spectacular, Adam, absolutely spectacular." She felt better knowing he was out there watching her every move. She wasn't as alone as she felt.

"There it is," said Connor, reaching his hand out and pointing off to their left. Because of the way the hoods worked, Grace just saw his hand hovering in front of her, his arm invisible to her. Looking past it she saw the clearly defined Pod wreckage. It didn't look too badly damaged but it definitely wasn't going anywhere. It had crashed head first into a giant boulder, probably half a mile in length, and had embedded its nose into the rock face. It was sobering to remember just how easily they could have befallen the same fate, just how easily they still could, either in the ISC or their own Pod.

"Are you going to try to make AV contact again, Cary?" asked Connor.

"I've been trying since the moment we left the Pod, but I think their transmitter must have been destroyed. We were lucky to get the message when we did."

That annoyed Grace. They had been close to not receiving the signal at all, to not having to go through with this mission. Now they were risking their lives when they should be back on the Pod, protecting their siblings.

As they inched their way towards the craft it became clear that the damage it had suffered was much more significant than it had first appeared. The children could see where the metal of the Pod had been bent, buckled and ripped apart as it hit the rock; it must have been travelling at some speed at the time of impact. Clearly Cary – who would have been piloting at the time – had been unable to slow down before the collision.

"I don't understand how the living quarters could have survived that kind of impact. I mean, surely the hull was breached? They can't have any air in there," said Grace.

"The living quarters are very well secured within the Pod. There are several separate metal hulls between you and space. The Pod has been designed to keep everyone onboard safe, almost regardless of what happens to it," confirmed Cary.

"So Renee and Isaiah will be fine in there?" asked Grace.

"There are no guarantees, Grace, but yes, looking at the crash site I don't think that any harm will have come to them."

Because the crashed Pod's transmitters had been destroyed, Cary couldn't log into the ship's systems remotely, which meant he couldn't open the dock doors. Instead, he had to search for an alternative entrance. Cary manoeuvred the ISC alongside the rear of the crashed Pod and stopped. Connor and Grace could see a panel perfectly flush with the exterior of the hull but could see no way to open it. They watched as Cary extended a thin, cable-like arm across the space between the two vehicles. The three-fingered hand on the end gently pushed against the panel, which popped open to reveal a computer terminal. Cary plugged the hand into a socket in the panel and the console screen to Grace's right lit up with a stream of text. Connor noticed it as well and immediately enquired as to what it meant.

"The whole computer system is down," explained Cary, "but fortunately most of the electrical systems are working to some degree or other. I can control most of them from here, but only while I have the hardlink up and running."

"What does that mean for us?" Connor asked.

"Well, I can let you in from here, but if I drop the connection, everything shuts down."

"You can let us in from here?" exclaimed Connor, alarmed, "How far away are the doors?"

Cary shone a spotlight in front of the Pod and directed the beam upwards and to the left. There, about fifteen metres away, they saw a door slowly open.

"And you can't get us any closer than this?" asked Grace.

"This is the closest terminal, I'm afraid."

"So we've got to clamber our way around to that door, through space?" Grace was outraged, "I don't think so!"

"Hey, we've come this far, I'm not giving up on them now," said Connor. He was terrified to the core but he wasn't going to turn down another chance to get one over on Grace.

"It's ridiculous, Connor," Grace replied, "You can't expect us to jettison ourselves into outer space to save two people who we don't even know are alive. It's far too dangerous."

"We can do it, Grace, it'll be easy. We tie a cable to the ISC and ourselves, kick off in the right direction and if we miss we reel ourselves back in. Simple."

"Hmmm. Well I don't like it," she said.

"That's no surprise," Connor retorted.

"Shut up," said Grace, shooting a withering look in his direction.

"Connor's right," said Cary. It was music to Connor's ears. "We can make sure you are both totally safe as you float across."

"Fine then," Grace spat out.

*   *   *   *   *

The flight to the crashed Pod had taken almost an hour and, while Adam, Evelyn and Max were variously intrigued, excited and terrified for their siblings, they had also grown restless watching the slow path being woven through the ring. Adam had returned to his room, eager to check on Isaac's progress.

He had found his little robot hanging from the ceiling. The machine was learning quickly about the skills Adam had given him and was busy testing out some of his abilities, in particular, his capacity to change the surfaces of his hand and feet. He had discovered that if he created thousands of tiny suckers all over them he could climb walls and walk across ceilings.

Adam hadn't spotted the robot when he first came in, not expecting to see him swinging somewhere above his head, but it hadn't taken him long to discover him. He was very impressed when he did, for while Adam had already thought about Isaac's capacity for climbing during the design process, he had no idea the robot would learn so fast or master the task with such ease.

"Wow, Isaac, you're doing brilliantly!" he said.

"Thank you Adam, I'm glad I've pleased you," the robot replied, still hanging upside down from the roof.

"Could you come down? I think we need to talk about a few things."

"Sure, Adam."

Isaac quickly evaluated the situation before swinging his body forward. He threw himself into a double somersault, bouncing on the bed, performing a back flip and finally landing on the floor facing Adam.

"Now that really was special," said Adam, laughing at Isaac's flair, "I certainly wasn't expecting that!"

"It's more fun than walking," replied Isaac, deadpan.

"I bet." Adam sat down on the chair at his desk, a more serious look on his face. He could see Isaac trying to interpret the meaning behind it but, though Adam had programmed some information about human facial expressions into his processors, this look wasn't one of them. Truth be told, it wasn't really Adam's strong point either. The robot would have to learn. "Now, things have changed since I programmed you, Isaac."

Adam proceeded to explain their current situation. Isaac had lots of questions, but Adam discouraged him from asking them. He didn't want to go into details about the attack or the explosion, though there was one question Isaac asked that caused Adam to think again.

"Where's The Shark now?" the robot had asked, but before Adam could answer Evelyn's face appeared on the wall.

"Adam, I think you might want to come back out here."

He raced back to the console, eager to find out the latest developments.

"What's happening?" he asked.

Evelyn shushed him, pointing at the monitors. "You've got to watch this," she said.

Adam looked up. There were three images to keep an eye on. The first was looking down on Connor and Grace's ISC airlock and the other two were from cameras in their respective hoods. They could hear the short sharp breaths their siblings were taking.

"They're scared," said Adam.

"Of course they are," replied Evelyn, "Terrified."

Grace and Connor were stood in the airlock. They were both breathing through the air canisters attached to their hoods; the air had already been sucked out, cables attached to their waists and they were just waiting for the doors to open. Grace was petrified. She much preferred to deal with the theory in situations like this, rather than having to do the practical, but she wasn't going to let a clown like Connor either mess this up or take all the glory.

Connor was just as scared as Grace, but the adrenaline was building up inside him, taking the edge off. Part of him wanted to get this over and done with while the rest wanted to try to enjoy the experience. He hadn't decided which it would be yet, he probably wouldn't know until afterwards.

The door inched up.

A shiver went up Grace's spine. Fear coursed through her body; she couldn't move a muscle. Fortunately Connor was standing in front of her and didn't look round because Grace knew that if he saw her face at that precise moment, he would never let her forget the expression of absolute terror.

Connor knew that the best way to deal with things you were scared of was just to dive straight in and get it over and done with. That's how it was when he was first jumping his vike and that is how it was right then. The fear was always worse than the experience itself so, with a short run up, he threw himself out of the airlock.

He immediately knew he had his aim slightly off as he could see he was flying towards the hull of the Pod about 2 metres to the right of the door. What was of more concern to him, though, was that he had put so much energy into his leap. He was flying at a pretty high speed and he knew that it was going to hurt when he collided. He didn't have too long to think about it though, a second or two later his fingertips touched the cold metal hull, rapidly followed by the rest of him. He was glad to discover that the flight suit he was wearing really did protect him as much as

Mr Mizar had told him back in his first, and only, ITC lesson.

Connor shimmied along the outside of hull and towards the door, the tips of the gloves and shoes he was wearing providing good grip on the sleek surface.

It was bizarre for Evelyn and Adam, watching Connor jump from three different perspectives. Their attention switched to Grace, who was standing stock still. Clearly she was petrified and things weren't going to get any easier for her. Connor had clambered his way into the door of the Pod and had now turned around to beckon to her to jump.

Adam didn't think she was ever going to move but Evelyn was convinced she would, only she thought that Grace would be heading back inside. Grace, though, managed to surprise them both. They watched Grace come alive and tentatively push off from the small ledge at the edge of the airlock.

In contrast to Connor's leap of faith, Grace was barely moving, but she had got the direction spot on and was slowly gliding in a perfect line towards the centre of the doorway. Connor tapped his foot impatiently, making fun of her slow progress.

"Come on, come on, we haven't got all day," they all heard him say over the radio.

"Be quiet. I just wanted to admire the view."

As she crept towards the doorway she flexed her legs, manoeuvring them underneath her so she could just gently put her feet down on the inside the airlock of the crashed Pod.

"Nice landing," she heard her brother say.

"Thanks, Ad," she said, glad she didn't realise he was watching her earlier or she'd have been far too self-conscious to go through with it.

Connor and Grace each untied the cables that attached them to the ISC and Cary shut the door of the airlock behind them, shutting out all the light and sealing them inside.

Chapter Eight
Speed Of Light

Ten seconds is a long time to be standing in unfamiliar surroundings in pitch black, and both Connor and Grace appreciated it when Cary finally managed to get the lights working. They were stood in a cramped, featureless airlock; the walls, floor, ceiling and doors were all a dull grey colour and it made Grace think she almost preferred the darkness.

"I've managed to get lights and cameras functioning on most of the ship," said Carrie, "but I still want you to go slow and look around you all the time. I'll be watching from the cameras mounted in your visors."

"Can you see Renee and Isaiah, Carrie?" asked Grace. She wanted to get this over and done with as quickly as possible so any help would be greatly appreciated.

"No," said Carrie, "but the cameras are all down in the main living quarters and two of the bedrooms."

"Great," said Grace dejectedly. Her hopes of being in and out in ten minutes were rapidly slipping away. "Well let's get things started then."

Carrie opened the door into the Pod and the children tentatively stepped through, Connor leading the way. They listened carefully to each and every footstep, aware that the floor might be damaged and could give way at any moment. In the absence of the ambient noise of the engines in the background, each step echoed eerily off the metallic walls. The only other thing they could hear was their own heavy breathing. They were both still connected up to the oxygen supplies as Carrie didn't want them to risk falling prey to a hull breach. It was something that both reassured and concerned them at the same time.

The corridor they had walked onto circled the perimeter of the Pod, with multiple entry points into the main internal structure and stairways leading down to the flight deck and store rooms. It was split up by several doors which kept each area air tight in the event of any breaches in the outer walls; the front section had been crushed on impact with the rock face but the doors meant that the craft's overall integrity had been maintained. Connor and Grace gradually crept around the gangway, treading softly at first before trusting the ground beneath their feet with their whole weight. All the while they looked around, noting that everything still appeared to be pristine. Carrie monitored every image being fed back by the cameras in their visors, as well as the security cameras onboard, for the first sign of danger as she guided them towards the living quarters.

Adam, Evelyn and Max watched everything beamed back to them almost as intently as Carrie. They had an advantage over their siblings as they could also see the images from the onboard cameras and were able to observe the path Carrie had laid out. It was strange, seeing Connor and Grace slowly sneaking along when everything seemed so calm and safe.

Adam was desperate to get himself involved somehow but there was nothing he could say or do that would help, and while he obviously didn't want any harm to come to Grace or Connor, part of him was hoping he could spot an impending danger before Carrie so he could shout out his warning.

Max, on the other hand, could barely watch. He kept covering his eyes with his hands but couldn't resist taking peeks between his fingers. Every time he did so he immediately had to cover his eyes again, terrified of seeing something he didn't want to see and of missing something important at the same time.

Eventually it all became too much for him and he had to run back to his bedroom. Evelyn went to follow him but Carrie stepped in and said she would talk to him instead. She didn't want Evelyn to overburden herself, and while the young girl was reluctant to leave her brother, she was also relieved that she would have a little time when she didn't have to worry about him.

Max was still emotionally raw. They all were, but Max had taken everything harder than anyone else. He couldn't begin to comprehend what had happened or why and when he got back to his bedroom he curled up on the bed and started to cry again. He looked up to Connor so much and, having already lost his parents, he didn't want to think about the danger his brother was putting himself in.

Carrie appeared on the wall opposite the bed. "Maxxie," she said softly. She had never called him that before, but she knew that his mother did and felt that it might help somehow. "Maxxie, do you want to talk?"

The boy looked up at the wall, blinking the silent tears away. "No," said the boy, "Not to you, anyway." He turned away and coiled himself back up into a ball, wrapping his arms around the back of his legs. He had never felt so alone or so frightened; he began to sob, gently letting his grief roll out of him.

Carrie understood. There were only two people he would really want to talk to right now and both of them had gone with The Magellan. There was only one thing she thought she could do that might offer him some comfort, and so she began to softly sing.

"Twinkle, twinkle, little star,
Shining your light from afar.
What you've seen I'll never know
But where you've been I long to go.

The skies are there to explore,
And every star is a door,
To a world where hope comes true
And adventures begin anew.

We are searching for the key
To unlock your mystery.
So twinkle, twinkle, little star
I will find out what you are."

The new version of the old nursery rhyme had come into being shortly after the Magellan had left the Earth. It was something parents would sing to their babies to hush them to sleep. No one knew who had written it, it just seemed to evolve naturally and it quickly spread across the ship. Carrie hoped that it was gentle enough to reassure Max and that its message of hope would sink in a little too. She sung it over and over, slowly altering her voice until she was no longer herself but had become Maria Moran singing to her own son.

Max stopped crying and closed his eyes, which were now red raw, and fell asleep listening to his mother's soothing voice.

Cary opened the door to the living quarters on the crashed Pod and Connor and Grace got their first glimpse of the kind of havoc that had been caused by the crash. Furniture had been thrown around the room and smashed against the walls, it looked like a hurricane had hit the room and torn it apart. But it was worse. While there was no sign of life, there was movement.

The lumi-firma walls were malfunctioning and turning themselves on and off throughout the room in a seemingly random sequence. A bolt of lumi-firma was powerful enough to slice almost anything in two and neither Connor nor Grace wanted to test whether that included humans. However, there were still two bedrooms that Cary had been unable to check and now they were here they were going to do all they could to make sure they saved anyone who needed saving.

Evelyn and Adam were still watching them intently back on the Pod, or rather they were watching everything their siblings were watching. As the cameras were out in the living quarters the only video feeds coming through came from the visors the children were wearing.

"How are they supposed to get through there?" asked Evelyn of no one in particular. To her great surprise it was Grace who replied.

"I don't know, but we'll think of something," she said, "We have to."

They all stood in silence, starring at the flashing lights in front of them, hoping that one of them would spot some way of solving the problem, but the more they looked, the harder the task appeared to be. There were over forty panes of lumi-firma flashing on and off throughout the room, all at different intervals.

After a couple of minutes, Adam broke the silence.

"OK, I've got it."

"Got what?" said Connor, his voice filled with scorn.

"The pattern and the route you're going to have to take," he said, ignoring Connor's tone.

"What do you mean? It's random, a death-trap," said Connor. He was desperate for the smart-arse boy to be wrong, just once. He was silent for a moment while he reflected on that. He realised that, as lives could be at stake, this probably wouldn't be a good time for that to happen. "Alright then, what's the pattern, where do we go?"

Adam called up a map of the living quarters on which he marked the lumi-firma panels, grouping them together. Six of the walls were blinking on and off at steady intervals and would be easy to pass. A further nine were flashing so fast it would be impossible to get past them. The remaining twenty-seven were illuminating seemingly at random and entirely unpredictably.

However, Adam realised that the problem wasn't that they were random, just that the period of repetition was so long it was difficult to spot it was happening at all.

The other pattern he noticed was that each pane was one of a set of three. When one was on, the other two were off. He marked all this onto the map, writing in the approximate time frames for each sequence. He asked Cary to check the video to verify his calculations were correct. As usual, he was spot on.

"OK, Grace, Connor, this is what I suggest," said Adam, delighted to be playing this pivotal role, "Carrie can superimpose a green light over the panes when it's safe to go through, change it to amber when you've only got three seconds left to get through and then red at one second. That way you know when it's safe and when to hold back."

"Sounds good, bro," said Grace, proud of her little brother and glad to see him get one over on Connor.

"Bro?" sneered Connor, "You don't sound cool, you know, I bet that's the first time you've ever called him that."

Grace ignored him. "Can you put the colours up then please, Cary, so we can get on with this thing."

Suddenly their visors lit up like an array of traffic lights. It was all a bit confusing, too many lights flashing here, there and everywhere.

"OK, Cary, can you tone things down a bit?" asked Connor, "How about you just show us the colour of the next wall on our route, eh?"

The rainbow that had flooded their visors disappeared, leaving each of them with just one brightly lit wall. Cary picked out their routes, isolating one bedroom for each of them to check. They took their first tentative steps into the living quarters.

Immediately inside the entrance were three walls boxing them in, one straight on, one to the left and one to the right. They belonged to the third category that Adam had identified, those with the seemingly random sequence. For the moment, they were flickering far too fast to be able to pass.

The routes that Cary had identified meant that the two children started off in opposite directions, Grace to the left of the entrance, Connor to the right. The computer was glad to have an opportunity to separate them.

Suddenly the flashing walls stopped, settling on the central position. The positions either side of it were bathed in green light indicating it was safe for the children to move off. Carrie also overlaid a small clock in the corner of their visors, counting down until their passage would no longer be safe. Cautiously, they both moved off on their journey through the seemingly innocuous but potentially deadly maze.

They each picked their way through, making sure they didn't trip and fall over any of the destroyed furniture that littered the floor. Some of the panels only gave them a small window of opportunity so Carrie added a second timer to their visor display that counted down until it was safe to move. She whispered in the ears of the two children to reassure and encourage them. As Connor and Grace each became more confident they moved more swiftly and with greater purpose, reaching their respective goals far faster than either had expected.

Grace was the first to arrive, but she quickly found that the door was shut tight. She didn't know what to do. Surely they hadn't come all this way to be defeated by a simple locked door?

"What do we do, Carrie?" she asked, more hoping for a solution than expecting one. A waiver in her voice betrayed her fears.

"Don't worry, Grace," was the supportive reply from the computer, "These doors all have a manual backup system just in case something like this happens."

Grace started looking blindly around the door, not knowing what she was looking for or where it might be.

"Grace."

She didn't hear.

"Grace, stop," said Carrie, more forcefully this time.

The girl froze, awaiting further instructions.

When Carrie was sure she'd finally got the girl's attention she said, "To the left of the door, just above waist height, there's a panel, push against it gently."

Grace did as she was told. It was difficult to find the panel because, as had been the case on the exterior of the Pod, it was flush with the surface, almost invisible to the naked eye. However, Carrie's directions were enough for her to get her hands on it at the third attempt. She pushed lightly against the metal surface and the panel eased itself open with a barely audible click. She pulled it back and inside was the most rudimentary of devices – a crank. She pulled the handle towards her, out of the wall, and started to turn. Ever so slowly the door slid open. Grace was starting to work up a sweat; the handle was quite stiff and each turn only seemed to open the door a millimetre. Eventually the gap was wide enough to be able to squeeze through but, even before that point, she was concerned. If Renee and Isaiah had been inside she was sure they'd have seen the door moving and would have been calling out to her, trying to get out of what would have been a prison cell for them.

Her fears were confirmed when she made it inside, there was no one to be seen. Grace reasoned that this wasn't wholly negative. They must be in the room Connor was heading to. The relief was that she hadn't opened the door to find them dead.

"Connor, they're not here, they must be in your room," she said, the radio crackling in Connor's ear. Connor liked that news. He would get to be the hero in the eyes of Renee and Isaiah. He got past the last of the lumi-firma walls and ran up to the bedroom door while Carrie briefed him on the crank he would need to find to gain entry. His hands, now sweating inside his gloves, grasped at the handle, turning it as fast as he possibly could. This was it, the moment when he would be greeted as a hero. The door haltingly opened in front of him.

Evelyn and Adam were watching with bated breath. The tension had almost been too much to bear. They had felt a wave of relief rush across them when Grace and Connor had made it through the maze of deadly lumi-firma. Admittedly, the job was only half done but the fact that they had made it through with such ease allowed them to rest easy about the return journey. Now they were anxious to see inside the final bedroom, and to hear the excited voices of Renee and Isaiah when they realised they had been saved.

Grace had already travelled halfway back through the lumi-firma maze when Connor got the bedroom door open. She froze when he did, waiting to hear what he found on the other side of the door. Everyone held their breath; the silence was suffocating as the door slid back.

Nothing.

There was no scream of excitement, relief or joy. Connor could hear his heartbeat as the blood raced through him. The tension was unbearable, but the lack of voices made his heart sink. They were dead already, surely. He craned his neck to see into the room. Finally the door was open enough for Connor to snake his way through.

He looked around. Nothing. The furniture had been scattered by the crash, just as it had been in the living quarters, but there was no sign of life.

"Well?" asked Grace.

"There's no one here."

"What do you mean, there's no one there? There has to be!" she implored.

"I mean," said Connor, exasperated, "There's no one here. Not dead, not alive. No one."

"Well where are they then?"

"I don't know, do I?" said Connor, getting more and more

annoyed by the second. What could he tell her that he hadn't already? "Any ideas, Cary?"

"The cameras can see everywhere else," said the computer, "so I'm as stumped as you are."

Connor let out a big sigh of resignation. "So what do we do now?"

"We get out of here, go back to our Pod and get ourselves to Speropolis," said Grace, almost ordering.

Connor had started to look around the bedroom and immediately objected to both Grace's tone and her words. "While we're here we may as well gather some supplies," he said. He had already pulled one flight suit out of storage and was rummaging around looking for more.

"Connor's got a point, Grace," agreed the computer, "We could use some more food supplies, just in case of emergencies."

Grace seethed at being put in her place in favour of Connor, but she could see the point. "OK then, but let's make it quick."

Connor had finished his search and come up with nothing more than the flight suit. Still, he didn't want to be carrying too much for his journey back through the lumi-firma maze. He left the bedroom and started on the journey back.

Having suffered the disappointment of seeing both bedrooms turn up empty, Adam was turning his attention elsewhere. The treacherous nature of the ring of rocks and debris was causing him concern. Still some distance out, but bearing down at a rate of knots, was a giant boulder. It seemed to Adam that it was on a direct collision course with the meteor the crashed craft had embedded itself on. He immediately raised the issue with Cary, but kept it from Grace and Connor for the moment, not wanting to panic them if there was nothing to worry about.

Cary had noticed the danger too and was already trying to calculate the likely outcomes and timescales involved. As far as the computer could tell, the boulder would clip the edge of another rock, diverting its course away from the craft. However, there was no telling what kind of debris a collision of that magnitude might send out. Cary made a decision about the safest course of action, but he knew that it wasn't going to be a popular one with Connor or, especially, Grace.

Chapter Nine
Supplies & Demands

"I don't want you to worry children," said Carrie, instantly causing a jolt of alarm to run through Connor and Grace, "I just need you to take some precautions."

"What's wrong?" asked Grace, a barely disguised tremor running through her voice.

"You're going to go down to the flight deck and get in the Pod's ISC rather than returning to the one you came in," said Carrie, ignoring the question for the moment, "I was going to suggest this anyway, an extra ISC could prove useful, and you can gather some supplies in it too."

"But what is it that we shouldn't worry about, Carrie?" said Connor impatiently.

"OK, some of the debris is heading towards the ship. It's not going to hit, but it is going to strike another boulder and there's no way of telling what may happen. I need to get our ISC out of the way and that means disconnecting from the Pod."

"What?" screeched Grace, "You're abandoning us?"

"I'll still be in radio contact, and I'll be able to see everything you can see. I just won't be connected to the Pod's computers. Once I disconnect, I won't have control over the ship's cameras or doors. I'll be with you, just not as close as before," said the computer, trying to be reassuring, "I need you to go now so I can open the doors for you."

"How long until you disconnect?" asked Connor, taking it all in his stride.

"Ninety seconds."

"Ninety seconds!?" Grace was about to start arguing but Carrie cut her off.

"Grace, we can argue and run out of time, or you can get moving."

Connor grabbed her hand and pulled her down the corridor at a brisk pace, Carrie opening the doors as they reached them and shutting them once they were through. They reached the steep stairs down to the flight deck with 30 seconds to spare. For the first time on the run, Connor let go of Grace's hand and ushered her to run down the stairs in front of him.

The stairs were too steep for Grace to manage at such a pace and she stumbled and fell as she neared the bottom. She landed harshly, her arms buckling under her weight and her forehead connecting solidly with the metal deck. She was momentarily stunned and Connor had to hurdle her when he reached the foot of the stairs, before pulling her out of the way of the final set of doors. Carrie's last act while connected to the Pod was to lock the children in.

Carrie disconnected the cable from the side of the crashed Pod. The video feeds from inside all went blank. Back on their Pod, Evelyn and Adam watched as they lost every internal image apart from the two coming from Connor and Grace's visors. While effectively nothing had changed with regard to their siblings' safety, the lack of video suddenly made them feel more remote and isolated. Carrie navigated the ISC back towards the Pod. There was nothing left that she could do by staying close.

Grace was winded and desperately trying to catch her breath. She was beginning to panic, fear coursing through her veins. She looked up in search of some support from Connor and saw that he was already off and looking for supplies to take back with them. She could feel the anger rising in her and before she knew it she had her breathing back under control. She took a moment to compose herself before joining him, and contemplated the path that had led her to this point. It was all such a nightmare, and there was no end in sight. She closed her eyes, hoping that she was asleep and that if she screwed them up tight enough, when she opened them she would wake up. But she didn't. She was faced with the same picture as before; the cold metal flight deck beneath her, the ISC standing 10 feet from her, the dull gray doors to the storage compartments lining the walls. She started to think about The Magellan, the explosion, The Shark and she could feel the fear that she had papered over coming to the fore. Before it had a chance to take over and paralyse her she leapt to her feet, eager to do anything to distract her from the enormity of her reality.

"Connor, what have you found?" she asked.

Connor had winched one of the storage compartments open and was pulling crates from the shelving units, searching for any supplies that might prove helpful.

"It's all scientific equipment, nothing useful," he said, disappointed.

"Hey, scientific equipment can be really useful," shouted Grace, running towards him, annoyed with his attitude.

"OK, well if you can explain how a load of Petri dishes and test tubes are going to aid our survival, I'll happily take a box, but I'm looking for either food or tools," said Connor indignantly.

Connor had a point and Grace decided she would have to wait before she dismissed him in future; she was letting him get the upper hand too often for her liking.

"Right, well that compartment's out then, so why don't you check that one," she said, pointing to the left, "and I'll check this way." She turned to the right and started winching the door open on the next compartment round. Connor started to push the crates he'd been examining back in. Grace took a breath, considering whether she should say anything. She decided it was safe.

"What are you doing? We've not got time to be tidy!"

Connor looked at her as though he was going to say something but thought better of it. He shoved the crates back through the door, sliding them into the back of the room with a crash, and then moved onto the next door.

Grace stood in her storeroom. On the front of each crate was a digital readout of the contents. She had no idea why Connor had had to pull those crates out. The crate in front of her apparently contained specimen jars. She decided to leave it where it was. Her eyes skirted across the rest of the crates – microanalysers, genetic decoders – there was nothing they needed anything more of back on their own Pod. She moved along to the next door.

Connor had hit pay dirt in his cupboard. There was box upon box of ISC parts. He didn't know what they might need but if they were being attacked and hiding out in dangerous meteor field he wanted to have a few spares. He pulled the box at the top of the pile. The moment he started to move it, he heard the whir of the crate's support thrusters start up. He gently guided it down to his feet and flipped open the lid to check the contents. Replacement circuit boards and body panelling stared back up at him. He shut the lid and gave the box a shove in the direction of the ISC. He wasn't sure how many useful crates they were going to find, but this seemed like a good place to start. He pulled the next box down.

It wasn't until the fourth compartment she came to that Grace found something useful – food. Crate upon crate containing pack upon pack of food of every variety. She saw the labels on some of the packs and they were enough to get her salivating: roast pork and apple sauce, Szechuan chicken noodles, penguin pizza. Delicious, she thought to herself. Of course, it wasn't real meat. Animals had become far too scarce on earth before The Magellan left for them to be able to eat the real deal, and while they had successfully farmed cows, pigs and sheep on board, they had rarely been for eating. No, these meals contained no real meat. They were 100% synthetic, but indistinguishable, so she was told. Of course, she would never know if that was the truth. Regardless, she was getting hungry and the quicker she finished scavenging the sooner she could tuck in. She followed Connor's lead, shoving the crates on the cushion of air under the thrusters towards the ISC.

Back on the Pod, all the attention was on the impending collision between the two meteors. Evelyn and Adam found it difficult to appreciate the size of the rocks involved but Carrie had seen them up close – they were massive. Now, as they inched their way across the screen, the two children awaited the impact.

Grace and Connor had selected three crates of food and three crates of spare parts to load onto the ISC when Cary's voice came over the radio waves again.

"You need to get out of there now!" He didn't dress it up this time. The computer had always tried to keep the kids calm, to avoid panicking them, but this time he was all business and wasn't going to enter into a debate.

"You both connected your oxygen, right?" He didn't wait for an answer. "Grace, I need you to go and decompress the room, the controls are by the door you came in through." Grace, her heart in her mouth, immediately started running to the control panel while the computer continued with the instructions. "Connor, once the deck is a vacuum I need you to open the dock doors manually." The boy sprinted as fast as his legs could carry him to the dock bay doors while Grace was trying to figure out how the control panel worked.

Fortunately, Cary quickly spotted that Grace was struggling and so made the buttons she needed to press flash on her visor. As Grace navigated her way through the menus, Cary gave the children another warning, "When the decompression has been activated, you'll need to hang onto something. The air's going to get sucked out of here and I don't want you to be blown off your feet."

Connor quickly found some pneumatic pipes to wrap his arms around while Grace diverted her eyes from the screen to see something she could grab when she was done. A ladder just to her left would do the trick, so she hit the last few buttons and hung on tightly.

Carrie's voice rang out across the deck, but not the warm version the children had got used to back on The Magellan and appreciated since their departure. This Carrie was cold and mechanical.

"Decompression in five. Four. Three. Two. One."

Grace closed her eyes and held the ladder tighter than she'd ever held anything before. She felt a wind rise, pulling at her limbs. She relaxed when she realised it wasn't going to suck her out too, but it was still stronger than any wind she had ever encountered before.

Connor kept his eyes open. He'd been hoping to see something, but the only visual sign that anything was going on was a slight rippling over the tight clothing that clung to his legs and torso. Otherwise, nothing.

Not more than ten seconds later, Carrie's cold voice rang out again. "Decompression complete."

Grace was momentarily dazed and Cary had to prompt her to get her running back to the ISC. Connor, on the other hand, was immediately trying to get the doors open. The computer panel wasn't having any of it and he quickly realised what Cary meant when he told him to open the doors manually. Just like the bedrooms in the living quarters, he'd have to crank a handle to get these doors open. Cary flashed up a guide arrow on his visor and he quickly located it. He took a deep breath and threw himself into turning the handle as fast as he possibly could.

Grace sat herself down in the ISC, breathing hard, and finally had a chance to consider what might be happening. The truth was, she had no idea and she didn't know whether that was a good thing or a bad thing.

Adam watched in awe as the two meteorites collided and splintered into millions of shards, scattering in every direction, and thought to himself that it was a very good thing that Grace and Connor didn't know what they were facing. He stared in disbelief as a rock twice the size of the Pod had broken off and headed straight for the crashed Pod his sister and Connor were on. There was no question in his mind that if they didn't get off that Pod as soon as possible they would be crushed and flattened by the incoming projectile.

Carrie processed every possible outcome of the impact as it happened and the instant she recognised the danger she was on the radio to the children. She didn't discuss it with Adam, she didn't make an announcement, she just got on with it. With the decisions that had been made before it was important to let the children have their input, but sometimes she just needed to act without consultation. As things were, her only concern was their safety.

Adam's eyes flitted between screens and settled on the view from Connor's camera as he slowly opened the dock bay doors. Getting off the Pod was going to be tight. He needed to open the doors wide enough to allow the ISC to squeeze through, then get back to the ship and fly out. The doors were massive and were inching open at a frighteningly slow rate.

Connor was almost out of breath, but his adrenaline was pumping and he hoped it would see him through. Up until this point, despite the various setbacks, he had remained positive about their chances, but something about Cary's voice had told him this was the most serious danger they had faced and it was no time for slacking off.

He kept pushing and pulling at the heavy handle and the doors slowly offered him a view out into space, out into the meteor field. It was a little scary to think that one slip and he would be drifting out there with no control over his speed or direction, no chance of pulling his way back in. But at least thinking about things like that stopped him from thinking about just how tired his arms were feeling. The burn in his muscles was intense. He closed his eyes and pushed on, his back starting to ache now too. He tried to divert his mind to anything that would distract from the pain spreading through his body. He thought about the Magellan, his vike, his parents, all the things he would never see or do again. And then he thought about The Shark, the reason they were where they were, the reason he'd never see or do any of those things. His anger built up again. He was determined to get his chance for revenge. His arms were pumping faster as his mind filled with aggression. He imagined getting the chance to destroy The Shark the way it had destroyed the Magellan, blowing it into billions of pieces.

He was pulled out of his fantasy by Cary's voice.

"The doors are open, Connor."

His arms stopped pumping and for a moment he was still, as though his job was done. And then he snapped out of it and remembered. He ran to the ISC, leaping through the door and into his seat, strapping himself in. The ISC remained dark and silent, there was no power.

"Come on Cary, get this thing out of here," he said expectantly.

"The computer on board that Pod is dead, Connor, you've got to fly it out yourself."

Grace remained pushed back in her seat, eyes closed. She didn't know what was going on but she had no control over it. She just wanted it all to be over.

Connor was taken aback. "What? I can't do that."

"Sure you can." Cary flashed arrows and highlighted buttons to push, guiding Connor through the ignition process. "You flew the ITC brilliantly in your lesson," the computer said, trying to build his confidence.

Connor was following the instructions Cary was giving him. "Yeah, my lesson, Cary. One lesson. That's all I've had. And I didn't get to take off or land."

"Well, you're going to get your chance now."

And with that, the dashboard of the ISC came to life, and Connor's visor lit up with all the dials he'd first encountered for real less than two days ago.

He manoeuvred the controls to lift the craft from the deck and inched it towards the open dock doors.

"Once you're through the doors, I want you to follow the path I light up at full speed, OK Connor?"

Connor was concentrating too hard to reply. This wasn't like his lesson where he had been relaxed and cocky. Back then Cary could jump in and save him if he did anything stupid. Now the responsibility was all his. His movement was slow and clumsy, not natural and fluent.

Grace could feel his unease through the movement of the ship and decided she had to say something.

"I may not like you, and I may think you're ignorant and obnoxious," she said, keeping her eyes closed. Connor was starting to wonder where she was going with this. "But if there's one thing I know you can do, it's fly this thing out of here and get us to safety. I have complete faith in you Connor." And she did. Because without it, she thought to herself, she'd lose all control, and she couldn't let herself do that. Not in front of Connor.

And it was with those words that Connor summoned the inner strength and courage to ease the power up on the throttle up and move the ISC towards the doors and towards safety. As the craft sped up, Connor gained confidence in his ability. He was flying straight and level, he knew he could do it. The doors, instead of looking like an impossibly small gap to navigate through, were looking wider and wider. He could feel his pulse rate starting to come down as he felt more comfortable with what he was doing. His eyes focused on the route that Cary had lit up on his visor and he readied himself to steer into it the moment he was through the doors. He had such control it felt like everything was in slow motion. But it was one slight moment of hesitation that cost him.

Chapter Ten
Rock & Roll

As Connor steered the ISC through the doors and out to freedom, he couldn't resist. He was about to steer onto the path Cary had mapped out for him, but he needed to see what it was that they were running from. While Cary had planned a course that headed almost straight below them, Connor decided he needed to crane his neck upwards. And that was when he saw the frighteningly huge boulder spinning out of control and only metres from them. He couldn't believe it was so close. If he had just steered the moment he had left the Pod they would have been safe. The momentary glance upwards, the fraction of a second it took to take in the sight, to process it and to react, was time they didn't have.

He reacted as quickly as he could, he pushed forward on the controls, forcing the nose downwards, and he put all his might into the throttle, willing the craft to go as fast as possible.

The rock struck the Pod first, crushing it almost instantly. The Ishiguro Scouting Craft was much luckier. It was only on the receiving end of a glancing blow. The tail end of the boulder ripped off and flew in their direction, striking the back of the ship. Without seatbelts Connor and Grace would have been thrown around their small cabin. Instead their limbs were almost wrenched from their sockets, their necks were jarred, the wind knocked out of them, as the craft was sent spinning through space.

Connor's reactions were quick. He was immediately

grabbing at the controls and trying to wrestle the ship back into straight flight. The ISC was having none of it though. The blow from the rock had destroyed much of the controls, steering was nigh on impossible and the thrusters were malfunctioning.

When he realised he was fighting a losing battle, he concentrated his mind on working out what was going to happen. He looked around. He found it difficult to get his bearings; they were spinning so fast that figuring out which direction they were travelling in was almost impossible.

It took him a moment, focusing on a point and turning his head to follow it, but he managed to work it out. At first he was relieved. His first fear had been that they would be hurtling straight into the face of another of the meteorites that made up the belt, but from what he could tell, they were heading into empty space.

But it wasn't endless space. The space came to a rather abrupt end. They were spinning out of control, directly towards the giant acid planet Zulfura.

Max had woken and decided to join his sister at the monitors. He was still half asleep when he reached her, rubbing his red eyes and stumbling forward. He reached for her hand to hold. Evelyn flinched a little at his cold hand, before wrapping both her hands around his to warm him up; Adam barely noticed his arrival. Max looked up at the screen to see what had caught their attention so completely and at that precise moment the collision happened.

The three children stood on the bridge aghast at what they had just seen. None of them knew what to say. They just stared at the screen, mouths wide open in shock. They looked at each other, looking for confirmation that what they had just seen was real, hoping they would be proved wrong. Blinking, they looked back at the screen, waiting to see Connor regain control of the ISC and bring it back towards the Pod.

Max couldn't stand it. He was so traumatised by everything that had happened already, he couldn't stand to see anything else go wrong. He ran from the console, bypassing the bedroom this time, running out of the living quarters. He wanted to find a secluded corner where he could be on his own and ignore everything that was happening. Evelyn went to follow him but Carrie called her back.

"He needs space, Evelyn. Leave him be. Trust me, I'll keep an eye on him."

Evelyn was torn. She trusted the computer, of course she did, but she hated seeing her little brother so distraught and just wanted to offer him a shoulder to cry on.

"What do we do, Carrie?" she asked.

"We send our ISC after them, of course," said Adam confidently.

"Is that the best thing to do? How badly damaged are they?"

"I'm just trying to assess that, Evelyn," said Carrie. In truth, she already had. The ISC had completely lost control; the omnidirectional thruster system was almost completely destroyed. There were no two ways about it, the ISC was going to crash into Zulfura. What Carrie was actually trying to work out was where the craft would crash. The results of this calculation would determine the children's chances of survival.

First of all, the ISC had to avoid landing in one of the planet's acid oceans. Fortunately, the surface of Zulfura was only around ten percent liquid so the chances were slim. The next issue was which side of the planet they touched down on. If the ISC crashed on the dark side, facing away from Tau Ceti at the centre of the solar system, the cooler atmosphere would be less acidic. Under these conditions the hull of the craft would survive for several hours, allowing ample time to stage a rescue mission. However, if they crashed on the light side where Tau Ceti's heat would have warmed the atmosphere, the air would be thick with corrosive acid which would eat through the hull in mere minutes. A rescue mission wouldn't stand a chance.

Grace finally opened her eyes. The spinning of the ISC had slowed and it was much easier to focus on the direction they were travelling in. Zulfura loomed large and was growing rapidly. It appeared that they weren't plunging straight for the centre of the planet, but would be skimming the edge of the atmosphere before entering and being sucked down by the planet's gravitational field. Grace just sat and watched. She couldn't say anything. She could barely think anything. She was paralysed.

"I'm sorry, Grace. Really, I am," said Connor. He sounded like he meant it.

Hearing his voice eased the paralysis which held her mind and body. Grace turned to him. "It's not your fault." The words surprised her, let alone him. They bounced around inside her head. She still wasn't convinced this wasn't just a bad dream. She tried to work out if she had just said that, and if she had, did she really mean it?

"It was my idea to come here. I..." He paused. He didn't know what he wanted to say.

"It was your idea for you to come here," replied Grace, "I didn't have to. I said it was a bad idea and I still came along." She would have loved to have blamed him, but she knew she had made her own choices and what was the point in making him feel worse now?

Connor's guilt wasn't solely based around making the journey in the first place, despite what he'd said. He felt guilty for taking his eye off the task at hand, for looking for the threat rather than just turning the moment they left the landing bay. He didn't want to admit it to himself, let alone Grace. What would it achieve? He decided it was pointless now. Maybe he'd tell her when they got out of this. If they got out of this.

"Carrie?" said Grace, "Is there any music stored on this computer?" She wanted something to take her mind off things. If she couldn't do anything she wanted to be able to close here eyes and escape it all.

"No, Grace, but I can play you something down the radio. What do you want to hear?"

"Whatever, Carrie, you pick."

The computer knew Grace's taste and so picked something appropriate. She heard the familiar strains of ABBA starting up and shut her eyes.

"Oh God," said Connor, "Not classical music."

"Shut up and listen," said Grace, "You might actually enjoy it."

"I'm launching our ISC," announced Cary.

It was what Evelyn and Adam wanted to hear. It meant there was hope, it meant Cary had done the calculations and there was a way out of this.

"Do you want any help?" asked Adam.

"You're not going," said Evelyn and the computer in unison.

"And I wasn't suggesting I should," said Adam, "I'm offering Isaac."

"Your robot? Is that thing even working?" asked Evelyn.

Adam called Isaac through from the bedroom. The robot almost sprinted out to join them.

"He's not even a metre tall, how much help is he going to be?" exclaimed Evelyn. The robot looked up at her, frowning. He didn't understand what she meant but he knew he was being berated and he didn't like it.

"He's quick and strong and clever. He could do all sorts of things. And zirgenesium won't dissolve in the acid atmosphere either."

Evelyn wasn't convinced.

"Look – what harm can it do to send him along?" asked Adam, and Evelyn had to admit that he had a point - his presence certainly couldn't make anything any worse.

Adam sent the robot down to the flight deck to get onboard

the ISC before Cary launched it down to the imposing red planet.

Carrie shut down all the screens and monitors as the ISC passed into the atmosphere of Zulfura. Moving from the vacuum of space into a gaseous atmosphere caused intense heat and light which could easily blind them. The scouting craft had been designed to withstand the heat with ease, indeed, for Grace and Connor, the ambient temperature didn't change a fraction.

Once the ISC had crossed the atmospheric boundary of the planet, Carrie had to prepare them before revealing images from outside. In space, because there was little to mark against, speed was very difficult to gauge. The difference between travelling one hundred, one thousand or one hundred thousand miles an hour was almost impossible to tell. However, when in close proximity to a planet, the speeds were much more apparent. Because of the initial impact and the gravity on Zulfura, the little scouting craft was travelling at well over a thousand miles an hour and as they descended their speed would become more and more noticeable, and more and more scary.

The first images of Zulfuran landscape they saw were of a huge mountain peak appearing and disappearing past them at a frightening pace. It was clear that if they hit any kind of rock face at this speed there wouldn't be much left of them. Grace closed her eyes and kept listening to the music, which had now moved on to Aretha Franklin. She let her mind drift away with the soaring vocals.

Connor was examining everything he could about the alien landscape. It was the first time either of them had seen real solid ground in their lives and not just pictures fed back from exploration missions. He found himself fascinated by the undulations, the randomness of the structure of it all. Having lived his life in the highly structured environment of The Magellan, the raw and wild surface of this terrible planet took his breath away.

Carrie interrupted the music to brief them both. The ISC

was not on course to hit any mountain ranges. In fact, they were about as lucky as they could be given the circumstances. They would be crashing into a vast plain at a shallow angle. Carrie's calculations suggested that the ship's hull would not be breached meaning that a rescue mission should be straight forward, and she had launched the other ISC after them. Connor and Grace both breathed a sigh of relief. There was, however, some bad news to go along with the good. It would still be daylight at the time and place where the craft would first impact with the surface. From that point on, Carrie had no idea how far the craft would bounce, tumble and roll; there were too many variables to calculate. What Carrie had managed to work out was that they would need to travel a further twenty miles in under 90 seconds in order for the acid in the atmosphere not to critically damage the hull. With the speed at which they were currently travelling this should not prove to be a problem, but she had no idea how rapidly the ship would decelerate once it hit land.

The other problem was protecting the children in such a violent impact. The seatbelts and their flight suits would provide some protection, but they were unlikely to be enough. The children would have to use airbags.

Max blinked his eyes in the dark. He had been asleep for he didn't know how long but something had woken him. He sat there for a moment trying to remember where he was. He couldn't see anything, that was for sure. He tried the latch on the door he'd come in by but it was locked. He tried to stand up properly but sat back down as he banged his head on the low ceiling. He was puzzled. And puzzling him even more was the fact that the floor appeared to be moving. Not dramatically, just a slight swaying this way and that, rocking.

"Carrie?" he said, his voice echoing in the small metal chamber he found himself in. The computer didn't answer. Strange, he thought. He'd never known of anywhere outside of the computer's range before.

He tried to look around for any source of light but there was none. He was in perfect darkness. Then he heard a beeping and immediately remembered the watch on his wrist, tuned to ship time. He looked down, feeling with his fingers for the buttons on the side. Pushing one he managed to illuminate his secret little bunker. He could see that a locking mechanism was keeping the door he had entered by firmly shut, so he decided it was best to examine other possibilities. Eventually he found another exit, just a panel with a simple latch, behind him and above his head. Once found it was easy to click open and push the light sheet of metal up and away. Light flooded in. He looked around and could finally see where he had been curled up. It was a narrow, low storage chamber. He remembered why he'd chosen it – he thought no one would ever find him in there, and he was probably right given that he couldn't even seem to contact Carrie from inside. He turned back to the gaping, light-filled hole above him and was rather startled to see the plain, upside-down head of a curious looking robot staring back at him.

Each airbag was no bigger than a golf ball. They were soft and squidgy, ready to absorb any forces thrown at them. Cary had filled the cockpit to the brim and Grace and Connor braced themselves for impact. They were not strapped into their seats as Cary had decided that the airbags would provide greater cushioning. They had never been tested in an impact generating as much force as this one would, but then neither had seatbelts. They were both breathing through their visors as the airbags left little room for any breathable air. It was a risk, but so was everything and Cary was convinced this was the right thing to do.

The music was still playing through the headphones and Grace had shut her eyes to everything else that was going on. Connor couldn't though; he was busy looking out at the planet flying past their ship. It was the first time in his life he had seen actual solid ground, and he was taking every detail in. The parks of The Magellan had been beautifully sculpted but they didn't have the same rough, sharp edges presented by the rocky surface of Zulfura. Part of him wanted the opportunity to take his vike out on the surface, no matter how impossible that was. In the corner of his visor, Cary had put a clock counting down the seconds until they would first touchdown on the alien world. It had reached ten.

Carrie had told them to relax, not to brace themselves. They could injure themselves much more if they tensed their muscles as they got thrown around. Seeing the clock tick down though, Connor found it very difficult not to stiffen himself in preparation of the impact. The ground was now flying past the cockpit at such a rate that Connor couldn't look any more. He closed his eyes, continuing the countdown in his head. Five. Four. Three. Two. One.

The first touchdown made it all seem so easy. The ISC just seemed to bounce back up. Connor wondered what he had been worrying about and opened his eyes. Grace was keeping hers shut no matter what. When he opened them it seemed as though nothing had changed. The ship descended to touch down again and Connor relaxed, expecting a second gentle bounce into the air. He wasn't so lucky this time round. An horrific scraping, scratching sound tore at the base of the ISC. Connor thought it was going to be ripped to shreds. It felt like slow motion as the cockpit pitched forward before tumbling end over end, the planet rotating in a blur. Connor got a nauseous feeling in his stomach. He fought back to neutralise it, shutting his eyes and telling his brain that this was normal, but nothing about his first encounter with natural gravity was normal.

Grace was dealing with the experience much better. She remembered taking a trip to The Magellan Fair and going on the Gravity-Coaster. It worked on the same principals as the old roller-coasters they had back on Earth but instead of having a carriage moving and throwing you around against gravity, you sat in a fixed position and gravity was pulled around you using rotating AGUs. The different strengths and directions mimicked the effects of the roller-coaster. She had been on it twice, the second time very much against her will, but she had survived and it was that experience she was falling back on. She blocked out all the sounds around her, concentrating on The Kinks that Carrie was now playing for her.

Carrie was monitoring the ISCs progress and saw that, for all the sickness it may have been causing in the stomachs of the children, the craft was easily going to push on into the darkness of night that would guarantee the children's safety from warm acidic air.

The airbags were working perfectly, cushioning every bounce and blow and protecting the children exactly as the computer had hoped they would. She monitored their vital signs, getting readings from their suits; they hadn't even registered a bruise.

After 72 seconds of bouncing and bowling over the rocky landscape the small craft bounded its way over the light threshold and into darkness, and still it rolled along, though finally showing noticeable signs of slowing down. Evelyn and Adam breathed a sigh of relief. The craft was no longer flying up into the air after each impact. Instead it had started to roll along the ground, taking a lot of the bumps out of the journey. Connor had managed to relax and his stomach was no longer churning. Grace had even managed to open her eyes for a couple of short periods before deciding that she was, indeed, best off keeping them shut.

The ship gently slowed and, just as everyone thought it was going to stop, started to pick up speed again. Their momentum had just tipped them over the edge of a large valley and they kept rolling until they reached the floor. For nearly a minute they spun head over heels before the ship finally came to a halt on its left side. Fortunately, one of the systems still working was the automatic self-righting mechanism. Legs eased their way out of the side of the craft, pushing the machine back onto its base with a crunch.

And then everything was still.

Silent.

Eerie.

Chapter Eleven
Tyrannosaurus Acidicus

As soon as it was clear that the ISC had definitely stopped for good, the airbags deflated allowing Grace and Connor to move again and check themselves for injuries. Remarkably, neither of them had suffered so much as a bruise. The computer then talked them through the safety checks they needed to do – air quality, hull integrity, engine systems. The hull had proved very sturdy and, though dented and damaged, it had not been breached at any point. This, in turn, meant that the air within the craft was perfectly safe to breathe. The children removed their breathing apparatus and sat back in their chairs. Connor reflected on the fact that they had survived such a harsh and mammoth impact. Grace's mind couldn't help but wander onto what lay ahead of them rather than what they had already come through.

The engine was fatally damaged; there was no way it would get them off the planet. It might be possible to fix it but that would take a lot longer than they had before Tau Ceti rose and filled the atmosphere with corrosive gases. Cary reassured them that help was on the way, and that meant that, for now at least, all they could do was sit and wait.

Max introduced himself to Isaac and the two prepared for their rescue mission. Carrie explained they were just going to the planet to pick up his brother and Grace and then leaving right away; there was nothing to be scared of. Max sat himself at the front of the ISC and was eagerly watching their journey, the fear that had devoured him before seemed to have completely left him. He relaxed as Carrie explained the simplicity of the mission and was even excited about being able to see his brother. He hadn't seen the crash but Carrie showed him the ISC still in one piece. When she explained how they would just attach some cables and haul them out, Max relaxed back into his seat and enjoyed the journey.

Grace and Connor lounged back in their seats, listening to the music that Carrie was still piping through – it was The Monkees now. Connor was even starting to enjoy it.

"This is good," he said to Grace, "It's got an interesting rhythm."

"What do you mean?" she asked, not thinking the rhythm was anything special.

"That kind of tapping sound, I don't know what instrument it is."

"Tapping sound?" she muttered to herself. "Carrie, stop the music."

The music stopped where it was, but the tapping sound continued, it clearly wasn't anything to do with the music.

"You mean that?" she asked.

"Yeah," Connor replied, "but if it's not part of the music, where's it coming from?"

They both started looking around the cockpit. It wasn't coming from inside.

"It must be something on the outside of the ship," said Connor. It wasn't until he'd said it out loud that he realised what he was implying. The children froze.

"If it's coming from the outside..." said Grace, not able to finish her sentence. They looked at each other, afraid of the words neither of them could say. Grace tried to think it through.

They looked out through the cockpit's screen. While Zulfura

didn't have a moon, the light from Tau Ceti reflected back off the meteorite belt surrounding the planet. The dim arc in the sky looked like a monochrome rainbow and provided a gloomy illumination across the rocky, desolate landscape.

"It could just be something waving in the wind, tapping on the hull," she said.

Connor nodded in agreement. That was the most likely thing. They sat back in their seats and looked out across the planet, breathing a sigh of relief that they had worked it out.

The tapping continued.

And it moved.

Slowly it moved from above their heads forwards, towards the screen at the front of the cockpit.

And then they saw.

A long, thin, spiny leg appeared, tapping on the screen in front of them, and they held their breath.

Cary had shut the video feed from the ISCs down prior to the crash and, despite Evelyn and Adam's pleading, was refusing to put the images back on screen. All he would do was confirm that Connor and Grace had survived the impact and were waiting to be picked up. He told them that it would probably take several hours to complete the rescue and, rather than spend the whole time watching the screen helpless, they would be better off saving their strength and getting some rest. They reluctantly agreed.

"What about Max?" enquired Evelyn, concerned for her little brother.

The computer hadn't yet told them of Max's whereabouts, he was embarrassed at his oversight in allowing the child onto the ISC and didn't want to scare them any further.

"Don't worry. He's curled up on his own," he lied, "Go on, off to bed with you. I'll wake you when they're on their way back."

This didn't satisfy either Evelyn or Adam. They went to Evelyn's room where she lay back on the bed and he slumped into a chair.

They both felt like they wanted to discuss everything but neither of them knew where to start. They sat there in silence trying to filter everything, find a starting point, and as they did they began to realise that maybe Cary was right. They ran their minds over all the events that had occurred to them in the last 48 hours and slowly their eyes began to shut and their minds began to drift and before they knew it, they were fast asleep without uttering a word.

The ten legged creature walked across the screen in front of them and strode onto the rocks in front of the ISC. It was like nothing either of the children had ever seen before. Its body was at least two feet across with its legs making it almost two metres in diameter. Each of its legs was long and thin, with a silver sheen; at the end was a foot covered in tiny suckers allowing it climb up almost any surface. As ugly as they were, it was the body that was really scaring Connor and Grace. It was covered in devastatingly sharp spines, a warning to anything that might attack it to beware. Its mouth sported a wealth of pointed teeth that it was gnashing together. Above these sat eight large black eyes, giving it almost comprehensive vision. At the moment, all eight eyes were staring straight at the children.

The creature bobbed up and down and from side to side, sizing up its target. Connor and Grace were peering behind the screen, trying to get a closer look, when it stopped. It had its back legs pushing up, tilting its body forward, and it stood there, perfectly still. Connor and Grace inched closer and closer. As the first humans ever to set sight on this alien animal, they couldn't help marvelling at it. They were scared but ultimately curious.

Their noses were almost touching the front of the craft when suddenly the animal launched two of its spines at high velocity straight at them, one hitting the screen in front of each of their faces. The spines weren't just there for defence, they were there as a weapon. They bounced off, unable to penetrate the front of the ship, but they left behind two tiny indentations in the screen. Connor and Grace both jumped back into their seats, shocked by the speed and venom of the attacks.

The creature fired another six darts in quick succession, all ricocheting off the screen, and then ran towards them. Before it had crept around, investigating, but now it was in attack mode and its speed was quite breathtaking. In no time at all it was at the screen, inspecting the damage it had done. It appeared to be sniffing and then attempted to bite. Its saliva touched the screen and a puff of smoke appeared. Whatever this creature was made of, its bodily fluids appeared to be as dangerous as the planet's atmosphere. The smoke startled the creature too; it jumped away from the screen before creeping back up for another close inspection. This time it spat at the screen and backed off rapidly, obviously a little afraid of the reaction it was anticipating.

This time the screen sizzled and smoked as the larger quantity of caustic saliva burnt away at the surface of the screen. It was clear to the children that if it kept attacking like that then it wouldn't be too long before it had made its way into the cockpit so it could attack its prey. Them.

But it didn't keep attacking them. Instead it just stood in front of the ship, staring.

"What do you think it's doing?" asked Grace.

"Maybe it's afraid of the smoke, it doesn't realise what it's doing," said Connor, hopefully.

Grace was looking straight into the creature's eyes.

"No, it knows what it's doing," she said, an air of puzzlement in her voice. They were silent for a moment. "But what's it doing with its back legs?" she asked.

Connor looked and, sure enough, the animal appeared to be twitching its legs at great speed. They both became transfixed by the action, trying to figure out what on earth it was doing.

A thought came to Grace. She turned on the intercom in

the hope that it was still working and she might be able to hear outside. Remarkably, with a crackle, the sound came through to fill the cockpit. A high-pitched humming sound.

Connor hadn't caught on yet. "What's that sound?" he asked.

"The creature's making it."

"Why?"

"Communication. It's calling other creatures to us," she said, the fear audible.

"What for?" asked Connor, realisation dawning on him halfway through asking. Grace shot him a look telling him exactly how stupid she thought he was.

That was when they heard a second sound. A low rumble. Not quiet exactly, more like it was a little way away. Gradually it grew louder until the children could see where it was coming from. Several dozen more creatures appeared over the horizon and were running towards them at high speed.

"Oh drek," said Grace quietly.

"That does not look good," said Connor.

Max was strapped into one of the seats in the cockpit while Isaac bounced around the cabin excitedly. They had entered the atmosphere of Zulfura, descended to mere metres above the ground, and were flying quickly through the gloom to get to Connor and Grace as soon as possible. The jagged rocks and hillscapes whipped past them in the electric green glow of night vision. Cary was displaying a map in the corner of the screen and Max followed their progress devoutly.

They were speeding along the floor of the valley, approaching the crash site, when Cary brought them to an abrupt halt. In front of them, and making a beeline straight for the crashed craft, was something that sent a chill down Max's spine like nothing else. The enjoyment he was getting from the flight dissipated immediately. He shrank back in his seat, trying to hide.

Max wasn't the only one sitting terrified. Connor and Grace were also frozen in their seats, staring out at an army of the spiny spider-like creatures. The original creature appeared to have merely been a scout, possibly mobilised to investigate the noise of their crash. These others he had invited along were almost twice his size, and there were hundreds of them, lining up to get stuck into their prey.

As the others stood and watched, the scout approached the screen and spat on it again. This time when it backed off, it appeared not to be in fear of the reaction but in order to show the others the effect. A horrible chattering reverberated between the creatures. "Are they discussing what to do?" wondered Grace. They started taking slow, purposeful steps in the children's direction.

And then they stopped. Frozen. Almost reflecting the lack of movement within the craft.

Max didn't know what it was so he called it by the one name that he thought was appropriate: dragon. The armour-plated scales on its back were a dark red hue, possibly allowing it a little cover against the backdrop of the red, rocky landscape, though how this huge creature could hope to remain hidden for any length of time was impossible to understand. Its tail split three ways, each end finishing in a coil it could use to wrap around and hang on to anything it desired. Its front legs also appeared to be useful for more than just walking, the seven toes on each having elongated into finger-like talons capable of gripping or slashing. Finally, its slavering mouth was packed with teeth jutting out in all directions ready to tear or crush any flesh that came its way.

In all ways this dragon was a creature to be feared. Fortunately it hadn't spotted Max, Isaac and their ship, but it did seem very interested in Connor and Grace's.

The dragon fell forward onto its front feet and upped its

pace to a gallop.

Grace and Connor felt their ship shake as the ground rumbled beneath them.

"What's that?" asked Connor, panic running through his voice.

"I don't know. An earthquake maybe? Whatever it is, it's stopped them" replied Grace, nodding her head towards the army of tormentors sat stock still outside.

Connor thought for a moment before asking, "What's an earthquake?"

"Don't you pay any attention in Earth History, it's when..."

Her voice trailed off. The creatures were running away, but that wasn't why both children had diverted their attention back outside. The dragon had suddenly appeared before them, scooping up 2 spiny-spiders in its toothsome mouth, crunching them up and gulping them down. It chased after the rest of the army, clearly mightily hungry.

"Carrie," whispered Grace, "What the deuce was that?"

"I don't care what it was," said Connor, "Just get us out of here."

"Nearly there," the computer reassured them.

The dragon was still chasing and had not looked back. The children were breathing a sigh of relief when they heard another sound echo through from the roof of the craft. Connor and Grace looked at each other and read each other's minds. Grace let her hand fall from the arm of her seat and Connor silently took hold of it, giving her a squeeze of reassurance. Again, whatever it was tapped its way to the front of the craft before dropping down on the screen in front of them. It was Isaac, Adam's robot.

"Cripes!" exclaimed Grace, "Carrie, you could have warned us, I nearly had a heart attack."

"Sorry," said the computer as she landed the other ISC in front of them, "I didn't mean to scare you."

"So what do we do, are we coming to you?" asked Connor,

already up and out of his seat.

"No," said Cary, "These ships may be fine in this atmosphere, but the suits you're wearing would dissolve before you got on board. No, Isaac is attaching some cables so we can pull you out of here."

"Well get a move on before that thing comes back then!" said Grace.

Isaac had already attached three of the five cables required and was busying himself attaching the fourth to the base of the ISC when Grace saw the dragon turn back towards them.

She unleashed an ear-piercing scream as the beast started to run in their direction. Cary mobilised the ISC but now that it was tethered to the crashed craft it had lost its manoeuvrability. Rather than being able to act as a fast moving decoy to distract the dragon's attention, it was a slow moving guidance beacon, beckoning the beast towards them.

Max was on the edge of his seat at the front of the ISC. Carrie had promised him this would be a simple rescue mission, in and out. This was not what he was expecting. "What are we going to do, Cary?" he asked, his voice wavering with fear.

"We need something to distract it."

"Why don't we shoot it?"

"We don't have anythi... Wait a moment," the computer exclaimed, "Max, you're a genius."

"Why? What did I...", he said, before Cary interrupted him.

"I need you to take hold of that joystick in front of you and aim this target," the computer said, as a small, white box appeared on the screen, "straight at the dragon. When it turns red, push the button on the top."

Max leapt to his task, training the white square on his target while Cary communicated with Isaac. The robot was finishing securing the fifth cable to the crashed ISC and Cary was preparing him for the next stage in the rescue mission.

The moment the final cable was attached Cary fired up the

thrusters to lift both machines up from the planet and away. The dragon was getting closer by the second, so close that Max desperately wanted to hit the fire button but he followed Cary's instruction and waited for the target to turn red.

The creature bowed his head, swooping down to take a bite from the hovering ISC.

At the same moment, the cables attaching the two ships drew taut, but Connor and Grace remained firmly stuck on the ground.

The target turned red and Max hit the button. A powerful jet of water fired from water cannons on either side of the ship, hitting the dragon full in the face.

The dragon recoiled, its face burning with pain. It stumbled past the twin ships, shaking its head to get rid of the water. Max couldn't keep the target on it as it disappeared out of his sight.

Cary realised that one of the legs on Connor and Grace's ship was wedged in the ground. With the dragon still a threat and the water canon not guaranteed to last, they needed to get out of there as soon as possible. The computer alerted Isaac to the problem and the small robot leapt into action.

At the same time, Cary kept watch over the dragon. He manoeuvred the ship so that Max had a clear line of sight to the beast and let the boy fire again.

The dragon had recovered from the initial burst of water. The substance was clearly highly toxic to the creature on this alien acidic planet as its face was scarred and inflamed, but it wasn't about to run away. It paused a moment, focusing its eyes on the craft moving around in front of it, before lunging forward.

Max hit the fire button and launched another flood of water straight into the creature's eyes and then down to its chest. It let out an horrific shriek. Max, Connor and Grace had to cover their ears it was so loud and terrifying.

Isaac jumped to the ground and started digging at the rock and dirt that had buried the leg of the ISC. The robot formed one arm into a shovel to clear space, the other into a pick-axe to smash through the rock. It was a difficult job but he was making progress, and far faster than any human could have.

The dragon, blinded by the toxic water in its eyes, was swiping at its face with its front legs, desperately trying to wipe away the liquid but only burning itself more. Max could see the flesh on its chest blister and bubble. He almost felt sorry for the creature, before remembering it had been attacking them without remorse. It was no longer interested in either of the craft, only in its own survival, but it was still just as dangerous; a creature that large unaware of its surroundings could do some serious damage.

Max stopped spraying the creature but Cary encouraged him to fire again, to force the creature to leave them. The boy did, hitting the legs and torso. As its feet got coated, every step the dragon took caused more and more pain. It lurched from side to side before spinning round, out of control, but still it wouldn't run away. As it span, the children all looked on in horror. Its tails were swiping closer and closer to the trapped ISC, threatening to pulverise it at any moment. Sensing the danger, Isaac clung to the leg of the ISC. Just then the dragon stumbled to his right and his tail gave the ISC an almighty whack. Connor and Grace fell in the cockpit and were terrified about the damage that might have been done.

Max was also pulled from his feet. His ISC was still connected to Connor and Grace's and the sudden force shook him. When the children had had a moment to gather their thoughts, they realised the dragon had done them a favour. The ISC was no longer embedded in the planet, but had been wrenched free.

While the dragon still staggered around in searing pain, the children made their escape, rising just as the sun started to peek over the horizon. The rescue mission had taken the whole Zulfuran night but at last they were safe. The journey back to the

Pod would take a little time so Cary cranked the music back up for Grace. The Monkees were still playing.

"What are the rules about naming places, Cary?" asked Grace.

"First come, first served, normally," replied the computer.

"So we can name the places we go to then?"

"Seems only fair."

"I'd like to name that valley," she said, surveying the land they were departing, "after this song."

For the first time, Connor focused on the lyrics to work out what Grace was suggesting. "Pleasant Valley Sunday?" he asked, confused.

"Well, just Pleasant Valley," she confirmed. Seeing his quizzical look she added, "It's ironic."

Looking behind them as Cary towed them back into space, the last thing Connor and Grace saw as they departed Pleasant Valley was a swarm of the spiny spiders attacking the collapsed dragon that had been treating them as lunch not so long ago.

Part Three
Begin The Sanguine

Travelling through space is just about the most exciting thing it is possible to do. The thrills of going where no one has gone and of seeing amazing sights that no one has set eyes upon before cannot be bettered. There is no rollercoaster, no bungee or parachute jump that can possibly compete with going into space the first time.

However, if you have lived your entire life in space, if you see planets and moons orbiting stars all the time and the places you go are just vast expanses of nothingness, it is most definitely not as exciting as it sounds. No, for someone who has spent every moment of their life in space – give or take a brief flirtation with a hostile world – the most exciting thing imaginable is making an inhabitable planet your home.

But just as a day out at an exhilarating theme park begins with an interminably long car journey, so the voyage to Baldr began with a seemingly never-ending flight, and one with no eye-catching landmarks to brighten the way.

Chapter Twelve
Moran Meets The Eye

Something was bothering Grace, and for once it wasn't Connor. She couldn't put her finger on exactly what it was though, and that bothered her even more. It was two months since their escape from Pleasant Valley and since then their lives had become routine.

Initially, Connor was constantly annoying Grace. Not on purpose, but whatever he did always seemed to rub Grace up the wrong way. To be fair, Connor felt much the same way about Grace but as far as she was concerned, that was his fault as well. If he had a little more intellectual capacity he'd soon see things her way and there wouldn't be a problem.

Connor had hoped the experiences they shared on the shipwrecked Pod and on the surface of Zulfura might help defrost their animosity, but it wasn't to be. From the moment they got back to the Pod she had made her feelings about him clear. After they docked, Adam rushed up to give her a hug, shouting "You made it, you made it!

"Just about," she replied, breathing a sigh of relief and, Connor was sure, shooting a withering look in his direction. "I'll tell you what though, even though I know we made it back perfectly safe, I wouldn't want to go through that again."

She never seemed to miss an opportunity to twist the knife a little, and while Connor acknowledged it was his fault they got into that situation, they had come through it and, in doing so, earned themselves more food and supplies, and an extra ISC. All in all, not bad. He couldn't work out why she couldn't get past it.

When it became clear that they just weren't going to get on, Connor had disappeared from view, and that's how Grace knew it wasn't him that was bothering her. She was still no nearer figuring out what was, though, so she decided to find out what Connor had been doing with himself, and maybe offer some kind of olive branch.

She found him on the landing deck, on his back beneath the broken ISC they'd shared on their eventful voyage.

"Hey Connor, we haven't talked in ages, what are you working on?" She put a smile in her voice and hoped that he heard it. Her hopes were dashed when all she got back was a grunted acknowledgement of her presence. "Connor, I'm trying to be nice. What are you doing?"

He pulled himself out from under the ship. Grease and oil covered his hands, face and overalls, Grace could even see it streaked through his hair.

"I'm just trying to get this ship ship-shape again. It's still a couple of weeks away from flying." He made sure his voice conveyed the fact that he didn't appreciate the interruption.

Grace, for her part, made sure she didn't show any signs of annoyance with his tone. She told herself to take the high road.

"Wow, I didn't know you were so mechanically minded, that's really impressive." And she was genuinely impressed. Even if his attitude stunk and he had the manners of a boar at least he was proving himself useful.

"Well, I'm learning while I work. Cary's teaching me how to put it all together. Still a long way to go though." He was trying to get the message across that he wanted to get back to it but Grace just wasn't biting.

"That's excellent, Connor," said Grace, "I think it's really good that you're training yourself up for the good of the crew."

He was doing it for two reasons and neither of them involved the good of the crew. One was to stave off the boredom which had rapidly settled in once they had returned to the Pod, and the other was to escape from Grace's patronising ways. He decided it was best not to share that with her though.

"So what's this?" Grace asked, kicking her left foot out in the direction of a large, grease-covered metal box that was sitting beside the ISC.

Connor sighed. It was clear she wasn't going to get the hint to move along, and was instead going to question him. He decided he had to do something about it. "It's the artificial gravity unit. I had to take it out to get to some of the mechanical parts that weren't working. Anyway Grace, I need to get back on with this, I was in the middle of something."

"Oh sure, you go ahead," she replied. But she didn't move away. If anything, it appeared she was going to watch him work. He sighed again and pulled himself back under the ship.

Grace stared at the various tools and spare parts lying around, picked up a clean rag and cleaned off the edge of the gravity unit. She had seen what looked to be a plaque on the side of it and, her curiosity piqued, decided to find out what it said.

"Moran Foundation Mini A.G.U."

"Moran Foundation? You're so lame." She turned on her heel and started to walk away, part of her hoping she'd struck enough of a nerve to...

"What? What are you talking about?"

Yes, it appeared she had.

"Your plaque on the AGU, so lame, you didn't make it." She almost spat the words out.

"I have no idea what you're talking about." He had pulled himself out from under the ship and was stood, hands on hips, looking at her like she was crazy.

"There," she pointed, "there on the side, you've attached a plaque, Moran Foundation."

He looked down at the unit. He had done no such thing; he hadn't even cleaned it off. "That's weird," he said. He picked up the rag and cleaned it further, revealing a further inscription.

"Model: 8G-4-16"
"Unit Number: 27F46-06F47-9D76-TVC15"

"Wow. It looks like I share a name with the people who made this. That's cool." He shrugged his shoulders and turned back towards the ship.

"So you didn't..."

He turned and shook his head at her in a pitying manner.

"Carrie!"

"There's no need to shout, Grace," said the computer.

"The Moran Foundation didn't really make this, did they?" She was telling the computer rather than asking a question, delighting in the moment she'd get Connor caught out in a stupid lie.

"No, they didn't make it."

Grace almost stuck her tongue out at Connor, she was so pleased to get one over on him.

"They invented it and licensed the design. Well, he did."

"What?" Grace was incredulous. Connor just looked up at her, smiling smugly; he didn't have to say anything.

"Yes, Professor Marco Moran invented the artificial gravity unit and sold the technology. Every product he invented would have his name and logo on it, it was a gold standard."

Grace didn't know what to say. She looked like she was going to explode with rage, but she didn't want to give Connor the satisfaction. She only had herself to blame. She stood for a moment as if on the verge of bursting before turning on her heel and storming off. Connor watched her go, taking a silent victory from every one of her stamped footsteps, before lying back down and sliding himself under the ISC to finish his day's work.

Now Grace knew what was bothering her, and this time it was Connor. Well, maybe not him directly, maybe herself, her misguided attack on him and the way she had allowed him to get under her skin. She sat down in her room, turned the lights down low and got Cary to play some classical music for her. She tried to free her mind and release her frustrations. She failed. Connor's smug face was all she could picture, and she needed to get rid of it.

She called her brother.

*   *   *   *   *

Two weeks after the children had fled Zulfura, Max was doing little but eat and sleep. The exhilaration of his victory on the planet's surface and the rescue of his brother and Grace had been short-lived and he soon found himself with neither the energy nor the motivation to do anything at all. After all, what was the point? His parents were gone, and he was stranded in a small ship in the middle of space, millions of miles from anyone except his four ship-bound companions.

Evelyn had done her best to rouse him but he wasn't interested. She had tried devising games, found his favourite music and movies, she even tried dressing up in a rudimentary clown costume for him but he barely batted an eyelid in her direction. Looking out for Max was her way of making sure she didn't end up like him; it was a welcome, and necessary, distraction.

However, no one could have guessed what it would be that would finally get the boy out of bed and smiling again.

The Pod kept a clock in sync with The Magellan's earth-based time-cycle and the children had, for the most part, slept at 'night' and been awake during the 'day'. Max had not. He had been sleeping and waking in patches, whenever the feeling took him. At 5am one day, long before anyone else was up, he opened his eyes and found himself staring at a shiny metal dome peeping up over the edge of the bed. It took him a moment to focus and another moment to realise what it was he was looking at. It was Isaac.

He hadn't seen the robot since he returned from Zulfura. In fact, he had completely forgotten about its existence, hence his delay in recognising the machine. His face lit up.

"Isaac," he said, a note of delight in his voice.

"Hello Max," the robot replied.

"I haven't seen you in ages, how are you?"

Max sat up on the edge of the bed to continue the conversation. He asked Isaac about everything Adam had been teaching him, about what he liked and disliked on the ship, and about what everyone had been doing. He didn't know why but he found it easy to talk to the robot. He knew he wasn't being judged, and he certainly wasn't being pestered like his sister always seemed to. He knew she meant well, but he hadn't wanted her attention, he'd just wanted to be left alone. But something was different about talking to Isaac. He was able to relax, and as he did he felt a weight being lifted.

Isaac was more than happy to talk with the boy. Normally overnight he was bored, no one was awake and, while it could be fun to test out all the different skills Adam had given him, he preferred interacting with people. Eventually he remembered some of the manners Adam had tried to teach him and asked after Max.

"So how have you been, Max?"

The weight descended back down on Max. He had been enjoying himself and had managed to forget a lot of his troubles. With that one simple question, he'd been reminded of everything that had been bringing him down. He was silent for a moment, before deciding that it would be rude to ignore Isaac after he had been so nice in talking to him for the past half an hour.

"I've not been very happy," he said, and as he said it he felt a little better.

"Why not?" Isaac asked, his face frowning in concern.

"Adam told you about the Magellan, right? Our home." Isaac nodded and Max continued, "Well, my parents died when it blew up, and I've been missing them."

The weight was lifting again. He began to realise that maybe keeping all this stored up inside of him was part of the reason he was feeling so miserable. He started to explain everything that he'd been thinking and feeling since they'd returned from Zulfura. He explained to Isaac exactly what parents were and what they had meant to him. Isaac was confused at first but then Max explained that Adam could be thought of as his father, the robot started to understand what that kind of loss could mean.

Max told him about why his parents were special and told his favourite stories about the fun they had had together. Isaac just listened, taking it all in and nodding or asking prompting questions when necessary. Adam had tried to teach him everything he was capable of doing and about his environment and their trip, but now he felt he was learning more than ever. He was learning about being human. He was learning what friendship and family and love meant. These were things that couldn't be programmed, for a robot they could only be taught through experience and observation, and Max was providing a perfect lesson for him.

Isaac could see that Max was becoming more animated, his mood was improving and by the end of his storytelling he was positively beaming. His mind was filled with happy memories of his family and he just couldn't stop himself from smiling. He was still sad that they were gone but he was thankful for the fun they had enjoyed together.

*   *   *   *   *

Since the journey to Speropolis had begun, Evelyn had slowly retreated into herself, almost mirroring the behaviour of her younger brother. Back on The Magellan she had always been outgoing and adventurous but she'd never been in any real danger. The events since The Shark had appeared had brought into harsh reality how much danger they were truly in. Now she was painfully aware of the inherent risks involved in anything she did. Upon their initial arrival on the Pod she had distracted herself by caring for Max but as he hid himself from reality she was only left with herself for company. The images of the engine rooms exploding and the poor engineer falling to his certain death kept appearing in her daydreams and nightmares, and slowly she cut herself off.

When she wasn't haunted by the horrific visions of her home being destroyed, she was thinking about what her life was and how it had changed. She thought about Dex and everything they used to do together. She thought about school and her other friends, but most of all she thought about her parents and she still blamed herself. If she and Dex hadn't gone off exploring, maybe her parents could have saved themselves instead of having to rescue them. Maybe then they'd have been onboard the Pod, or better yet, could have done something to ward off The Shark. There were so many ifs and maybes, but all of them came down to the fact that she had been irresponsible and that, if she hadn't been, everything could have been different.

Her train of thought was distracted one morning when Adam came barging into her room unannounced.

"Have you seen Isaac?" the boy asked, without even so much as an 'excuse me'.

"Who?" She couldn't even remember the robot at this point, let alone its name.

Adam impatiently described Isaac before realising that the lack of recognition clearly meant she can't have known where the thing was. He turned and made his way back out the door.

"Adam?" she said, halting his departure, "Do you ever think that if you'd done things differently, maybe none of this would have happened?"

He contemplated her question for a moment. "No. The Shark was too powerful. Nothing anyone on board could have done would have changed things." And then he left.

Evelyn sat and thought on what he'd said. She still felt guilty, but what if Adam was right? Her parents were smart and important. If they hadn't been spending their time saving her, maybe they could have done something. She debated this for a while before following Adam out of the room.

When she got into the main living quarters Adam was leaving Max's room and wasn't looking happy.

"Adam, I..." her voice trailed off, not wanting to ask her question after seeing Adam's face. "What's wrong? Did you find Isaac?"

"Yes, he's just spending some time with your brother."

"Connor?"

"No, Max. They seem to be having fun."

"Well that's good," said Evelyn. She was pleased Max was actually doing something now.

"Yeah, I guess so," said Adam reluctantly.

"So why don't we do something?" She could see that Adam needed cheering up and, as she was in need of company herself since Max had shut himself away, it seemed like the best solution for everyone. Before he could reply she grabbed him by the hand and dragged him towards the bowels of the Pod.

Over the next few weeks Evelyn and Adam spent more and more time together. Evelyn saw Adam as a project, something to keep her mind away from where it had been. Every so often she would probe him for more of his thoughts about The Shark and his answers always reassured her. Her guilt gently ebbed away and she began to enjoy herself. She was also regaining her confidence and adventurousness.

Adam could never have been considered an action man, but he enjoyed being lead around the corridors and vents of the Pod by Evelyn. He was doing things he had never imagined he would do, but in doing them he was learning things. He got to see firsthand how the engines worked and he spent some time explaining it all to Evelyn. She didn't understand any of it, but she could see how he came alive when he started talking about the technical details and so she let him go on. It made her happy that he was happy and that was what counted. They were an odd pair, with seemingly nothing in common, but in these extraordinary circumstances they were a huge help to each other.

Evelyn was waiting for Adam at a place they called The Lookout – a small area of decking by the main thrusters. A window let them look out into space, surveying everything they were flying away from. They could spend hours sitting there, talking. Adam was running late when Grace called her brother in to see her.

"What is it, Grace?" he asked wearily as he walked through the door.

"Do you know who Marco Moran is?" she replied, cutting straight to the point.

"He's only one of the greatest scientists and inventors ever. Come on sis, you've heard of him. He's up there with Da Vinci, Newton and Einstein."

"Oh no." She hadn't just made a mistake, she'd made a massive mistake. This could get humiliating.

"Why? Do you think the others are related? That'd be so cool."

"No, I..." She hadn't considered it before, but now she was filled with dread. What if they were? She'd already made a complete fool of herself with Connor.

"Carrie, are the others related to Marco Moran?" asked the boy.

The computer only took a moment to come back with the answer.

"He's their great, great, great Uncle. Well, enough greats to go back three-hundred years. Eight greats to be precise." And Carrie was rarely anything but.

"Cool! We've got to tell them," shouted Adam.

"No, no, no, no, no," said Grace, trying to hide herself from further humiliation but Adam was already summoning the others to the bridge.

Chapter Thirteen
Star Man

"To call Marco Moran a one-off would be an understatement. It has been said that he alone moved science forward two-hundred years, solving problems people thought impossible."

Carrie had found a video in the archives that explored Marco Moran's life and career and everyone was paying rapt attention, even if Grace tried to hide it. Back on The Magellan, Connor would have been bored by the history lesson but the combination of circumstance, his relationship to Marco and the anguish it was clearly putting Grace through made the video all the more enthralling.

"Dubbed the Miracle Man, his prodigious talent was noticed very early in life. At age four he was already correcting his teachers and textbooks. He was at Cambridge University studying quantum physics aged eleven but never completed his degree."

A wild- and white-haired man in his thirties appeared on the screen. A caption announced him as "Marco Moran, interviewed in 2284".

"There really wasn't any point in continuing," he said. His voice carried a strange inflection, occasionally wavering between high and low. There was something almost other-worldly about him, aided by his strange, almost mystical, differently-coloured eyes. "A year into my degree I sat down with Professor Goodwin, my mentor, and discussed what I planned to do. We agreed there and then that I would cease studying and begin research. I never completed a formal qualification."

"Within two years," the voiceover continued, "he had completed work on the world's first artificial gravity unit."

Professor Mordecai Goodwin, an elderly gentleman with a big, bushy white beard, filled the screen. "That first AGU was huge, far too big to be practical. You couldn't take it into space, no, no. But the point was, he had done it. No one thought it possible to create an artificial gravitational field. It just, it just blew everyone away. To put it into context, it was another ten years before anyone else even understood how it worked."

"Another two years later, aged 16 now, and he had shrunk the AGU down so it would fit in a shoe box."

The smaller AGU was presented on screen and Connor immediately saw the similarities between it and the one he had removed from the ISC.

"From that moment on, the media scrutinised everything he did. Suddenly he had made the impossible possible and everyone wanted to know what was next on his agenda."

Professor Goodwin again, "Marco hated the intrusion, he just wanted to be left to work. With the money the AGU generated he set up the Moran Foundation and adopted more and more idiosyncratic methods. If he needed parts built he would subcontract different things to different companies so no one would be able to figure out what he might be attempting. His staff were kept in the dark, they just did as they were told. He was the quintessential mad scientist.

"He invited me to his labs about once a year. He never showed me anything I could comprehend, you understand. But then I'm not sure he was working on anything that would have made sense to me, even if he'd tried to explain it, it was such a... a quantum leap."

A nineteen year-old Marco walks out onto a podium in front of a large crowd of journalists. Even at that young age, the crazy hair is perfectly obvious, though not yet the white of his thirties.

"I realise that in the three years since I finished work on the AGU there has been intense speculation about my next project. I can now reveal that, subject to governmental approval, I intend to have a fully functioning space elevator in place by the start of 2272."

A ripple of amazement went around the audience along with a few gasps.

"Pause," said Connor, and the film did. "OK, what's a space elevator?"

"Well," said Adam, getting ready for a long and detailed explanation before being cut off by Grace. She wanted to reassert her intelligence. Plus she knew that Adam would get far too in-depth and technical for anyone else.

"Essentially," she said, "You have a long cable stretching from a planet's surface to some kind of counterweight in geostationary orbit."

"And what's that?" asked Evelyn.

"It's where an object or satellite orbits a planet directly above one point, so that, relative to the planet, it's not moving. So anyway, the space elevator enables the easy manoeuvring of people and objects from the planet's surface into space and back again."

"Well can't we easily just use an ISC or whatever for that?"

"This is 300 years ago, they didn't have ISCs back then." Grace's impatience was showing. "Right, can we get back to the video now?"

"You've missed something out, sis," said Adam. Grace did not appreciate his input. "They built one back in the 21st century. It worked perfectly for 3 years but then the cables snapped. Thousands of people were killed by falling parts that were being taken up into space. No one had even thought about attempting anything like it since, that's why it was such a big deal."

"Fine. And back to the video now?"

Carrie started it playing again.

"Once the space elevator is in place," Marco Moran continued once the noise in the auditorium had quietened down, "I shall be able to complete my research into D.M.E., at which point I shall be able to reveal to you my findings."

And after that short speech he left the stage leaving the assembled masses to ponder what on earth – or what in space – D.M.E. was.

Newspaper headlines flashed across the screen - "SPACE ELEVATOR MAKES MORAN THE STAR MAN" - "MORAN GOES TO SPACE AND BEYOND!" - "WHAT IS DME? IS MORAN CROSSING DIMENSIONS?"

More footage from the interview in 2284 followed. "Everyone was so desperate to know what I was working on, so I told them. Anything more would have been like trying to explain the internal combustion engine to a Roman."

The interviewer asked a question from off-screen, "But you could have told them, told us, what your inventions would do, you didn't need to explain how they worked."

"But it was all hypothetical. I didn't know whether they would work or not. Not for certain." A smile crossed his face. "And besides, the beauty of them is how they work, not what they do. If anyone would have understood the 'how', I would have happily explained it." And he let out a laugh, his face coming alive, making him seem like a different person.

"Well is there anything you can tell us about what you're working on now?"

"All I can say is that I've nicknamed the project The Dream Genie."

"You won't say anything more?"

"Do you know what a Gordian Warp Loop is?"

"No, I... No I don't."

"Then you wouldn't understand."

The film continued to explain DME, or Dark Matter Engineering. 96% of the universe is composed of a combination of what scientists call dark matter and dark energy. It was called dark because nobody could find it, but it had to be there for the forces in the universe to work. People had tried to find it and failed for so long that some wondered if anyone ever would. Until Marco Moran showed up, of course. Then the question became not if, but when.

Marco's work produced large ships that could fly the length and breadth of the solar system in days and weeks, not the decades that it previously took. Along the way, Marco invented many new materials, including the zirgenesium Adam had used to build Isaac and the cloth used to produce the flight suits Grace and Connor had worn when they left the Pod. In fact, it turned out that virtually everything on board owed some debt to the work of Marco Moran.

However, after listing all the ingenious breakthroughs Marco was responsible for, the documentary took a more sombre tone. There was no video footage of Marco subsequent to the 2284 interview, pictures were in black and white, people were more downbeat in what they had to say.

"In 2290, when he was 40, Moran married a woman who had studied under him, 25 year-old Simona Silmenkova. Again, media speculation was intense. No one had heard Silmenkova's name before. Would she hold this genius back, distract him? Would she inspire him to even further greatness?

"These photographs," the voiceover continued, over pictures Moran and a short and equally wild-haired woman being showered in confetti, "were the first photographs of Simona Silmenkova and the last photographs released to the public of Marco Moran. After the wedding, the pair disappeared into his laboratories and worked in isolation of the rest of the world. Were they working on the Dream Genie that Moran had so enigmatically referred to in his last interview, conducted six years earlier? No one will ever know.

"Moran had had next to nothing to do with his staff in the previous 18 months, but at the beginning of March 2292, he had sent them all on paid leave, meaning that only he and Simona were left working in the building. Vendic Coff was the last man to see Moran alive."

A young man in a white lab coat sat surrounded by equipment which, to the eyes of the children, looked outmoded. "He would have us build pieces and deliver them. We'd rarely speak to him or even see him. We never knew what they were for, but there was palpable excitement building. We knew that, whatever it was, it was almost complete. When he came and told me to move everyone out for the foreseeable future, there wasn't fear or concern in his eyes. He was excited. It was like seeing a little kid get his first hover bike. He was about to test whatever it was we'd all been working on and he wanted privacy for those tests."

The voiceover picked up the story once more, "On the 15th of March, 2292, a huge explosion ripped through the Moran Foundation's laboratories. Whatever the Dream Genie was, it had been an experiment too far and it had taken his and his young bride's lives. Investigators examined the site for wreckage but it appears everything involved had been vaporised. Moran's last project will forever be a mystery."

"Wow," said Connor. "And to think, we're related to him." He looked over to his siblings, then Grace, and smiled.

"What do you think the Dream Genie was?" said Evelyn.

"I think it was something that could read your dreams and bring them to life," said Max. "I mean, what else could it be with a name like that?"

"Bring them to life? That would just be dangerous. What if you dreamt of snakes or dragons or something?" said Evelyn.

"And there wouldn't be enough room in the universe to fit

everyone's dreams into," said Grace.

"Maybe it could just film your dreams," suggested Connor.

"Well, why would that blow up and vaporise everything?" asked Adam. "I don't think it had anything to do with recording your dreams. He liked teasing people, I bet it had nothing to do with that."

"Oh, you bet, do you?" said Connor, "Well seeing as we're never going to find out, I think you're money's safe." He gave Adam a fake smile just in case the sarcasm wasn't enough.

"Oh shut up, Connor," said Grace.

"You're just jealous because we're related to him and you're not."

"Oh, will you two please stop bickering!" pleaded an exasperated Evelyn. "All the time you're going on and on at each other and it's soooo boring. You're supposed to be the mature ones. Max is more mature than you."

"Yeah, I'm more mature than you two!" said Max.

Grace and Connor looked at each other and stormed off in opposite directions. Adam, Evelyn and Max all burst out laughing at them. When the laughter eventually died down, Max asked, "What does mature mean?"

Chapter Fourteen
The Mother Ship

As the days turned into weeks and the weeks turned into months, life on board the Pod became the norm for the children. They obviously missed the space the Magellan granted them, but they adapted to their surroundings and even came to like them.

Evelyn and Adam explored every inch of the ship. Adam made a mental inventory of all the equipment and technology on board and took pleasure in pointing out to Evelyn just how much of it had been invented by her great uncle Marco. The Lookout was still their favourite spot though, staring out into the depths of space.

They dangled their legs from the end of the platform while Evelyn admired the myriad stars lining the infinite darkness. "I almost don't like thinking about how many there are," she said, "It's scary to think the universe is that massive."

"You know, back on Earth, hundreds of years ago, they used the stars for navigation," said Adam. "They knew which stars you should see from different parts of the planet at different times of year and from that could work out which direction they needed to head."

This was how many of their conversations would go; not quite talking to each other, but certainly not ignoring each other.

"Really? So just by what they saw in the sky they knew where they were and which way to go to get to the shops or to school?"

"Well, not quite. It was more for boats travelling from one

country to another. Big journeys."

"That's still pretty cool though," said Evelyn.

"Yeah. They'd travel for years across seas in boats to find new places and they'd have to find their way home again."

"A bit like us, I suppose." They both sat in silence, pondering the similarities. "But how did they know which star was which?"

"They'd look for groups of bright stars that made a shape or pattern and give them names based on what they looked like, like the plough."

"So what are they called?" She pointed out a constellation twinkling away at them.

"They don't have a name. They only named the patterns they could see from Earth." They sat and stared at the stars a little longer, soaking up the magnitude of their view. "So what do you think they look like then?" Adam asked her.

"I was just trying to decide that. What about you?"

"They remind me of a molecule of nitrogen dioxide."

"That's what I was going to say," Evelyn said, tongue firmly in cheek, "but I don't think it's a very good name, do you?"

"Probably not."

Evelyn traced her finger along the lines created by the seven stars she had identified as her constellation. "Hmmm..." A picture was forming in her mind's eye. "I suppose... it kind of looks like... oh, what's it called?" She took her mind back to school, struggling to place the name of the creature. "I know! It looks like an eagle."

Adam gave her a sideways glance. He didn't see the similarity himself.

"No, really. That one, top left, is the head," she said, pointing it out to him. She drew the shape of the body, then the wing and the leg and it became clear to Adam.

They sat in silence again. Evelyn was looking for more constellations that she could name but she was failing to draw another coherent picture. Adam was trying to think what other fascinating facts about stars he might be able to impress his new friend with. He was more successful than Evelyn was with the constellations.

"People used to think that they could predict what would happen to them according to when they were born and where the stars were."

"That doesn't make any sense. Why would the stars tell the future?"

"I think it was from when people didn't understand the universe."

Adam didn't really know the answer but he liked the role he had with Evelyn as the font of all knowledge. She had a lot of questions and he was more than happy to try to answer them. In turn, it comforted her to know there was someone on board who could.

"Do you think there's any way to know the future? Not by the stars or anything stupid like that, but, you know, some way?"

"What do you want for dinner tonight?"

"What are you talking about?"

"Seriously, what do you want for dinner?"

Evelyn was confused. Adam would always set his mind to her questions, not ignore her completely. "I don't know, pizza?"

"OK, so what if I told you you'll have fish."

She scrunched up her nose. "I don't like fish."

"But that's your future, that's what you're going to have."

Evelyn shrugged her shoulders and turned away from him. "I'll just choose something else."

"So you'd rather live in a world where you can choose what happens, rather than know what happens, whether it's bad or good?"

She turned back, suddenly understanding what he was getting at. "I suppose." She thought about it for a moment. "But if I knew something bad was going to happen, couldn't I just change it? Do things differently?"

"Well if that were the case, you wouldn't know the future, would you?"

She thought again, before shaking her head.

"I don't believe in destiny," he continued, "because I want the things I do to have meaning and for me to have a choice. If you know the future, you have no choice and no meaning."

Evelyn looked back out into space, pondering Adam's words. She wasn't totally certain she had understood him – after all, what did he mean when he said you'd have no meaning? – but she certainly didn't like the idea of not having a choice.

Adam looked out and surveyed the stars too. "This way, we can still visit any of those stars. Anything can happen."

Connor was taking pride in his handiwork repairing the crashed ISC. He felt he had learned more in the short time on the Pod than in all his years in school. Finally he was developing some practical skills. He was more than a little nervous the first time he piloted the machine back out into space but everything worked absolutely perfectly. He even started thinking about making some upgrades to both ISCs, increasing their speed and handling. And since Evelyn's dressing down, he'd actually started to get on with Grace. Granted, they weren't bosom buddies, but they could tolerate spending time with each other. He'd even taken Grace out for a few lessons in piloting the ISCs. She hadn't been bad. She hadn't been good either, but she hadn't been bad and Connor had to give her a little bit of respect for that.

For Max, things were a little different. While he had made friends with Isaac, he was still finding it difficult with the others. At first he even shied away from Evelyn and Connor, he didn't want to answer their questions and deflected their concern. They stopped trying to interrogate him and slowly he came out of his shell with them. Adam and Grace were still eyed with suspicion though. Evelyn tried to convince him to come exploring with her and Adam but he refused. In the end a swap was performed –

Adam got Isaac back while Evelyn would show Max their latest discoveries.

Connor enjoyed spending time with his brother and sister too. Back on The Magellan they had tended to spend time with friends of their own ages and minimal time with each other. Now they were taking the opportunity to catch up. Connor naturally had to show off his work on the ISC and happily took them out for flights whenever they wanted.

Grace, on the other hand, had tried to spend time with her brother but he only seemed interested in working on Isaac or running off with Evelyn. Outside of the occasionally uncomfortable time she spent with Connor, she was pretty much left on her own. In many ways, it was like being back on the Magellan. She had never had many friends and was always trying to get ahead at school, but at least there was a world around her. Here she was so much more isolated. She still read and still gave herself lessons but she was much more aware of how cut off she was. She would sit and stare out of the windows for hours, her eyes would glaze over and, instead of contemplating her position, she just felt. Tears would roll from her eyes and she would wallow, blocking everything else out. And when the spell was broken and she brought herself back to reality she would hide her tear-stained cheeks and puffy eyes from the others.

They were closing in on Speropolis when Grace finally realised what she needed to do. At first it was just a vague idea. All she knew was that she wanted to commemorate her parents somehow. Like a statue or a plaque or something but she couldn't put her finger on what form, exactly, this memorial should take. Of course she knew that ultimately it would be a futile gesture. It wouldn't actually *do* anything. She knew that her parents would live on inside her whether or not a piece of metal on the wall bore their names. She had dwelt on the subject for nearly a week, trying to work out exactly what was to be done, and also trying to work out why she felt it was so necessary. In the end the answers came at exactly the same time. In fact, they came in the same sentence.

Carrie had been cajoling Adam into spending more time with his sister for some time but the boy had been revelling in his new friendship with Evelyn and had declined all invitations. He finally relented when Max plucked up the courage to ask if Isaac could join him on the next stage of exploration. In truth, Isaac had been keen to see more of the ship too but it was Max who made the request. Adam was left on his own and, without prompting, decided to pay his sister a visit.

He didn't knock or announce himself, he just marched straight into her room catching her unawares. She had adopted what was, for her, a familiar pose, chin resting on the palm of her right hand, staring out at Baldr in the distance, a tear rolling down her left cheek. She didn't notice him until he broke the silence.

"Hey sis, what are you looking at?"

She jumped, embarrassed, and wiped her cheek. She sniffed, trying to cover her emotions. "Oh, you know, just looking out at our final destination."

"Are you cry... Why are you crying?"

"I'm not." She sniffed again, and realised that must have sounded ridiculous. "I was just thinking about mum and dad. And home. I was thinking about home."

"This pod is our home now, Grace," he said, moving to her side, "and you have to put everything else behind you and accept that."

If there was one thing that Adam could be relied on for, it was to be direct and to the point. Grace laughed, even as more tears sprang from her. "How old are you? Twelve? And here you are giving me this worldly advice." She leaned into him and gave him a hug. She knew it would make him uncomfortable but it was what she needed. He knew it too, and he gave her a hug and a squeeze back. And that was when it came to her, what the answer was.

Two hours later, the whole crew were seated in the lounge, waiting for her announcement. With the exception of Adam, none of them really wanted to be there but Grace had insisted they all sit down together and listen to her.

"We've been living on board this Pod for nearly four months now. It's our home, at least until we reach Speropolis." She saw some eyes roll and figured she needed to cut to the chase. "I think we need to name this pod, make it truly ours."

She saw the others perk up. They actually seemed to like the idea.

"And I suppose you've got an idea for what we should call it," said Connor.

"Well," said Grace, and again noticed Connor rolling his eyes, "I kinda thought we could maybe name it in honour of our parents."

"That's a great idea, Grace," said Evelyn. The mood changed and now they were all buying into the idea, even Connor, though he wasn't quite as enthused as the others.

"So we've got four names," he interjected, "how are we going to turn that into one name for the ship?"

"Well I don't know. I thought we could discuss it, come up with some ideas together," replied Grace, finally feeling part of the crew.

The children batted ideas around between them. Naturally each family tended towards their own parent's names being more prominent in the final choice – the Leungs' parents were Lucas and Anna, the Morans', Laurie and Maria. They ruled out a single name early on, they were never going to get agreement on that, but it was so difficult to find something that sounded right and honoured both their families. Connor's suggestion of Lauria, a combination of both his parents' names, was laughed out by all of them, while Max's sweet offering of "Mum & Dad" was turned down in a slightly more diplomatic fashion.

"I know," said Evelyn, "What about The Anna-Maria? It's

both our mums' names together."

The suggestion got some nods around the table. It was certainly the best idea so far but no one was completely sold on it. They all sat in silence, pondering it.

"You're onto something," agreed Grace, "but how about swapping it round?"

"The Maria-Anna? That's stupid," said Connor.

"No, The Marianna. One word. I think it's perfect."

They all looked at each other, nodding their heads in agreement. The Marianna it was.

They started to get up to leave, happy with the resolution they had come to, when Adam cleared his throat and asked "What about our dads?"

They all stopped, mid-move, before sitting back down in silence. They all knew they should try to do something for their fathers but they were completely stumped as to what it should be. And then it came to Connor.

"We've got two ISCs, we could name one after each."

It was agreed. The ships were all named and everyone was happy with the outcome.

Three days later, Connor took it upon himself to summon everyone to a meeting of his own, but this one happened down on the flight deck. He was grinning to himself at the surprises he had in store as they slowly trudged their way down to meet him. He greeted the five of them (Isaac had come too) behind the two ISCs, which were both pointing towards the doors. They all knew he had kept himself busy over the past few days but no one knew what he had been up to.

"Ladies and gentlemen," he announced, bowing, "Welcome to a very special day for all of us." The children all looked at one another, wondering what on earth he was talking about. "I could dress this event up with a lot of fancy words..."

"No you couldn't," said Max. He was feeling much more

at ease with every day that passed and he enjoyed the hearty laughter that greeted his joke.

Connor didn't appreciate the interruption. This was serious. "Anyway," he continued. "You're wondering what I could possibly have called you all down here for. Well, if you would like to follow me, and without further ado, it gives me a very great pleasure to present to you all..."

They had followed him round to the front of the ISCs and for a first time saw what he had been up to. He was now stood between the two ships and hanging on the front of each, above the windows, was a piece of red cloth. In each of Connor's hands he held a piece of thin rope connecting to one of the pieces of cloth.

"... the newest members of Earth's Space Fleet, Laurie and Lucas." And with a flourish he pulled the ropes and the cloth came down. On the front of each craft he had attached a golden name plate, elegantly decorated and seemingly hand engraved. None of them had expected him to have produced such a beautiful statement in honour of their parents and they all applauded his effort.

"Come on then, who wants to come for a ride?"

The doors on each craft opened and Connor gestured his brother and sister into Laurie, and Grace, Adam and Isaac into Lucas, families together. Laurie, the craft named after Connor's father, was also the machine that Connor had rebuilt. It still bore the dents and scratches from their trip to Zulfura, but in Connor's mind they only added to the character. Mechanically, it was a fine machine and he felt only right that it should be his.

Once they had all sat down and buckled themselves in, the doors to the flight deck opened and the craft set off. Connor was piloting Laurie and Grace gingerly took command of Lucas. Connor lead them out and flew round to the front of The Marianna where the children all saw what he had managed to do. A piece of cloth hung on the front of the ship, with a length of rope attached.

His voice came over the radio, "Grace, would you like to do the honours?"

She was confused. "Er, how?"

"Cary, give her control of the arm."

A mechanical arm extended from the front of Lucas a few feet and then stopped.

"Grace," said Cary, "you can now control the arm."

Grace gripped the control stick and tried to guide the arm towards the rope. She wasn't as smooth as she would have liked but she made it there. The hand on the front grasped the rope and Grace gave a short, sharp tug on the stick, dislodging the cloth which seemed to flutter away from the ship as if caught in a breeze, even though that was impossible.

From behind the cloth, the final part of Connor's elaborate work was revealed, another large nameplate declaring the ship to be called The Marianna. Once again, it was beautiful work. Grace even had to brush away a tear, she was so overcome with emotion.

The children sat on board Laurie and Lucas for some time, remembering their parents and admiring Connor's work, none of them wanting to be the one to break the spell.

*   *   *   *   *

There was only one person who could ask the question that Carrie had been dreading, and that was Adam. He was the most logical and direct of the children. As such, he would probably be the one to take the news best, but the others would have to know too and before long the computer would have to deal with a very serious situation.

Adam sidled up to the main console and started checking the star charts and maps. They were only two weeks away from arriving in Speropolis, the end of their journey and their new home, and, as he periodically did, he wanted to check on their progress.

"Carrie?"

The computer could tell from the tone of his voice that the time had come. "Yes, Adam?" she said.

"Have you made radio contact with anyone in Speropolis yet?"

"I..." she started, but she was cut off.

"I mean, they need to know what's happened, they need to be expecting us and they need to know about the danger out there."

"Yes Adam, I..."

"I should have thought of it a while back. I mean, we really should warn them in case The Shark turns up there, too."

"Adam, please," the computer pleaded. She paused. It was though she was taking a deep breath even though, as a computer, she had no need to. "I've been trying to reach them. I've been trying for weeks. There's been no reply."

"You've been trying for weeks? And you didn't say anything?"

"Of course I wanted to, Adam, I just didn't know how to raise the subject, how to tell you. Tell all of you."

Adam was shocked. He didn't know what to say. He let the news sink in. He had been so preoccupied spending time with Evelyn he hadn't even thought about contacting the city.

"Well," he said, pausing, still collecting his thoughts, "Well, what do we do now?"

"We need to tell the others," said Carrie.

It came as no surprise that none of the children took the news well. They had all been excited to be arriving in Speropolis; a new city to explore, and, for the first time in their lives, a home that was a real planet with a real sky above their heads and real solid ground beneath their feet.

"Do we even bother going there?" asked Grace, "I mean, what's the point?"

"We have to go there," explained Carrie. "We have food, but it won't last forever. We need to get to a place we can restock and there's nowhere else that's in range."

"Is Speropolis even still there? Or has it been destroyed like The Magellan?" asked Connor.

They all looked at each other. It was a very valid question, and a very scary one. If all the humans and all the technology that was within reach had been destroyed then that was it. It was over. It would just be the five of them, stranded forever.

Carrie quickly reassured them. The city was still standing. She showed them all live pictures of the dome of the city poking up above a huge forest like a colossal egg.

"So they could still be alive," said Evelyn excitedly.

"Well yes, in theory they could be," said the computer, "but it's very unlikely that their radio equipment would be unable to broadcast."

Adam took over. "Carrie's right, we have to accept that in all probability there's no one on that planet to meet us, but there's loads of technology there, we'll be able to contact other settlements, replenish our supplies and plan our future. We've got to make the best of this."

They all sat in silent contemplation. They each knew that while Adam was right, they had to accept that their chances of ever seeing another human were getting slimmer.

Part Four
The 'H' Word

The City of Speropolis was not built in a day. It was on September 19th, 2556, that the first human set foot on Baldr, more than 20 years before the children arrived on the planet, and it had taken six months to construct the massive dome on the planet's surface. The city was contained entirely within the dome, allowing the new residents of the planet the opportunity to settle in exclusion from the local flora and fauna. Having learnt the lessons of humankind's mistreatment of Earth, the plan was to ensure that the impact of the settlers was kept to a minimum.

The dome – the city – offered an ideal self-contained world in which those left behind could start afresh. It was built between a lake, an open plain and a forest, a location chosen due to the ideal opportunities afforded both human life – a fresh water supply being vital – and scientific research. As time went by and the new residents settled, the intention was to come out of hiding and explore further afield. If other, even more suitable locations were not found, Baldr would be a good location to start again, but the hope was that, ultimately, it would merely be a stop on the way to a planet even more perfect for human colonisation.

Baldr itself was a significantly larger planet than Earth, and initial explorations had revealed that the wildlife tended to be significantly larger too. This presented a major concern to anyone venturing outside the confines of the city walls as it meant that there were many potential predators viewing their human visitors as a wholesome meal, or even just a tasty snack. Even 20 years after the establishment of the settlement, the only people to venture outside were the plumbers and the scientists.

Plumbing was perhaps the most dangerous job on the planet. Nerves of steel were required to venture into the waters of Lake Speros to attend to the water plant that supplied the whole of the city because the lake was home to many large and ferocious creatures. Even the less ferocious ones posed a risk as they could still swallow a man without knowing it. The plumbers had come to jokingly call the lake Loch Ness because of all the monsters that lay in wait.

The scientists, on the other hand, tended only to venture out onto the plains and, once in a while, enter the edges of the forest. They collected samples and monitored the behaviour of the creatures they came across, broadening their knowledge of the planet on which they now resided. The biggest danger came, not from the large predators that viewed them as lunch, but the tiny ones that viewed them as a home. The germs and microbes on the planet needed to be analysed before any human exposure could be allowed. Something very innocuous to any indigenous creature could potentially have a devastating effect on a human, and until the bacteria were understood, no one was to leave the dome without a protective suit.

The city had become a vibrant and growing community but from the outside you would never know. From inside, the roof was completely transparent, letting all the inhabitants see the brilliant blue sky above them, but from outside it was impossible to see through. Unless you saw the scientists or plumbers on their missions, you would never believe anything was living inside.

And you would never know if there was nothing left at all.

As The Marianna approached Baldr the children looked on in wonder at the sight before them. The planet glowed blue-green, slowly growing to fill the screens. It was truly beautiful to behold. It was pure and unsullied, the vast bodies of water cool, crisp and inviting, the land rich and verdant. They gently orbited the planet taking in the glorious snow-topped mountain peaks that glistened, reflecting the light from Tau Ceti back up at them. It was all they could hope for in a new home. It was everything Zulfura wasn't and so many things The Magellan could never be.

Baldr promised to be the beginning of a fresh new chapter in their lives.

Chapter Fifteen
The Paucity Of Hope

Connor stood at the computer terminal by the entrance and tried to activate it again. Nothing. The gate to the city loomed over him. The colossal metal doors were impenetrable; the children had tried to do something, anything, to the first set they had encountered and they hadn't even left a mark. This was the third set and they weren't even going to bother trying.

There were six gates into Speropolis from the outside world – three from the plain, two from the water and one from the forest – and the children had just run out of easy options. They collectively deflated.

"So what do we do now?" It was the question they had all been deliberating but Evelyn was the only one who dared to vocalise it.

"Three down, three to go," said Connor.

"I agree." The comment surprised the other children. Grace wasn't known for taking Connor's side, after all. They stared at her, waiting for the kicker. "What? I do. What else are we going to do?" She had a point. "I mean sure, we can camp out here, try and survive with dwindling supplies and no real idea of what we're doing, or we can try to sort this mess out and get some kind of resolution."

Connor was disarmed by her agreement and almost instinctively reversed his position. He knew there were issues that needed discussing, he just thought Grace would be the one to bring them up. Now it fell to him, even if he was just playing devil's advocate.

"Of course, we've got to bear in mind what Carrie told us. Our options are Loch Ness and the unknown forest. It's not exactly safe either way," he said. A moment later, almost as an afterthought, he added, "And we have to accept that there's a chance that there's no one inside. I mean, there's no sign of life, no radio contact, the doors are locked."

"Are you now saying we shouldn't go?" asked Grace.

"No. There are still supplies in there. And maybe answers. I'm just saying that we shouldn't expect to find everything we've hoped for."

The gravity of the situation brought out the best from the two eldest. They didn't know what to do and were terrified of making the wrong decision, so they did the fairest thing of all. They sat everyone down and debated the situation and their options.

They had descended to the surface of Baldr in the two ISCs, Laurie and Lucas, while The Marianna remained in orbit. However, the journey to any of the remaining doors would have to be carried out in the open. The forest was too dense to bring the ships through and the gates in Loch Ness were in the middle of the water plant and impossible to reach in a vehicle as large as an ISC. Neither option was particularly appetising but they all acknowledged with no argument at all that something had to be done. The finer details of the mission were something else though.

"I don't think we should all go," said Connor, and Grace agreed with him immediately.

"I thought the same, you and I should go," she said.

"No. I'm going by myself," he said, "We should keep as many of us safe as possible."

"What, so if we don't hear from you, someone else goes in, then someone else, until there's no one left? No, there's got to be at least two of us."

Connor knew Grace had a point, but he had something to

prove himself. He had got them into trouble on Zulfura and he wanted to make amends and be the saviour. "No, Grace, I really think…" But he was cut off.

"I'm going too." It was Evelyn. Despite all of Adam's reassurances otherwise, she still felt she carried some kind of debt for her stunt back on The Magellan. And besides, she was an explorer at heart and it was time to put herself to the test.

"No, you're not, Evie," commanded Connor, but Evelyn wasn't listening.

"Fine. If I'm not going with you, I'll go on my own." And with that, she stood up and set off in the direction of the still distant forest.

"Evie," he called, but she didn't stop. "Evelyn! You don't even know where the gate is. Come back and we'll talk about it."

She stopped for a moment and thought about it, before turning back and retaking her place in the loose circle. "So I can come with you then." It was definitely a statement and not a question.

"I said we'll talk about it."

"No, I am coming."

"Well, if she's going, so am I," said Max.

"No you're not, Max-honey," said Grace.

"Hey, don't talk to him like that," complained Evelyn, taking exception to Grace meddling in Moran family affairs.

"Yeah, don't patronise him Grace," said Connor softly, "But no, Max, you're not coming."

"Yes I am. If Evie's going, so am I. I'm not staying with them," he said, turning to Grace and Adam, "No offence."

Connor couldn't help but let out a laugh. "Hey, don't be cheeky," he told his brother, but the admonishment lost a little amidst the giggles.

"You can take Isaac if you want," offered Adam.

"Really? Brilliant," exclaimed Max, "See, I'll be fine Connor, I'll have Isaac to protect me."

"OK, now listen both of you," said Connor, "If you do come with me – and I'm not saying you will – you'll live by my rules, OK? If I tell you to do something, you do it. There's no messing about. It could be dangerous. I need you to promise, OK?"

They both nodded and said "Yes Connor", though he was a little concerned about the authenticity of their promises.

"Right," said Grace, "I need to talk to your brother alone now, so just stay here with Adam, OK?" She beckoned Connor to leaves the others. They walked away from the makeshift camp out onto the plain, muttering quietly to each other.

"What do you think they're talking about?" asked Evelyn.

Adam ignored the question. "Why do you want to go into the forest?"

"I'd rather be doing something than waiting around for someone else to do it. Wouldn't you?"

Adam thought about it. It was an interesting point, but the idea of all the strange and dangerous creatures that he could come face to face with put him off. "No. No I wouldn't," he said.

"Are you sure about this?" Grace asked.

"No, are you?"

"I'm not the one contemplating taking my brother and sister into that forest."

"Hmmm," was all he could manage in response. It was a big decision to make and not one he could ask Evelyn and Max to make for themselves, despite their desire to go. He felt they were too young to fully appreciate the danger they might be putting themselves in. No, this was a decision he had to make on his own.

He looked back at their primitive camp. Adam, Evelyn and Max were sat facing each other, talking quietly. Behind, the city dome dwarfed them. He turned and surveyed the plain. It stretched out for miles, flat and featureless, mountains rising in the distance.

"Look at this," he said, "There's nothing out there. Nothing. How dangerous can that forest be?"

"Well..." said Grace, but she wasn't allowed to finish her thought.

"We can do this," Connor declared. "We can do this," he repeated to himself.

It was too late in the day to start their journey through the forest so instead the children prepared for the great adventure the next day. Carrie plotted the shortest route through the forest and the children made a base-camp close to their starting point.

Connor wanted to know what he and his siblings should expect so the three of them embarked on a brief walk before Tau Ceti set. But before they could set foot in the forest there was the problem of the undergrowth. From a distance, the bushes and shrubs at the foot of the trees had looked as though they could easily be stepped over, but as they closed in they realised the forest loomed hundreds of feet above their heads and the bushes they had thought merely rose to knee height were actually a knotted, tangled mess several metres tall. Connor was going off the idea of trekking for nearly eight miles if it as going to mean he'd have to hack through such dense vegetation the whole way.

He grabbed a lumi-firma knife and strode purposefully towards the nearest greenery, his brother and sister jogging to keep up. He slashed the knife forward with all the strength he could muster and was taken aback when the blade just slid through the branches. Just a few more hacks and he had fashioned a hole through which they could clamber. He led the way.

The undergrowth, while dense, was not deep. A metre and a half and they were in the forest. The difference was amazing. The ground was almost as barren as the plains outside, but the canopy of the trees blocked out nearly all the natural light.

Evelyn stepped through after Connor and looked around.

"Wow," she said, astounded by what she saw. The treetops were so far above her she couldn't see the branches. Max followed. He had picked up one of the branches Connor had hacked down and was too busy studying it to react to the forest itself. For a moment, they all stood still, lost in the perfect silence. It was unbelievable that there didn't appear to be a single living creature within earshot.

"Connor, what's this?" asked Max, holding out the branch he was carrying and indicating something shining at its core.

"Hmm?" said Connor, distracted. He turned and took the branch from his brother. At the centre there appeared to be a thin rod of metal – or a metallic substance – running along the length of it. "Well that's strange," he acknowledged, but he didn't offer an answer to Max, because he didn't have one.

The radio link to Grace and Adam crackled to life. "Guys, you might want to take a look behind you," said Grace.

The three children turned and watched as the hole Connor had carved slowly closed, branches growing and entwining like a hideous mouth closing. Max looked momentarily panicked but Connor reassured him. "We cut through easily enough, we'll be able to do the same on our way back out." He turned back and looked deep into the forest. "Right, let's explore," he said, "But remember, if I tell you to do something, you do it."

They slowly edged into the forest, Connor first, Evelyn bringing up the rear with Max in the middle, now using the stray branch as a make shift walking stick. The dead leaves and branches cracked and crunched beneath their feet, echoing around them eerily. Connor's senses heightened and he looked and listened closely, taking deliberate steps. Somewhere amidst their footsteps he thought he was picking up the sound of shuffling and short sharp breaths, but when he held up his hand signalling to his brother and sister to stop moving and be quiet, silence surrounded them.

"Just my nerves getting the better of me," he told himself,

before continuing the journey. It wasn't long until the snuffling and shuffling was back. He held his hand up again and shushed the others, determined to figure out where it was coming from, but to no avail, silence was everywhere.

No sooner had they started again and the sound was back. Perhaps it's Evelyn or Max, he thought, but before he could think about anymore, the radio crackled to life. "...t can y.. .ee? Is ev..... ing a..ight?" said Grace. The reception was terrible.

"What?" asked Connor. "I can't make anything you're saying out."

He waited a moment for the reply. ".e c.n't hear y... May.. ... ..ould co.. back."

While the message wasn't clear, it was clear enough. He turned on his heel and was about to tell his siblings to do the same when he saw it. He saw it and he shrieked.

Grace and Adam hovered over the radio. The signal may have been bad but there was no mistaking that for anything but a scream.

"I knew this was a bad idea," said Grace. She wasn't blaming Connor. If anything she was blaming herself for not stopping them.

"Do you think Evelyn's OK?" asked Adam.

"I hope so. She sounded pretty spooked."

It had an inquisitive face perched on the end of its long, slender neck, its four eyes blinking independently, looking straight ahead, up, and to both sides all at once. It sniffed the air through its squat nose, assessing these new creatures invading its territory. Four short, sturdy, but most definitely not stumpy, legs supported a body about a foot in length and covered in the most gorgeous, silky dark fur. Until, that is, Connor spun round and screamed, startling it. It curled itself up into a tight ball, its sleek fur transforming into tens of thousands of sharp quills, and left just the one eye on the top of its head visible, keeping watch.

"Connor!" admonished Evelyn, "You scared it."

She got down onto her stomach and gently reached out a hand, letting whatever it was see she wasn't a threat.

"Hey, it scared me," said Connor, getting his breath back and stating the obvious. "Be careful, it could be dangerous."

"It's not dangerous," she said, as it poked its nose out and sniffed the tips of her fingers. "See?"

Slowly it unfurled its body and its fur returned to its natural, silken state. Evelyn leaned forward, reaching out to pick it up but it backed away from her, its head rocking from side to side as if to say 'no'. Evelyn stood back up and all three of them stood still as they were considered by the unusual animal. It shuffled towards them again and Connor instantly recognised the noise. Evelyn's feet were being given the once over by the creature when something caught its right eye. It stopped mid-sniff and slowly turned its head as if it was trying not to startle something. Connor and Evelyn followed its eye line. It seemed to be staring at Max, or rather, at the branch Max was still leaning on.

Evelyn tried to catch his eye.

"Branch," she whispered, gesturing he should throw it to her. He looked back blankly. "Throw me the branch," she hissed. It was like Max had just woken up or snapped out of a stupor. He did a double take at the branch in his hand before gently tossing it to his sister.

She held the tip down to the animal's mouth. It sniffed before taking a bite out of the end. Then it looked up at her, as if to ask permission to continue.

"Go on then..." she said, shaking it a little. The animal took another large bite before grabbing the branch in its front paws and giving it a tug. Evelyn held firm, she wasn't going to let the animal take the branch and disappear forever. Instead, she patted her chest, inviting the creature to jump up into her arms. It looked around, weighing up its options, before leaping from the floor and clinging to Evelyn's shoulder. It didn't wait for Evelyn to offer the branch, grabbing it from her hand and tucking in. Evelyn didn't mind, she had what she wanted. She ran her hand over the creature's beautiful coat, she had never felt such a glorious texture. It wasn't like any fur she'd felt before. It was like it wasn't even there, like it was liquid.

"Oh, wow, this is amazing," she said, almost melting on the spot. "You have to feel this."

Max walked over and gingerly touched his fingers to the strange coat of the happy animal. He couldn't believe it was the same fur that had turned into the deadly looking quills just a minute before.

"Right, come on kids, we've got to get back," instructed Connor.

"I want to stay with him," pleaded Max.

"No, come on. You know the rules, if you come into the forest you do what I say."

"Oohhh!" said Max, stamping his feet.

"If we're going back he's coming with us," said Evelyn.

"Yeah, ha ha Connor, he's coming too."

"Fine, whatever. Grace can tell you we're not keeping him. Come on."

He made a beeline for the edge of the forest, Evelyn and Max following slowly behind, cooing at their new friend.

"He's adorable."

It wasn't the reaction Connor was hoping Grace would have. He rolled his eyes and walked past the doting triumvirate. His arms were filled with branches he'd cut from bushes and he dropped them between the two ISCs. He was intending to build a fire for the evening but Adam stopped him before he could light it.

"Err, what do you think you're doing?" Connor asked.

"Err, stopping you before you burn us all alive," Adam

answered sarcastically. He took Connor's hand, dragged him back to Lucas, pulled out some tools and proceeded to instruct Connor on how to build a fire pit. "These aren't trees like on The Magellan or on Earth, we don't know how they'll burn. The grass may be highly flammable," he lectured. "If you want to do this, do it safely."

Connor dug a shallow hole in the ground and circled it in rocks before throwing the branches in.

"No, no, no, you've got to do it properly," said Adam, pulling the branches out then assembling them into pyramid structure in the centre of the pit. "There. You see?"

Connor had to admit Adam had built a pretty good fire. "And now to light it," he said. He bent forward with the lighter and introduced the flame to the wood.

WHOOSH!

"Ow!" screamed Evelyn as the terrified creature leapt out of her arms and curled into its small, prickly defensive position.

The moment the flame had gotten close to the branches it went up in a huge purple and yellow fireball. Connor stumbled backwards, taken aback by the reaction. The initial flame quickly came under control and danced in front of them, crackling its way across the branches.

"What on earth was that?" shouted Grace, running over to the boys.

"We were just lighting a fire to keep us warm over night," said Adam.

"Well you need to be more careful," she said, spinning to confront Connor, and then she burst out laughing. Adam looked up too and joined in. Soon Evelyn and Max had joined the circle laughing at their brother.

"What?" he said, totally confused.

"Your face," said Max, before resuming his uncontrollable laughter.

Connor wiped the sweat off his forehead with the back of

his hand and he realised what they were laughing at. The back of his hand was covered in damp purple soot. "Oh yeah, ha ha," he said sarcastically, "You can cut it out now, I get it."

"No," struggled Evelyn. It was almost painful to speak. "No, you don't."

"What then?" asked Connor, groping his face, trying to feel what was so funny. And then he really did get it. His face seemed to be missing something it used to have. Eyebrows. His heart sank. He felt like a complete donut. He backed away from them, heading back to the ISC to wash his face off and see exactly how bad the damage was. It was bad. They were completely gone. He cleaned his face up and returned to the group who were now gathered around the fire, warming their hands as the air took a chill. The sky was darkening and the fire was looking like a good idea.

"Much better," said Grace when she saw his clean face.

"I don't know, I think I preferred him purple," said Max, to the amusement of the rest.

"Yeah, very funny. At least you're enjoying the fruits of my sacrifice," he said, gesturing to the fire.

"Yes, a very good idea," said Grace, patting the grass beside her. "We were just saying we should have a cook out."

Connor sat down and rubbed his hands together, enjoying the warmth. "Great idea. Evelyn, go and get some sausages," he said.

"Why do I have..."

"Come on, I'll help you find them," said Adam. The pair went on their little mission, returning laden down with a wide variety of sausages and burgers to cook on the fire. They even managed to find some strong wire to use as skewers, and so the five of the sat around their camp fire, cooking, eating and laughing at Connor's expressionless face.

By the end of the evening, much important business had

been conducted; the children had all been well fed, Connor and Grace had devised a plan for the journey the next day, and their new friend had been given a name - Gordon. The others had protested, especially Evelyn, but Max was adamant that that was his name.

"Why Max? Gordon's a stupid name for a pet," Evelyn complained.

"No it's not," he replied, "It's a very sensible name."

"That's what I mean," she countered, "It's the kind of name an accountant has, not a cute little pet like this fellow."

"Why Gordon, Max?" asked Grace softly.

"Because I was going to get a dog and call him Gordon, but mum and dad wouldn't let me," the boy said.

"But why Gordon?" she pressed.

"Because that was going to be the dog's name. I just said. Don't you listen?"

No matter what they said, he wouldn't budge, and so Gordon it was. At the end of the day it was a minor thing and Max was so attached to the name it seemed foolish to push him on it. They had bigger issues at hand. The radio interference was not a good situation; they needed to keep in touch in case anything happened. The plan concocted by Grace and Connor was to plant small radio transmitters whenever the signal started to deteriorate to relay their messages back and forth. All in all, it turned out to be a pretty successful evening.

Max, Evelyn and Adam were all feeling the effects of the day and retired to the ISCs to sleep soon after Tau Ceti had disappeared over the horizon. Grace and Connor stayed up talking as the fire slowly died down.

"You know what I realised today is?" Grace asked him.

"What's that?"

"My birthday. I mean, I know it's not important, and I know that a year is something that only really means anything on Earth and we've never even been there. But, you know, I just thought it was a strange coincidence, our first day here..." She trailed off, not really knowing where her thoughts were taking her.

"Well, happy birthday Grace. I hope you've enjoyed it."

"I've had better," she said, "but yes, it was good, nice. I got to hear you scream like a girl and see you burn your eyebrows off. What more could a girl ask for?"

"Hold that thought," he said, standing and running to Laurie. He came back carrying a bottle of wine and two glasses.

"Where did you...?"

"It was on the Marianna. I thought we could celebrate when we got into the city but this seems a much better reason. Plus the others won't keep pestering us for some."

"We're fifteen, Connor, we shouldn't be drinking."

"We're on a strange planet, possibly stranded light years from the nearest human, just the five of us. Our families and our home are gone, and it's your birthday, I think we can handle a glass of wine each."

"OK then, just the one," conceded Grace and Connor poured two generous glasses.

"To Grace, happy fifteenth birthday," offered Connor.

"To your journey tomorrow, may it be quick and uneventful," countered Grace.

"To Speropolis, a fresh start in our new home."

"To family. Old and new. Where would we be without them?"

"To family," agreed Connor. They looked over to the ISCs where their siblings slept and then up to the sky, as if hoping their parents may catch a glimpse of their gesture, and then to each other. They smiled, clinked glasses and took a sip, before exploding in a coughing fit.

"Ugh, that is not nice," said Connor.

"Is it supposed to taste like that?" asked Grace.

"I don't know," said Connor, taking another sip. This time he tried to savour it, to see what it was that made so many adults like this drink. He still didn't understand it but he vowed to persevere.

Grace followed suit, not wanting to be lose face.

They sat in silence for a moment, pondering the new world around them. Grace looked over at Connor, his face still looking a little flushed in the flickering purple light of the fire, and smiled to herself. "You're not so bad, Connor," she said. "I mean, you're a bit of a donut sometimes, but you're alright. I'm sorry I gave you such a hard time before."

"Hey, I'm sure I deserved at least some of it."

"Oh, you did." They both laughed gently before returning to silence. Neither of them quite knew what to say so they continued sipping at the wine and admiring the stars shining above their heads. Neither of them had experienced anything like it before, a true natural silence, fresh air, the elements. They were marvelling at the world around them.

Eventually, Grace plucked up the courage to break the tranquillity. "What happens tomorrow, Connor..."

"Hmmm?" Connor had been in his own little world.

"What happens tomorrow if we can't get into Speropolis? Or we do get in and everyone's dead?" It was the great unasked question. They had all been surviving on the hope that Speropolis would hold the answer. They didn't want to consider the possibility that maybe it wouldn't.

"We're going to get in," he said confidently, "We'll get in and they'll be there."

"But what if they aren't?"

"Then there'll be something else, Grace. We aren't destined to spend our lives here on our own."

"How can you know that?"

"I don't know that. But if I didn't believe it then I'd give up. I mean, what would be the point? The five of us stuck here, alone, forever? No, that's not how it ends."

"That's why we need you, Connor," said Grace, emptying her glass. "That wasn't so bad after all." She held it out for refilling.

Connor duly obliged, and topped his own up while he was at it. Grace felt a warmth grow from her stomach as the wine made its way into her system. She was starting to feel a little light headed.

"So, Connor," she said, noticing a little slur on her words, "You seem pretty stellar at that flying lark, what's the secret?" She had no idea where it came from – after their trip to Zulfura she wasn't too impressed with his flying – but it seemed like a good thing to ask right now.

"It's really not that difficult, once you get used to it. It's just practice, I guess," he said, a little taken aback.

"No, but you are really good, and you only just started out."

"Yeah, but I practiced a lot before I started actually flying."

"You're too modest."

Connor was feeling a little uncomfortable, but the wine was taking the edge off it. "Well, I suppose...Hmmm... You've just got to... People normally freak out over the simple things. There's not much complicated to do. Just take it slow and steady and don't panic. It doesn't take much to go where you want to go. Make sure you know what you want to do. You're smart. Just think about it and then do it. It'll soon become natural."

"Thanks Connor." She smiled, but it soon became a massive yawn. It was getting late and they had a long day ahead of them. "I think," she started, before finishing off the remains of her second glass of wine, "I think it's time I hit the hay."

"Me too," said Connor, stifling the yawn he'd caught from Grace. "Me too." He watched her walk back to the ISC as he finished his own glass, and then he left Gordon curled up in front of the dying embers of the fire and took the slow walk back himself.

Chapter Sixteen
A Long Day's Journey Into Hope

THUMP.

Bright light from the star, Tau Ceti, pierced Connor's eyelids and brought him painfully awake.

THUMP, THUMP.

His head was throbbing and he could hear his heartbeat pounding in his ears. This was not how he wanted to feel the morning of his great expedition.

THUMP, THUMP, THUMP.

He closed his eyes and wrapped his arm across his face to prevent his retinas from being seared any further.

THUMP. THUMP. THUMP. THUMP.

He tried to summon the strength to move, but failed. He couldn't even think. The only thing going through his head was...

THUMP, THUMP, THUMP, THUMP, THUMP.

Grace didn't feel much better. She felt like she was having an argument with her stomach and was losing. The seats in the ISCs folded flat to serve as beds and she was woken by Adam laughing at the large slick of drool that had made its way from her mouth, over her shoulder and down onto the headrest. It was far from her proudest moment and she immediately swore her brother to secrecy.

She had, at least, risen, and had proceeded to drink a lot of water. It appeared to be what her head was crying out for, but her stomach wasn't quite so keen. She had ended up retching behind the ISC they had named after her father. She shuddered at the thought of what he would have thought of her at that moment. Fortunately everything was still peaceful in Laurie and her episode was missed by the Moran clan. By the time Connor had struggled out into the fresh air she had recovered enough to appear unaffected by the night before, quietly ignoring the rumbling coming from inside.

She saw him gingerly exit the craft and she put a little bounce in her step as she approached him. "Hey Connor, how are you?" She said it a little too loud, making his head pound. The tone of friendship was almost gone; it was almost as if their conversation the previous night had never happened.

"I've been better," was all he could muster by way of reply. Grace's stomach growled and for a moment her face became transparent and her discomfort was obvious. "Feeling stellar too, I see," he said, catching her out.

Once the pretence was over, the two stumbled through the early morning, getting things ready for the journey and ignoring their siblings' muttered jokes and covered laughter. Adam's vow of silence had been broken the moment Evelyn and Max cottoned on to Grace's predicament and his revelations had provoked a bout of spontaneous giggles from all three. Grace had turned and given them a disapproving look but deep down she couldn't blame them. She just felt embarrassed. As far as she was concerned, the sooner they were ready to get moving, the better.

The cloudless blue sky allowed the bright yellow star, Tau Ceti, to beat down on their heads and they worked up a sweat as they packed up their camp and prepared for the journey ahead. Tau Ceti was, as far as they were concerned, the sun. Every so often they looked up to marvel at the heavens above. The blue sky was a constant source of amazement. They were so used to the black nothingness that had previously surrounded them, that the blue was almost unnerving. Max, in particular, kept checking that the view above him hadn't disappeared, as though it were some mirage and at any moment his brain would see sense and it would be stolen from him.

Evelyn was far more distracted by Gordon. He had seemingly become her pet and the two were now inseparable. He weaved between her legs like a cat and she was far more interested in stroking and playing with him than she was in helping prepare. More than once she got a sharp word from Connor, reminding her that she was only allowed to come if she followed his instructions and pulled her weight. She'd immediately pick up the pace, vowing to herself that she wouldn't get distracted, but inevitably, within ten minutes she was luxuriating in his fur or finding another branch for him to munch on.

Adam was the most focused, but that didn't stop him from making a nuisance of himself. He was providing a constant buzz around Connor, asking question after question about his venture into the forest the previous day.

"How light was it?"

"What was the terrain like?"

"Was there much foliage?"

"How dense were the trees?"

Connor's head would've been aching even without the previous night's alcohol, and it didn't take long for him to tell Adam to leave him alone. Adam was, at least, putting the knowledge he gained from Connor to good use, collecting all the appropriate equipment and clothing and briefing Isaac on his duties when he set off.

When the time came, Connor, Evelyn, Max and Isaac lined up in front of the forest. Clad in their protective flight suits and each with a rucksack of supplies on their backs, they waved goodbye to Grace and Adam. The trek was almost eight miles and, barring any unforeseen circumstances, should take them between two and three hours. While the children had been delayed by Connor and Grace's slow, hung-over preparations, they still had hours of daylight to complete their mission. Even if they failed to gain entry to the city, they should be back at the base camp in time for tea.

Connor sliced his way through the undergrowth and held it back to allow his siblings and the robot through. Evelyn had insisted on bringing Gordon with her and, after a brief discussion, Connor had conceded, mainly because it became perfectly clear that Gordon would follow his sister wherever she went anyway.

Max overheard the conversation and took particular interest in the outcome. "Is Evelyn leading this trip now?" he asked, with a cheeky glint in his eye.

"No... No, I still make the rules, and you'd better behave mister."

The more flustered he got, the more Evelyn and Max giggled at him. In the end, Connor was glad to get the journey underway, if only because it might focus them a little and give him some control back.

Once they were through the undergrowth, he turned back to Grace and Adam, still watching from their camp, and waved again as the branches grew back in place and cut them off once more.

Connor plucked a branch from the ground to use as a walking stick and Max dutifully followed his example. The moment they walked into the forest, the young boy's whole demeanour changed, there was no more laughing and joking, this was a serious mission and he wasn't going to take it lightly.

Evelyn picked up a branch herself, but she had no intention of using it as a walking aid. She waved it in front of Gordon's face and then threw it for him to chase down. She'd never been allowed a pet back on The Magellan, and while Gordon was no dog, it didn't stop her from playing with him as though he were.

Connor knelt down and pushed the first radio beacon into the ground. The dome only poked up a couple of centimetres but it did its job very effectively.

"Testing, testing, Connor to base, over," he said into the radio.

"Loud and clear, over" said Grace.

Connor smiled, satisfied with the arrangements. "We'll walk in a few hundred metres, see how the reception is. Over," he said.

"Sounds good, over," came the reply.

"Right guys, follow me," he commanded, and they did. Max tried to match Connor stride for stride but kept having to put a little jog in his step to keep pace, eventually dropping back and walking with his good friend Isaac. Evelyn was happy running around, throwing the branch for Gordon and getting it back. More than once Connor tried to rein her in, but to no avail.

The forest started out quite open but the trees rapidly became more populous and there were signs of undergrowth. Connor couldn't quite understand it. He looked around, surveying his surroundings. The edge of the forest had been quite light but Tau Ceti was already finding it difficult to penetrate the mesh of branches. The undergrowth seemed to thrive in the darker areas; quite the opposite of earthly vegetation.

Connor called them to a halt and issued his first serious instructions. He told his brother and sister to put on their hoods and engage the night vision. It took them a few moments to adjust their eyes to the harsh green glow, but when they did, they felt for the first time that they were looking at a truly alien landscape. A metal thread ran through each of the plants and trees and the heat it conducted turned the trunks, branches and leaves into a spiders-web of bright glowing green amidst the wood's darker shades.

Connor looked back to where they'd come from. He saw the occasional flash from the radio transmitter he'd planted and thought it was time he tried the radio again. Through the static he could just about make out Grace's voice but he certainly couldn't understand what she was saying. He knelt down and planted the second transmitter and immediately the reception improved.

"Is it working now? Over."

"Perfect, over."

"We've come in about five-hundred metres, but the forest is much more dense from here so I'll keep planting these every two-fifty or so. Over."

"OK, we'll be here. Keep in touch, over."

Connor noted that Gordon clearly wasn't having any problems with the light. He was still chasing after the branches thrown by Evelyn and tracking them down with ease. It unnerved Connor. If Gordon could see perfectly in the dark he wondered what else might be able to.

Grace and Adam sat on the steps of the ISC named after their father, keeping one ear on the radio.

"I'm not sure I can just sit here for the next two hours, waiting for a message," said Grace. She was nervous. Their whole future seemed to hinge on this one trip and there was nothing she could do to influence it. It was too much for her to deal with.

"What do you propose?" asked Adam. It was a fair question and one Grace didn't know how to answer. They sat in silent contemplation, waiting for inspiration or a message from Connor to distract them.

Grace closed her eyes and leaned back against the door of the ship. When she opened them she was looking straight up into the sky, and that's when she knew what she wanted to do.

"I want to practice my flying," she said. She had already got to grips with the basics on their way to Speropolis.

"That's great, Grace, but what am I supposed to do?" asked Adam.

"You can have a go as well. We've got two ships after all. And anyway, I saw you having a few practice flights coming here too. You were good."

"And what about the others? What happens when they radio in?"

"We can still reply. It won't stop us from talking. Carrie can always take over the flying if needs be." Grace had a point. Carrie would keep them safe and it was always going to be a useful skill to have. No reason why Connor should be the only one to hone his talents. She clambered up the steps of the ship, eager to make a start.

Adam wasn't quite as enthusiastic as his sister, but the idea was growing on him. He'd enjoyed flying in space a lot, even if he hadn't done that much of it. He wondered how different it would be now that gravity was involved. In space the only obstacle to avoid was the Marianna. Now they had a world of obstacles to test themselves on. He walked across to Laurie and climbed on board.

They had been walking for half an hour and Connor had just planted the sixth transmitter. He lent on his branch, catching his breath. It was far hotter in the forest than he had been expecting. The metal at the core of the trees seemed to suck the heat of Tau Ceti through their leaves and channel it down to ground level and Connor could feel quite a sweat building up under his flight suit.

"Cary, I thought these suits were supposed to cool us down," he said into the radio.

The computer's voice came back through the airwaves strong and clear thanks to the transmitters. "The only thing I can think, Connor, is that the trees are emitting some kind of electromagnetic radiation that's interfering with the suits' programming."

It was an answer but it didn't reassure Connor at all. Walking through the darkness with malfunctioning equipment was not how this was supposed to go. He took a swig of water from his flask and Max followed suit. Evelyn had the most energy and was still throwing sticks around for Gordon to chase, though she was starting to tire of it now.

Connor made a decision. He undid his flight suit down to his waist and pulled his arms out, tying the sleeves around his midriff, intent on marching on in just his tee-shirt. It could be construed as a risk but Connor figured they'd not seen a single creature aside from Gordon yet so hopefully there was nothing around to see his bare arms as a tasty snack. And besides, he really needed to cool down.

"Right, come on guys, we're only a quarter of the way there, let's get moving," he said, beckoning them on.

"Hey," said Max, affronted at the implication that he was holding Connor up, "We were waiting for you."

Flying above the surface of a planet was a significantly greater challenge than flying in boundless space and Grace was struggling with it. In space, direction was only relative to the position of the craft; up was always somewhere above your head, and down was always below you. On Baldr, up meant away from the ground and down, towards it, and the consequences of getting muddled up with your steering were far greater. It was much easier to pass off your mistakes in space as intentional manoeuvres because, unless you veered towards the Marianna, it really didn't matter where you went. Now she had to be far more accurate and precise with her movements and Grace almost had to go back to basics.

Adam, on the other hand, found it much easier. Gravity and solid ground imposed their own rules and limits on what he could and couldn't do and it was exactly this kind of structure that he needed to begin to master the controls. Soon he was flying this way and that, looping the loop and skimming the ground, much to the annoyance of his sister.

Grace had Carrie mark a series of points on the display of her hood and attempted to navigate her way there as simply as possible, but she always found herself having to undertake the journey one step at a time – first forward, then left and finally up – rather than combining it all into one sweet movement.

She remembered Connor's advice from the night before – know what you want to do – and stopped the ship. She closed her eyes and visualised the combination of moves that she'd need to pull off to get the ship where she wanted to. Miming the actions that would guide her, she stopped whenever she made a mistake and started again until she had managed the sequence correctly three times in a row. It took some time, but time was something she had.

She opened her eyes and concentrated on repeating the gestures. Very slowly, the ship started to move towards the marker Carrie had projected. She was doing it. A momentary rush of triumph flooded through her body and she gradually increased the speed of the craft.

The radio crackled to life. "That's nine. How's the reception out there?" It was Connor checking in at exactly the moment Grace wouldn't want him to. Her concentration was broken and the ship shot off course. She took her hands off the controls and it stopped almost at once.

"Dammit, Connor, I was just getting the hang of it."

"What? What are you talking about?"

"Flying. I'd just worked it out and you interrupted me."

"Well I'm sorry, Grace. Sorry to have got in the way of your larking about. We're just in the middle of a pitch black alien forest trying to find us a new home, but obviously some things are more important."

"Sorry Connor, but you don't understand. This is really difficult and I was getting it."

"Well that's great," he said, but it was obvious he didn't mean it. "I'll speak to you when we've planted number ten, OK? Over."

"OK, Connor, speak to you then. Over." The radio stayed

silent. "Connor?" Nothing again. "Fine, if you're going to be like that."

"Self-centred so-and-so."

"What?" asked Max.

Connor hadn't realised he'd said it out loud. "Nothing, nothing. Come on, let's get a move on."

The walk had been hot and boring and Evelyn and Max were beginning to regret coming. They had thought it was going to be a lot more interesting and exciting than this. No, this was just a long, tedious walk. Gordon sloped along behind Evelyn. She had given up playing with him, having realised the long slog ahead. Isaac was the only one seeming to get anything out of the trip at all, constantly running around, clambering up trees and somersaulting back down. Of course, the robot was the only one not at risk of dehydration. He was bringing up the rear, trying to entertain an increasingly disinterested Max.

They marched on. Connor's tee-shirt was now drenched in sweat and clinging to his body.

When they stopped to plant the tenth transmitter, Connor's concentration was interrupted by the first inevitable call of "Are we nearly there yet?" from his brother. He rolled his eyes. Now he knew how his parents must have felt. "We're about half way, Max," he replied.

"Oh drek," said Max.

"Hey, less of that language mister. Now, you asked to come along. I warned you," said Connor, starting to lose his patience a little. Max pulled faces behind his brother's back as they set off again.

The further the journey went on, the less interest Max and Evelyn had. They dropped further behind Connor, catching him up anytime he planted a transmitter. There was nothing to see but trees, no wildlife, nothing. Evelyn had hoped that, having met Gordon so quickly, the place would be bustling with alien creatures but no such luck. Nope, instead it was tree after tree after boring, boring tree.

They planted the eleventh transmitter, then the twelfth. Every step taking them closer to the city gate, but each one was becoming heavier and harder for the two younger Morans. As they approached the location for the thirteenth transmitter, Evelyn looked ahead at her brother, readying her own rendition of the "Are-we-nearly-there-yet?" chorus, when she saw something rather odd. She couldn't quite make out what it was, she was too far behind Connor to see clearly, but there appeared to be something clinging onto his left arm. It was probably a leaf or part of his flight suit – she really couldn't make it out – but she thought she'd ask him anyway.

She knew he'd heard her when she saw him turn his head and look down. He froze, staring at whatever it was for what seemed like forever, before toppling face first into the ground.

Evelyn couldn't quite believe what she saw and waited a moment before shouting to Max and Isaac to come quick.

Grace and Adam heard Evelyn's cries over the radio and immediately called up video from the hoods' cameras into the screens in the ISC cockpits. The view from Connor's hood was pitch black and they could see why. While the pictures from Evelyn and Max's cameras were bouncing around as they ran, Grace and Adam could just about make out Connor's body slumped face first on the forest floor. Their hearts were in their mouths. What had happened to him?

His sister's voice came through the radio in his hood. "Hey, Connor, what's that on your arm?"

He looked down, completely unaware and was shocked by what he saw. A giant fly the length of his forearm was perched on his left arm and he couldn't feel a thing. But then he realised what it was doing. It had sliced through the flesh, was using its legs to pin back the skin and appeared to be tucking into the meat underneath.

Connor tried moving his hand. His fingers closed into a fist but he couldn't feel it, it was completely numb. He saw the tendons and muscles twitching as his brain sent the message to his hand but there was no sensation at all coming back to him. For a moment he stretched and contracted his hand, rotated his wrist, amazed at the way his body worked, and then the reality of the situation hit him. The blood drained from his head, he felt dizzy. He felt sick.

Everything went black and he collapsed.

When Evelyn caught up with Connor his arm was splayed out in front of him and the insect was still enjoying its meal. She tried to pull it off but its legs seemed to have locked themselves into his flesh and couldn't be wrenched free. It didn't even stop eating.

Isaac was next on the scene. The robot turned his right arm into a blade and sliced through the creature's legs, cutting Connor's arm free from its grasp. The insect let out a pained screech before Isaac plunged his blade into its body and killed it.

Evelyn rolled Connor onto his back and tore his hood off. She checked his breathing. It was shallow but consistent. She breathed a little sigh of relief and called on to Max to hurry. He was carrying the medikit in his backpack and they needed it immediately. She pulled a torch from her own backpack while she waited and shone it down on his arm, pulling her hood from her face so she could see clearly. There was almost no blood around the wound; either the insect had been drinking it or it had cauterised the vessels as it opened him up.

As soon as Max arrived, Evelyn tore the pack off his shoulder and tossed everything out until she put her hands on the kit. Her father had made her take a first aid course back on the Magellan. Seeing as he didn't seem to be able to stop her getting into trouble, he thought she should at least know what to do if it became necessary. She had Max hold the torch while she scrabbled through the pack. She found what she was after, the tube of stembiotics, and squirted the cream straight into the wound. Next was the hard part. She was squeamish and really had to force herself to put her fingers inside the lesion. She rubbed the cream over every part of his butchered arm, being careful to trace her fingers around the edge of the skin flaps the fly had pulled back. She hated the tendons which felt like strings as she ran her hands over them. Connor's fingers twitched as she accidentally strummed them. Touching the bone was chilling too and she could feel the notches where the insect had tried to bite in. She kept telling herself "Just one more minute, one more minute" as she felt her stomach turn.

Finally she was done. She folded the skin back over the wound, grabbed a stembiotic bandage and wrapped it around his forearm. The moment she was done, she turned away and let go of her stomach, vomiting on the ground beside her. She pulled her water bottle from her pack and rinsed her mouth, spitting her acidic saliva back out. Turning back to her brother, Evelyn pressed her fingers to his neck, feeling for a pulse. It was still there, and strong. Reassured, she sat back on her heels and drank some water down.

Max had watched intently, highly impressed by his sister's skills, but when the wound was covered he turned his attention to the perpetrator of the injury. The fly had six wings and under the torchlight he could see what he never could through the green glow of the night vision; the creature was beautiful. The wings were a multi-coloured marble, shimmering and shining back at him. He gently reached his hand out to touch them and found the most delicate silk. A little too delicate – his fingers went right through. He had no idea how the creature managed to fly, the wings appeared nowhere near robust enough to support the weight of the fly in mid-air. Perhaps that's why it needs six, he thought. Its body, too, was an array of colours, but before Max could admire them any further Gordon had muscled his way in front and started attacking the insect, looking for a snack.

Grace and Adam had watched the scenes aghast. They had held their breath while Evelyn operated and finally let out a gasped sigh when she was finished and they knew Connor was going to be alright.

"Well, that's that then." Grace broke the silence.

"What do you mean?" Evelyn's voice came back through the radio.

"Well you can't go on now," said Grace.

"We're two thirds of the way there, Grace, we're not giving up now."

"But you can't take Connor with you, the state he's in."

Evelyn squirted some water on her brother's face and into his mouth, trying to revive him. He slowly came to and tried to push himself up into a sitting position. Feeling was returning to his left arm and it hurt. He almost fell back to the floor but managed to use his right arm to catch himself.

"He's coming round. I'll see what he says, but we're closer to the city than to the plain. We'll be better off going on," said Evelyn.

"And what if something else happens?"

"And what if we don't go on? We're just going to stay here on our own?"

"No, we'll..."

But Grace was cut off. "We're going on, Grace, so don't bother. Over and out."

The radio cut out and Grace harrumphed. She resented being talked to like that, though she had to admit that Evelyn might have a point. At the end of the day, they were on the ground and the decision rested with them. Or, more to the point, it rested with Connor.

"Come on Adam, let's head back down," she said.

"Why?" he asked. "What are we going to do?"

"Well, it's not really..." she tailed off. What would they do? "It doesn't seem right to be up here." She certainly wasn't convinced by her words.

"We might as well keep learning," he said before flying away from her and out over the forest. It was the first time either of them had ventured away from the plain and the area around their camp from the previous night.

"Adam..." she called after him, but when she realised he wasn't going to stop she dutifully followed on.

Connor was still feeling a bit woozy, which was only natural really, all things considered. His face was white and he was still trying to comprehend what had happened.

"Thanks sis," he said sincerely.

"Hold still," she said. She'd decided she need to play things safe and should give him a stembiotic shot too. Before he had a chance to react she had stabbed his arm and pulled the trigger, shooting the medication into his bloodstream.

"Ow," complained Connor, before feeling the rush go around his body. The stembiotics included adrenaline and the colour began to return to his face as his blood pumped the drug around his system at double time. "Wow." He tried to get to his feet again, but was still unsure of himself, despite the shot.

"I guess I should put my suit back on, eh?" he said to no one in particular. He pulled the sleeves on, covering up Evelyn's expert bandaging, and fastened it back up. "Right, shall we get moving?"

"Not yet, we won't," his sister told him. "We're going to sit down here while you have something to drink and regain your strength."

"Drek," he muttered as he sat back down and took the water bottle from his sister's hand.

Connor agreed with Evelyn that, having come this far, there was no point going back. He still felt groggy and he could feel his entire body pulse every time his heart beat, but his strength was coming back and he was sure he could make it to the city, he'd just be more careful for the remainder of the journey. Fifteen minutes later he was back on his feet and cajoling his siblings to get a move on. He was keeping everyone together from now on though. They were all to look out for one another and report even the slightest oddity they should see around them. Their pace was much slower now, partially because of their increased caution, but mainly because Connor couldn't go any faster.

*   *   *   *   *

It was half an hour since Connor, Evelyn and Max had set off again and there was good reason for Grace and Adam to be optimistic. There had been nothing to report the last time they had checked in and they must be within the last mile or so. The end was in sight. In the meantime, Grace had managed to get to grips with the controls. Since attempting several more gates that Carrie had set for her, she had found a natural rhythm for combining the controls and was now happily swooping and soaring above the treetops. Granted, she wasn't quite as fast or accurate as Adam, whom she had to admit was proving to be an impressive pilot, but she was still enjoying herself. In fact, she was enjoying herself much more than when she had flown in space. It was really quite a thrill to see the scenery fly by close-up. She could feel her pulse rise and the adrenalin pump as she pushed herself as close to the branches below as she dared, edging a little nearer each time, challenging herself more and more.

Her fun was cut short and replaced with fear by the next message from the Marianna.

Calmly and clearly, Carrie said "Grace, Adam, listen very

carefully..."

Chapter Seventeen
Can't Hope Won't Hope

It was certainly hot in the forest, but Connor still knew he was fevered. A wave of heat rushed through his head and chest and, perversely, sent a chill running down his spine. He paused a moment, pulled his water bottle to his lips and drained the last few drops from it. He checked his pack and found his next bottle was the last. He had to ration himself in case they needed to make the return journey. "This is not good," he thought to himself. "Perhaps we should have gone back, if only to get more supplies, be better prepared next time." It was too late now, they were almost there. He just hoped they made it in. He forced himself to continue walking. He didn't want to break for too long and let the others see him weaken. They were so close, he just had to force himself on a little further.

Evelyn and Max had remained vigilant, pointing out every tiny thing they noticed. Connor had lost count of the times they'd paused because Max thought he'd seen something move in the distant undergrowth. Still, it was definitely better to be safe than sorry.

Connor's feet were getting heavy and the flushes and chills were running through him more frequently. They'd definitely been too hasty hitting the path onwards. One foot in front of the other, he kept telling himself, and we'll be there in no time.

"Connor! Look out!" cried Max.

He'd been looking at his feet, willing them on. He looked up and the shape, whatever it was, hit him square in the chest, knocking him to the ground.

"What on earth was that?" shouted Evelyn.

Whatever it was, it was much bigger than the insect they'd encountered earlier.

"Grace, Adam. Listen very carefully, The Shark is back. You've got to..." The radio cut out. They stopped their craft.

"Carrie? What's going on? Are you there?" asked Grace. Silence. "Carrie!?" Still nothing. Grace's heart sank. Someone, or something, seemed determined to wipe them out. She felt like giving up. She caught sight of Adam's ship and it brought her back to the reality of her responsibilities. "Adam, what are you doing? We need to find some cover."

Adam was looking up at the sky above them, a sky now dominated by the enormous shadow of The Shark. Looming from above, it seemed even more terrifying than before. It blocked out Tau Ceti and threatened to destroy their world for a second time. Against the huge backdrop, Adam managed to make out four tiny dots of light. Four tiny dots that were growing larger by the second.

"It's too late for cover, Grace, we've just got to run." Adam hit the throttle in his ISC and made a beeline for the mountains on the far side of the plain. Grace wasn't as confident with the controls as Adam but, after gently turning the craft around, she followed Adam's lead, cranking up the speed and chasing after him.

The radio crackled to life again, but the reception was terrible. Grace and Adam could just about make out Evelyn's voice. ".. ne.. .... help. We're ....r attack."

It was some kind of bird and it was almost as big as Connor. It had a large, hard skull which it had used to butt him in the chest. As it flew on by, Max and Evelyn could see its strong, powerful beak and, as its four wings flapped up and down, the large, sharp talons on its feet.

Connor was winded and doubled up on the ground. As he uncurled, he looked up to the treetops above him and saw hundreds of these creatures lit up in bright green, circling them, waiting for their envoy to report back.

Gordon had rolled himself up in a ball, petrified by the creatures, and his fur had become needle sharp again. An eye on the side of his head was all that was visible of the creature underneath, looking out and surveying the area.

Evelyn and Max looked to Connor for leadership but he had no idea what to do, and neither did he have the strength.

"Grace, we need help. We're under attack," cried Evelyn into the radio. There was silence and then a very distorted reply. ".o ar. .e"

They exchanged confused glances, before Connor managed to decipher the message. "I think she said 'So are we'." They felt helpless.

Evelyn felt a tug on the leg of her flight suit. She looked down. "Not now, Gordon." He was pulling on her leg with his teeth.

"I think he's trying to tell us something," said Max. They all looked over in the direction he was dragging her and realised what it was. The roots of one of the trees had ridden up above the ground and created hollow. They started to run. Connor grabbed Max's hand and towed him along. He was using what felt like his last ounces of strength, but he was going to get there, he knew that.

Gordon got there first, followed by Isaac, the robot sliding through the gap in the roots. It was going to be a tight squeeze for Connor but he should be able to make it. Evelyn could feel the loose earth beneath her feet slipping but she kept driving forward, flying into the enclosure face first as she finally lost her grip.

Connor was pulling Max as fast as he could, keeping his

eyes fixed on his goal. He was rapidly closing in. Twenty feet... fifteen... ten... And suddenly he felt the strain on his shoulder grow inexorably and heard Max's muffled cries. He looked behind him and saw Max striving to keep hold of his hand. One of the birds had taken hold of Max's free arm and was trying to pull him up to the treetops. Connor stopped pulling and clenched his left fist, swivelling and punching the creature in the side of the head. Its beak opened in a silent cry of pain and it let go of Max. Searing agony reverberated down Connor's damaged arm, it felt like it was trying to break apart at the seams, and he let out an anguished scream of his own. His grip on Max's hand faltered and at that moment the bird took advantage and grasped his brother for a second time.

Connor scrabbled to grab either Max or the bird as they took off but he failed. He fell forward, the strength draining from his body as he looked up at his brother disappearing to the highest branches. Max was screaming, screaming for help, screaming for his brother, screaming in fear of his life.

Connor was broken. How could he let this happen to his brother? Another bird, and another, swooped down towards him. He scrambled to the tree, through the roots and to safety. The birds knew they had their prey cornered and continued to pepper the children with attacks, thrusting their beaks between the roots, trying to grab onto anything they could.

Connor collapsed at the back of the hollow, exhausted and burning up. He couldn't forgive himself for what he had allowed to happen but he no longer had any strength. He was crushed.

Evelyn and Isaac peered out between roots that made up the bars of their impromptu prison, trying to catch a glimpse of Max as he was carried up higher and higher into the treetops.

Grace and Adam reached the mountains ahead of The Shark's craft, but only just. The ISC was built for manoeuvrability, not speed, and the tadpole-shaped ships chasing them were considerably faster. They stayed close to the ground while they fled. As they reached the foot of the mountains and had to pitch their vehicles upwards, the realisation dawned on Grace that, without Carrie available, it was her and her alone that was controlling this craft. The thought unnerved her and forced her deeper into concentration. She wished she had never hit on the idea of taking a flying lesson.

As the ships scaled greater heights up the mountain they saw more and more snow and ice lining the ground. Whenever they flew a little too close, their movement carved a line through it and sent snow flying up into the air behind them.

Adam was leading the way. His brain was working overtime to combine the information pouring into him. His primary source was the mountainside directly in front of him, flying past him all too fast, but projected to the side of his hood was a computer visualisation of the mountain just around the next corner or past the next dip. The trick to flying the ship was gentle movements and being prepared for the next shift in direction. At the speed they were travelling, mistiming a turn could be disastrous – something Grace was constantly on the brink of discovering. She couldn't process everything like Adam and instead was relying on copying his movements. She wasn't as smooth and gentle as he was and her ship constantly clipped snow drifts, showering her screen with snow and rendering her momentarily blind.

Adam was also keeping an eye on their pursuers, looking out for any edge he could spy. Flinging the ship around corners he could see that their hunters were either slowing considerably or hitting the ground harder and heavier than Grace. Ahead of him, he saw the computer mapping out a deep crevasse and immediately knew what he had to do.

"Grace, I've got a plan, but you need to be watching the route, not copying me." He knew that if she just tried to copy him, the delay in her reactions could get her killed. She needed to react to the twists and turns in the ravine. "We can't afford to slow down."

"I don't know Ad." She was nervous. She had no faith in her own ability.

"OK then. When I go down, you go right and follow the edge of the mountain. Stay as close to the ground as possible, keep turning."

"What? Where are you going?"

"I'll find you." Adam pushed forward on the controls and dropped out of sight. Grace turned to the right as her brother had told her and pushed on around the mountain.

Two of the tadpoles followed Adam down into the crevasse, the other two following Grace. It was a tight passageway with sheer walls of rock and ice. One false step would send a ship to oblivion. Adam flung the ship left and right with a subtle movement of his wrist, taking the corners at breakneck speed. Behind him he could see the tadpoles struggling to keep up. With every corner they clipped the rock-face, sending showers of sparks flying. It was then that Adam knew his plan would work; he just needed to find the right moment to put it into action.

Grace had slowed down. Without her brother to guide her she was finding flying much more difficult, but she was managing to keep her trackers at bay by following Adam's advice. She wove whenever she could, finding rocky outcrops to bend her course around. She was flying aimlessly and suddenly found herself back out on the open plains. She knew if she stayed out there she would soon be caught so curved her path back towards the foot of the mountains. A few trees stood, lonely, on barren plains and gave Grace something to arc around. One whipped past on her left and she pulled the ship round past it to let one fly by on the right. Her monitors showed the tadpoles behind her and she saw one swipe the second tree and spin away, the tree collapsing under the weight of the damage. The tadpole regained control and resumed the chase. Now she understood Adam's instructions and, more determined than ever, continued to find corners to swing her followers around.

Adam was living by the skin of his teeth. The crevasse narrowed, giving even less room for error. He had given up watching the predators behind him; he needed to concentrate far too closely on his own movements. He just knew that if he got things right, he wouldn't need to worry about them.

It was then he saw his first opportunity arise. The scanners showed him what he needed to see. He took the first corner fast, flicking the controls to the left and back again to bring himself back on course. Then it was a right, a long, blind corner that didn't seem to end, but Adam knew it did. Abruptly.

He timed it perfectly, tilting the controls and guiding the ship straight up merely centimetres from the rock face. The first tadpole on his tail had no time to react and smashed headlong into sheer cliff in front of it. It exploded in a mighty fireball, the energy released forced the air out and upwards, giving Adam's ISC an extra boost on its way up towards the sliver of skyline above.

Adam checked behind him and saw the second tadpole emerge from the smoke and fire, but at the wrong angle. It had obviously been blinded by the explosion and whoever was flying it had lost their bearings. It clipped the cliff face on its way skywards, spinning and ricocheting from one side to another, dislodging chunks of rock and ice as it went. Adam increased the throttle and raced up out of the chasm as quickly as he could. Below him, the explosion and impacts were taking their toll and the crevasse was starting to collapse in on itself. Above him, he could see the walls crumbling, stones and rocks striking the front of his ship as he made his escape. The sliver of sky became larger and larger as he neared the top, but the collapsing walls bore in on him like a mouth closing.

And then he was out, free, and a rush of exultation passed through him. Behind him the crevasse fell in on itself, the walls burying the pursuing tadpole.

Adam looked around and gained his bearings. The gorge had taken him way up the mountain and the views greeting him were phenomenal. He let out a huge sigh, both in relief and admiration. In the distance, he could see his sister's craft, still being chased by the other two tadpoles. She was racing along the foot of the mountain range and flying onwards towards the lake. She needed help. Though she was managing to keep them at bay, she was doing nothing to get rid of them.

Max's arm felt like it had been wrenched from the socket. He had shut his eyes for the flight into the tops of the trees. It was way too high and he was terrified; terrified of what would happen if he was dropped and terrified of what would happen if he wasn't. The bird let go of his arm and he fell with a thud into its nest. He finally opened his eyes and looked around. Staring back at him were three chicks a matter of feet away. They pecked out in his direction and he scuttled back in the nest away from them. They were young and didn't yet have the strength in their legs to move in and attack him. They sat and squawked at their mother, begging her to feed them the fresh meat she had brought, but she wasn't having any of it. She flew off to try to scavenge them some dessert.

Left with just the chicks for company, Max looked around for some kind of escape. The nest was hundreds of metres in the air and yet there was nothing beneath him, only a sheer drop to the ground. He looked past the chicks, along the branch, to the trunk of the tree, but he knew he'd have no chance of clambering down to the ground. A shiver ran down his spine. He was trapped.

Shivers were running through Connor too. He'd given up and was curled at the back of their root prison. His strength and resolve were gone and he could think about nothing except how wretched he felt. Every beat of his heart echoed pain back from every organ in his body. He longed for it to be over, no matter what that meant.

Evelyn looked at her brother, sweat pouring from his brow, and felt helpless. It was down to her now and she had no idea what to do. The birds had circled the tree under which the children hid and periodically stabbed their beaks through the gaps, hoping they could catch a limb. Evelyn surveyed the options. Gordon sat quivering in fear. He had found their refuge but couldn't do anything to help now. Isaac was the only other option. She turned to the robot. "How strong are you? If you got to him, could you carry Max down?"

"Yes. If I can get to him," he said, "But it's a long climb, and there are a lot of those birds. I don't know if I could get there."

"Well, we've got to try." Evelyn reached into her rucksack. She had an idea. She pulled out an empty water bottle. "I can buy you a few seconds to get started."

Isaac set himself by one of the openings, and when Evelyn threw the empty bottle out he made a break for it. As Evelyn had hoped, the birds followed the object flying past them and Isaac had enough time to start clambering up the tree unnoticed. The birds' interest in the bottle quickly waned and they turned back to their cornered prey.

Isaac shaped his hands and feet into picks, stabbing them into the bark of the tree and propelling himself up at a rate of knots. All the while he was monitoring the birds below him with his omnivision. The creatures were still flying up and down from their nests and he knew it was only a matter of time before one of them saw his silver shape scaling the tree.

When it came, it swooped in from above, screeching to alert the other birds. Isaac swung his right arm, the edge tapered to the sharpest blade, and caught it across the throat, slicing deep into the flesh. A spray of hot blood gushed from the wound and the bird wheeled away, frantically flapping, panicking. It slowly fell from the air, careering closer and closer to the ground below.

The other birds heard its screams, smelt its blood falling from above, and prepared to attack their fallen brother.

It hit the ground with a thud. All strength lost, it tried and failed to stand. The others slowly closed in, eager to get their beaks on some fresh meat as their other prey was proving so elusive. The blood that moved its body now covered the ground, nothing left inside to keep it alive. It collapsed in a heap and they dived in, beaks and talons tearing the flesh apart.

"Where are the other two?" asked Grace.

"Don't worry, I got rid of them."

"What? You lost them?"

"Kind of, yeah."

Adam had caught up with his sister and her pursuers. He had the advantage of being able to fly in a straight line while Grace had dodged this way and that to keep them at bay. When he finally got there he announced himself by flying right across Grace's nose, something she did not appreciate in the slightest. She naturally veered to the right and out across the lake to avoid him, even though she was never in any real danger of hitting him.

The tadpoles split, one following each of them. Grace skimmed mere metres above the water's smooth surface, looking around to get her bearings now her brother was back on the scene.

"Grace, look out!" and she snapped her eyes front and centre. Rising from the water in front of her was a long-necked beast. Its head was bigger than the ISC and it was chomping its layered teeth in anticipation of the meal coming its way. Grace reacted immediately and instinctively, pushing the controls forward and diving head-first into the water, sending up a plume of water in her wake.

It took a moment before she could see clearly, the bubbles and waves crashing across her screen obscured her view. When they cleared, she was faced with an even more terrifying vision.

The creature she had so deftly avoided above the water had a second head lurking beneath the surface and its toothsome mouth was opening as she flew straight towards it. She veered right just as its jaws came crunching together, avoiding it by the skin of its teeth. The tadpole that followed her wasn't quite so lucky and ploughed headlong into the animal's face. Damaged and taking on water, the tadpole followed on behind Grace. They both pulled up out of the water and headed away from the beast as quickly as they could.

Adam circled around behind them, his pursuer in tow. The two long necks bobbed alternately as the animal chased after Grace and the damaged tadpole. It wasn't fast enough and Adam was quickly gaining on it. Seeing how the creature had gone for his sister, he had come up with what he hoped was the ideal way of losing the tadpole that was on his tail. He slowed a little and let the tadpole catch him before accelerating between the two nodding heads. As he'd hoped, the craft followed him. He wove from side to side a little, allowing the creature to gain sight of him and, at precisely the right moment, pushed himself up to top speed.

Adam saw the neck lunge towards him but he knew he was too fast to be caught; he just hoped that his timing was right. He kept his eyes on the monitors and saw the monster's teeth come clamping down on the tail of the tadpole as it tried to follow Adam's path. Perfect, he thought.

The creature slowed, delighted with its victory and its prey. The second head came round and grasped the body of the craft in its teeth, crushing it. The tadpole was strong but the metal began to buckle. Fuel cells were breached and a series of small explosions started to go off in the animal's mouth. It didn't like this one bit and decided the tadpole wasn't the meal it had hoped for. It curled its neck back and then tossed it forward with all its might, launching the ship into the air and across the lake. The jaws had caused too much damage and it was incapable of slowing or steering.

Adam watched, enthralled, as the creature gave up its pursuit. Its prey was too much trouble for too little reward so it dived back below the water. His eyes returned to the tadpole as it followed its inexorable path straight towards Speropolis, on the bank of the lake. It crashed near the peak of the dome and span up into the air, engulfed in flames, before disappearing into the forest on the far side of the city. The dome fractured, cracks seeping out from the point of impact, and the roof slowly fell away, leaving a gaping hole in the surface. A way in.

Grace only began to notice what else was going on when the tadpole pursuing her seemed to give up. It was clearly damaged and had been struggling to keep up or even fly in a straight line. Now it seemed to be returning to the mothership. She turned to fly towards her brother, only to realise that he was flying towards her as fast as he could.

"Adam, what are you doing, where are you going?"

"I've got an idea. I'll meet you at the city."

"What? But..."

"Don't worry. Just meet me there."

She gave up questioning him and flew towards Speropolis.

Adam was catching the fleeing tadpole, which had pointed itself up towards the sky, space and The Shark, resigned to defeat. As he approached, he prepared the ISC's water cannon and inserted a magnetic quantum transmitter into the water tank. He braced his finger over the trigger as he got closer and closer, trying to judge the right moment. He squeezed his finger and jets of water fired at the craft in front of him. He watched his scanners, waiting for the blinking light to leave his own ship and, hopefully, stick to the one in front of him.

The water was buffeting the tadpole but having little impact, but that wasn't what concerned Adam. It seemed to take forever but finally the tiny transmitter flew from the cannon. When Adam saw it had gone he stopped firing. It was now just down to whether it stuck or fell to the earth below. He watched the scanner intently. The depth didn't change, it was right in front of him. It had stuck. He gave up his pursuit and turned back towards Grace, safe in the knowledge that, if it went undetected back on The Shark, they would be able to track the ship's movement, wherever it disappeared to. Assuming it did disappear.

Isaac reached the top of the tree and surveyed the branches, searching for a glimpse of Max. When he couldn't see anything resembling the boy, he switched to thermal imaging. A hundred metres away he saw Max's outline cowering down in a nest, three small birds lunging and pecking in his direction. Still trying not to draw attention to himself, Isaac crept along a branch, staying as flat and as low as possible. Halfway along, the branch thinned and he had to leap six feet up to another. He felt the bark tear away in his hands as he struggled to maintain his grip. Feeling himself slip back down he quickly stabbed a hook on his right hand into the fleshy wood underneath. This time it held and for a moment he dangled before managing to swing his left arm over the top of the branch and clamber his way up. He froze for a second, making sure he hadn't been spotted, before slinking along the new branch.

Another fifty metres and he was looking straight down on Max and the nest. The boy was cowering, afraid to move for fear of encouraging anything's attention. Isaac dangled by his feet from the branch above, inching along to line himself up perfectly. Then, when he thought he'd got it right, he let go.

Max jumped out of his skin. For a moment he was convinced it was the mother finally returning to feed her chicks, but then he focused and saw who it really was.

"Isaac!" he shouted, before the robot gave him a hearty "Shhhh."

The chicks were squawking loudly at the intruder in their nest, desperate for their mother to come back and either get rid of this dangerous presence, or feed it to them.

"We need to get out of here, and soon," said Max.

"My thoughts exactly," replied the robot. The nearest trunk was twenty metres from them. If Max could hang on, Isaac could shimmy down, but it wouldn't be easy. He thought for a second before a plan evolved. "Put your arms around my neck."

Max did as he was told. Isaac used his flexible zirgenesium and moulded two loops and two handles into his torso. Max pushed his right hand through the loop on the left side of Isaac's chest and grasped the handle, before doing the same on the other side. He felt the loops tighten around his wrists, holding him tightly to the robot's body.

They turned towards the tree trunk only to see the pathway blocked. The mother bird had returned to the nest to check on her brood's pleas. In her beak she held some meat freshly ripped from the body of the bird Isaac had slashed on his way up. She was not pleased to see Max making his escape on Isaac's back. Slowly she moved in, looming over them ever larger. They inched backwards until Max felt his backside being pecked by the youngsters behind him. He gave Isaac a quick nudge with his knee to tell him not to go back any further, but with the mother homing in on them it just wasn't possible. Isaac glanced to either side of the nest in the hope that maybe there was a branch close enough to leap to, but there was nothing; just a two-hundred metre drop to the very solid earth below. The mother grew closer and closer. Max closed his eyes and buried his head in the back of Isaac's neck. He could feel the bird's breath.

Above them there was an almighty crack. Everyone and everything looked to see what was happening. A giant fireball crashed through the top of the trees. Max was blinded; his nightvision couldn't deal with the bright light. Time slowed down, a second took an hour. He couldn't do anything about his visor before he felt the branch start to give way beneath them. The fireball had torn through it and it was falling away from the trunk with them still on board. The bird in front of them took flight and tried to save her children as they tumbled from the nest. Isaac started to scramble back towards the trunk now their path was clear. His feet tore through the bark as he tried to gain enough momentum to launch himself at the shaft of the tree. He could see the branch was ripped clean from the trunk and as it fell it became a steeper and steeper climb to safety. When it became too much, he pushed away from the branch with all his might, launching himself and Max across the chasm to the trunk.

They hung in the air for what seemed like an eternity. Max regained his vision and immediately wished he hadn't. At first he thought they were falling straight down, his stomach rose up the back of his throat and he had to swallow down the acid. It made him cough and gag. It certainly wasn't what he wanted the last thing he ever tasted to be. As his perception came back to him, he realised they weren't falling down but were flying across and straight into a tree. In slow motion, he saw Isaac turn his hands into pickaxes and swing them violently into the flesh of the tree.

All of the air was knocked out of Max's body as they impacted with the tree. He struggled to breathe and he felt the acid rise in the back of his throat again. His hands lost grip on the handles on Isaac's chest and wrists wrenched against the loops holding him in. Isaac's right hand bounced back off the bark but the left tore in. He didn't have a firm grip but he scrabbled with his hands and feet and dug in. They slithered down ten, fifteen, twenty metres before Isaac finally managed to gain full control over their progress and draw them to a halt.

"You OK Max?" he whispered.

Max could barely reply, he still didn't have any breath in his body. "I... think... so..." he struggled to get out.

"Alright then. Next stop, ground floor..."

Evelyn was trying to track Isaac's progress but he was so far away it was nigh on impossible. Still she stared and, like her brother, she was almost blinded by the flash of light as the ball of fire crashed through the top of the trees. She had no idea if Max and Isaac were OK but she didn't have time to think about it before the fireball crashed only metres away from where they were hiding. She turned her head and reconfigured the settings on her visor before looking back.

It was some kind of ship, but it definitely wasn't an ISC, that was about all she could tell from the mangled flaming wreckage. She breathed a sigh of relief before she realised the danger they were in. She knew the trees burned well and as branches and debris fell she knew that they weren't safe to stay there.

"Connor, we have to get moving," she said.

He didn't move. She could see his chest rising and falling but otherwise he was motionless.

"Connor!" she shouted.

He opened his eyes and she saw that he had no strength left whatsoever. All his effort had gone into one movement of his eyelid. There was only one thing for it: another stembiotic shot. She knew there was a risk of an overdose, but without the adrenaline rush, there was no way he was moving and there was certainly no way she could move him herself. She grabbed her backpack and rifled through the first aid supplies, there was one shot left. She turned back to her brother.

"Connor, if this doesn't work, I'm sorry, but I have to try." She thought she saw a look of recognition, a look of understanding in his eyes.

She pulled the cap off the needle with her teeth and sank it into his arm. Nothing happened. Evelyn bit her lip. Last time the effect had been almost instantaneous. She resisted the urge to check his pulse, instead fixing her eyes on the rise and fall of his chest and listening for his breathing. She thought she saw a difference, a deeper intake, a louder sound. She checked over her shoulder. The fire outside was growing stronger and brighter. She needed him to hurry up. She looked back. His eyes were wider, his breathing far more controlled.

"Connor, we've got to go. I don't know what's out there, but I'm not going to burn up in here."

He tried to speak but his mouth was dry. He sat up and coughed. He ran his tongue around his mouth, trying to find some saliva. "OK", he finally managed to croak. He pushed himself forward and crawled to the root bars to their cell, his strength returning by the second.

"Where are we going?" he asked. It was a good question. Evelyn struggled to remember the direction they came from and where they were heading.

"Let's get out of here first," was all she could offer.

Gordon spotted they were on the move and readied himself to follow them. They lined up, ready to spring into action like sprinters on a start line.

"Three, two, one..."

Evelyn made a clean getaway but Connor was struggling. She reached out a hand to him and pulled him forward just as a flaming branch crashed down behind him. Connor needed to focus. His strength hadn't fully returned. He was feeling woozy, just like he had after the first shot. He felt his feet stumble and underneath him and he nearly fell, but he managed to catch himself.

They ran until they could no longer feel the heat from the fires and until Connor had run out of breath. He propped himself against a tree, wheezing, looking back at the wreckage. His mind finally cleared and he knew the question he had to ask.

"Where's Max?"

As if on cue, he felt a tap on his head. He looked up and saw his brother on Isaac's back. He moved out of the way to let them reach the ground. Isaac released Max's arms and the boy fell onto his back. He was exhausted. He just needed a moment to recover, but he wasn't going to get one. Connor and Evelyn both fell on top of him, hugging him, so relieved to have him back.

Max pushed them off and struggled free.

Evelyn sat back on her heels and surveyed the area. It soon became apparent that something was different. It took her a moment to realise what it was.

"The birds have gone," she said, to no one in particular.

"What?" asked Connor.

"The birds have gone."

"That's great news, Evelyn, but..."

"We need to get some fire to take with us, to ward them off," she said. "Come on Isaac." Connor went to push himself up but Evelyn gave him a gentle push back down. "You stay here and rest with Max. Me and Isaac can do this."

She and the robot trotted back off to the fire, collecting sturdy branches that would make good torches, while Connor and Max rested their aching bodies. Gordon sat at the feet of the brothers warily eyeing the darkness. Max's arms hurt terribly, especially his wrists. The loops and handles had saved him but they had chaffed. He shook his hands to try to get rid of the cramping pain, it didn't work especially well but he had to do something.

Connor sat and watched him, memories flooding back through his mind. He had forgotten what had happened to Max but all of a sudden it was at the forefront of his mind. He saw his brother being torn from his grasp by the giant bird and how helpless he was.

"Max, I..."

"It's OK, Connor."

"No, I'm sorry, I should never have let you come. It was too dangerous."

"No Connor. I'm alright. I'm fine."

"That's not the point. Next time, you're staying behind."

"Oh, Connor..." he whined, but before he could finish complaining, Evelyn was back. She and Isaac were carrying six suitable torches, one of which they had lit. Isaac held it like the Olympic beacon while Evelyn tucked the spare branches into one of the back packs. Then she took the remaining branches one at a time, lit them and passed them to Connor and Max, keeping one for herself.

They all stood ready, looking out into the darkness of the forest, the flames from their torches casting dancing shadows across the ground before them.

"Now, which way is it again?" asked Connor.

They looked at each other, all clueless.

Finally Isaac piped up. "Thataway," he said and they followed the direction he was pointing.

The radio buzzed and crackled to life and then Carrie's voice echoed out of it. "Children? Children, are you OK?"

"Carrie! You're back," said Grace.

"Where did you go?" said Adam, "What happened?"

"The Shark. It jammed all my outgoing signals."

"But... But you're back?" said Grace, not understanding.

"Well, The Shark's gone now..."

"What? It's gone? When? Where did it go?"

"I don't know. It just disappeared a moment ago."

"I don't understand what it wants. Why is it tormenting us like this? It tries to kill us, it leaves us alone, it tries to kill us, it leaves us alone..." said Grace, flummoxed.

"I wish I knew Grace. If we knew what it was doing..."

"Yes, Carrie? If we knew what it was doing then what?" asked Grace, but the computer wasn't allowed to finish her thought. Adam was already steering his way through the hole in the domed roof and was desperate to check out the city below.

"Come on Grace, what are you waiting for? There's a city to explore here!"

Hundreds of metres below them they could see the single- and two-storey buildings that had been raised. It was sparse for a city but it had been built for a population to grow into. It was always way too big for the 10,000 settlers that had been left there ten years ago.

They slowly moved their craft into the city limits, looking in every direction for any sign of life, but there was none. When the city had been colonised, farm animals had been left too but these were nowhere to be seen either. They city was silent and deserted. It was eerie. It unnerved Grace and Adam.

As they touched down they began to recognise the town. They had seen pictures of the city back on The Magellan, what seemed like a lifetime ago, and the low buildings were instantly familiar in a way they had not been from above. They had been built to cultivate the flora of the planet, allowing the plants to grow over each building. Each house had a different feel depending on which coloured flowers were blooming across the walls, and they all felt organic, as though they had grown out of the land itself, like the buildings were alive. Adam could see through the windows and doorways that inside they were as modern as anything on board the Magellan, at odds with their external appearance.

For a moment they admired their new surroundings. It must have been a monumental task to build the dome and everything within it. They looked up and, rather than the white structure they had seen from the outside, they could see the sky. The roof was clear and showed them brilliant views over to the mountains and deep into the forest. At the very outskirts of the city, though, the dome became white again, giving the feeling of being walled in.

"It looks like Connor was right," said Grace, a note of disappointment in her voice. "There's no one here, is there?

The question hung in the air. Adam wasn't sure if it was meant rhetorically, but regardless he didn't know what to say in response.

"I guess I knew it would be like this," she continued, "But I always hoped I was wrong. I hoped we would find an explanation and we could start again."

Again, Adam had nothing to say, but Grace continued her lament as they began to walk. They began to bandy about ideas as to what had happened; questions which ended only in one word: Shark. There wasn't time to dwell on it though because there was one task they had to do above all else. They started to run through the wide open streets looking for the gate to the forest, where they would hopefully be welcoming the others at any moment.

Chapter Eighteen
Feeling Hope's Pull

Grace was getting worried. The last time they had heard from Connor, Evelyn and Max was when the tadpoles had arrived and the message had been disturbing. They were under attack from something but she had no idea what. The radio connection still wasn't working, and there was no video feed either. She and Adam had been waiting at the gates for nearly an hour and, by her estimation, the Morans should have arrived at least half an hour ago. Something wasn't right, of that she was sure.

The first thing they had done when they reached the gate was check the computer systems. They appeared to have been hacked by someone from the inside, ensuring that nothing would be able to operate them from outside the gates. Adam rapidly reprogrammed the system and made everything operational again, but he was confused by what it all meant.

"I mean, why would the people in here want to make sure no one from outside could get in?" he asked Grace. She didn't have an answer. "It doesn't make sense," he continued, "There aren't any other people on the planet. Who were they trying to keep out?"

They sat in silence for a moment before Grace said the only answer that had come into her head. "Us?"

"Well that doesn't make any sense. They didn't know we were coming. And anyway, what advantage would that have?"

"Oh, I don't know, Adam. I just couldn't think of anything else."

Adam continued to theorise, dancing from one theory to the next, none of them making much sense. Grace blocked him out and eventually he got the hint and went to reinterrogate the computer systems. Grace sat herself down on a bench outside one of the houses and thought about the others. It was only a few months ago that she couldn't stand the sight of them; Connor had almost physically turned her stomach back then. Now she couldn't stop thinking about them.

She remembered how she had felt when they arrived in the Pod, when they had left the Magellan, when it had been destroyed. Her world had caved in and the only people around her were uncouth interlopers or her brother. She felt bad for dismissing her brother. It wasn't his fault; he'd always been disconnected. He just couldn't offer her the emotional support she had needed. The black hole that had opened up inside had almost swallowed her whole. Her bickering with Connor had been the thing that had pulled her through and kept her despair at bay.

It had been a long journey to Speropolis, but looking back, Grace realised she wouldn't have made it without the others, especially Connor. They had their differences but he kept her grounded and his bravery was invaluable. She hadn't noticed it at the time, but in the months since the attack, her black hole had receded, disappeared, and that was all down to the way they had moved forward and become a family of their own. A dysfunctional family, but a family nevertheless.

But now she was scared. Time was slipping away and they still hadn't arrived. Where were they? What was she going to do if it was just her and Adam left? It was no fun waiting, worrying, not knowing.

*   *   *   *   *

When they had set off, the birds had chased after them. They had swooped down, trying to scare the children, but the flaming torches thrust back in their faces had soon gotten the message across. They gave up, returning to their nests in the upper branches, but always keeping an eye on the children in case they ever let their guard down.

Progress was slow. Connor didn't have the energy to walk at full pace. In fact, he had to stop every ten minutes to catch his breath. His face grew paler and paler and Evelyn was getting seriously worried about him. They were out of stembiotics and their food and water supplies were getting dangerously low too. He managed to force himself onwards each time, thinking about how he'd be letting the group down if he failed. He couldn't bear to think what might happen to his brother and sister, but there was also Grace and Adam; they were relying on him to get them inside. He couldn't let them down.

This was how it had been since the day he had walked on board the Pod and introduced himself. One way or another, he and Grace had forced each other onwards. They had forced real thought and proper preparation to be put into decisions. There was no doubt in his mind that they wouldn't have made it as far as they had on their own.

He stood again, determined to finish the journey. He forced one foot down in front of the other, pushing himself on to complete his mission.

A rush of jubilation ran through the group when they saw the wall of the city in front of them and, a mere hundred metres away, the gateway, but by the time they reached it Connor was ready to collapse again.

When they saw the gates, Evelyn and Max had wanted to run, but they knew they couldn't, or rather shouldn't. Instead, they all walked side by side, a show of solidarity, even if they didn't know who they were showing it to.

Standing at the gates, Connor instantly leaned against the wall, holding on to whatever strength he could. He closed his eyes and breathed deeply. "I could just go to sleep right now," he thought. He was jolted back to reality by his brother.

"Connor, come on, open the doors."

His reactions were dulled and it took him a moment to comprehend the request. He pushed himself away from the wall and walked over to the computer.

"And what if they won't open?" he muttered. It wasn't really a question, but it was the thing that had been at the back of all their minds since it became obvious Connor wouldn't have the strength for a return trip. No one dared answer the query. No one knew what happened then.

Connor pressed his hand up against the screen for the scan to take place. The screen came alive instantly, an improvement on all of the other gates they had visited. The whir of the computer systems got the adrenalin pumping again. They were actually going to get in. "This is it," he told himself.

The screen lit up and he removed his hand, scan complete. They waited for what seemed like an eternity. The gates slowly swung open.

"Finally," said Max sarcastically, as they queued up, waiting for the gates to open enough to let them through.

Grace was just thinking about setting off in search of the others when she heard the gate mechanism kick in and start to open. She grabbed Adam and ran over to greet them, flushed with excitement. When the others were finally revealed, Grace leapt forward in delight, embracing Connor and, before either she or Connor knew what she was doing, planting a kiss on his lips.

"Eeewwww!" shouted Max, but Grace didn't care. She didn't know where it had come from but it immediately felt right to her so she continued. She'd never been this impetuous before, but she was glad she was now.

Connor, on the other hand, was still not feeling well and really did not appreciate Grace's attention. When his mind caught up with what was happening he struggled to break the embrace but he didn't have the strength. He managed to pull his mouth away from hers long enough to take a breath and say "Grace, I..." before he got a horrible feeling in the pit of his stomach.

Grace looked at him and took a pace back. Only then did she notice just how unwell he was. His face had been lacking colour but he was rapidly turning green. She could see what was coming next and he could feel it. He opened his mouth to say something, but only one thing came out. He fell forward and Grace looked down at her vomit splattered shoes.

"I always knew kissing was bad for you," Max said, a little too gleefully for Grace's liking. She could have died. She turned on her heel and ran. She didn't care where to, she just needed to hide somewhere until the embarrassment was gone, and she was acutely aware that that could take a very long time.

Evelyn ignored Grace and Max and went straight to tend to her brother. She was very concerned about him and beckoned Adam over to give her a hand carrying him.

"Is there anyone here that can help him?" she asked.

"There's no one. A ghost town," he replied.

"What about the computers?"

"They're all online."

"We need to hook him up to one, get a med report."

"Over here."

Every building in Speropolis could run medical tests and, for many ailments, offer treatment. Connor had returned to his ghostly white complexion and barely had the strength to move his legs. Evelyn and Adam were forced to drag him through the door of the building. There was a terminal in the lounge so they brought him to the sofa and laid him down. Evelyn mopped his brow and poured water into his mouth while Adam searched for the medikit.

Grace felt like she was standing on the edge of an abyss. She wanted to fall in, or dissolve, or in some way just disappear.

She felt like such a fool and couldn't begin to envisage a situation where she would want to see the Morans again. She screwed up her eyes as tight as she could and held her head in her hands as she sank to the ground. She kept reliving the experience. She could see with perfect clarity the looks she'd gotten and she could hear Max's comment ringing in her ears. She shuddered. It was too much to take and she could feel the tears forming in the corners of her eyes.

This was not how she had imagined her first kiss.

Connor had fallen unconscious. His body was shivering and shaking all over and he was sweating so profusely that the cushions on the sofa beneath him were soaked through. Adam rushed back in with the diagnostic sleeve, shooed Gordon out of the way and slipped it up Connor's arm. The motors quietly whirred as they pierced his skin and began to take readings of a variety of chemical levels in his blood stream. Adam had also found some stembiotic syringes and was ready to administer them if it proved necessary. They all gathered around their fallen shipmate, awaiting the readout that would tell them what treatment was required.

The screen on the sleeve lit up. They held their breath as it spelled out its answer.

"Healthy."

*　　　*　　　*　　　*　　　*

It sounded like an explosion on the far side of the city. Grace sat bolt upright, her heart in her mouth. She looked up through the roof of the city, searching the sky for a glimpse of The Shark but there was nothing. She had no way of communicating with Cary or the others. She knew she should go back and find them but they had their hands full with Connor. They probably hadn't heard it; it wasn't that loud where she was.

Getting to her feet, she decided to investigate. She ran through the streets in the direction of the noise, slowing as she got in the vicinity of its origin, poking her head around corners, trying not to draw attention to herself.

When Grace saw it, she had no idea what it was. It was a perfectly spherical... thing... sitting in a crater in the dirt, a sheet of dust still rising up around it. It was completely smooth and had a sheen to it, like a black mirror. She felt as though every heartbeat was audible within a hundred metres and she struggled to keep her breathing under control. She was fascinated and terrified at the same time. It was completely different to The Shark, and she was sure it had nothing to do with that terrifying monstrosity, but what on Baldr was it?

She listened carefully as a number of valves hissed and vents exhaled and then watched as some kind of door separated itself from the body of the craft. It pushed out and then fell forwards, hinged at the bottom. A cloud of smoke was forced out of some of the mechanisms and through the smoke and the dust she saw a figure walking down the steps and out of the craft.

She held her breath, petrified of what this might mean for her, for them. And then, as the smoke cleared, she started to recognise him. It must have been the shock of unruly white hair. He was older than she'd seen him before, but not by much. Which was remarkable given it must be over 200 years since the photo she'd seen was taken. She ran from her hiding spot.

"Marco Moran?!"

He looked only momentarily surprised by her cry. "Why hello there..."

"But how are y...? What's going...? Where did you come from? What's this ship? What are you doing here? And who's that?" She pointed to the ship, before realising the answer to her question. "Is that Simona? Who's she carrying?"

It was indeed Simona Silmenkova, Marco's wife, carrying a young baby in her arms. Before Grace could ask any more questions, Marco cut in. "Grace, calm down..."

"How do you know my name?"

"That's not important right now. Where are the others? We don't have much time."

"How can he be healthy? Look at him," cried Evelyn, petrified for her brother's life. Arriving at the gates, she had thought the worst was over, but if they didn't find out what was wrong with Connor soon, it would be too late. "So what do we do, give him more stembiotics?"

"You've already dosed him. How much has he had?" asked Adam.

"Two doses."

"If two doses haven't sorted him out, a third isn't going to do anything, except perhaps send him over the edge. In fact, I'd be worried the stembiotics are strengthening whatever's making him ill."

"So what are you suggesting? Doing nothing?"

"Exactly." He paused. "For now, at any rate."

"Look at him, Adam," she pleaded and they both turned to look down on Connor's ghostly appearance. His breathing was incredibly shallow and he was covered in sweat. Neither of them was comfortable with leaving him as he was, but it was well known that stembiotics were best in small doses.

"We might kill him if we inject him again," said Adam.

"Yes, and we might kill him if we don't."

"So you want me to guess? You guess, he's your brother."

Evelyn was getting frustrated. She had no idea what to do, but felt they should be doing something. She let out an exasperated sigh. "Oh, I don't know... What do you think?"

"You know what I think..."

"I know, I know, don't do anything. This is ridiculous."

Before they could go round in anymore circles, Grace burst in the door with Marco and Simona in tow. Evelyn and Adam spun around and instantly recognised the famous scientist. They were struck dumb, unable to comprehend how he was there or what was going on.

"Where is the sick boy?" demanded Simona, casting her eye around the room. She had a thick accent that the children couldn't place; they'd never met anyone who didn't speak the way they did. They were all too bemused by her arrival to give her a reply but she could see plainly enough where Connor lay. She handed her son to her husband and immediately knelt by Connor's side.

Max and Isaac ran in behind them all, suddenly aware of the commotion going on. He had been busy exploring the city, or at least a few of the streets nearby, unaware of Connor's deteriorating health.

"Who's that? Uncle Marco?" he shouted as he came in. Grace shushed him, conscious that there were bigger issues at hand.

"What is this drek on his arm?" she asked rhetorically, pulling the diagnostic sleeve off and throwing it to the floor. She pulled a syringe from a small kit of medical supplies she'd brought with her, and slapped the inside of Connor's elbow, trying to raise a vein. With Connor's pulse so weak, it was difficult to find one viable, but she managed it and inserted the needle swiftly enough to make the watching children jump back in alarm at the brutality of her skill. The vial attached slowly filled with Connor's dark red blood, his dim pulse preventing it filling any faster. When she was satisfied she had collected enough, she whipped off the vial and attached another; this one full of a swirling blue and yellow liquid. She pushed the plunger down, forced the liquid into Connor's body, pulled the needle out of his arm and stood up. "OK. This is done. He'll be walking in three hours. Leave him until then."

Evelyn walked towards her brother. She wasn't sure why. She wanted to say something, to squeeze his hand, to let him know she was there and thinking of him.

"I said leave him," said Simona sternly. "Come on, out, out." She gestured for everyone to leave the room. Evelyn was going to protest but she didn't even really know what she wanted to do. She decided Simona was clearly in charge so she dropped it.

"He's going to be OK, isn't he?" asked Max, who was confused by everything that had been going on around him.

"Oh yes, honey, he'll be fine if we give him space to recover," said Simona, dressing her voice up and babying him a little too much for Max's liking. He wasn't afraid of her hard exterior and happily let her know what he thought of her tone. "I am eight, you know, not a baby. Talk to me like an adult."

Simona just shrugged and laughed. "Oh, sweetie."

Once they got outside, Simona pulled Grace to one side and held out the vial of Connor's blood. She tapped something on the top and instantly the contests of the vial froze. "Take this, and when we meet in two years for the first time you give back to me. Then I make the medicine."

Grace took the vial and peered at the contents. She had questions she wanted to ask but Simona had already walked off to rejoin her husband. They sat down at a table and chairs outside one of the homes, Simona taking her son back from Marco. Evelyn, Max and Adam sat opposite them and began their interrogation. Before they got any answers to their questions, though, Marco had a question of his own.

"So you two must be Evelyn and Adam, then?"

Grace had arrived at the table and overheard the question.

"So hang on, you knew who I was instantly, you know Max too apparently, but you don't know them? What's going on here?"

"OK, OK. I guess we owe you some answers..." said Marco, before being interrupted by Grace.

"Yes, you..." said Grace rather forcefully, before seeing the look Simona was shooting her and deciding to change tack. "Thank you Marco, that would be good."

"Right. So first of all, yes, we have met you before, Grace.

And Max, and Connor. But Evelyn, Adam and Isaac were not there."

"When was this?" asked Grace, "I don't remember this."

"No, this is, ooh, about two years from now. We meet you for the first time for us, but for you it is about the fourth or fifth time, I think."

"So where were we? Were we OK?" asked Evelyn, getting scared that something went wrong for her and Adam in the future.

"Yes, you were, you were fine, you were just... somewhere else. Don't worry." Marco seemed a little flustered by the question and it didn't really put Evelyn at ease, but having said they were fine, and remembering Adam's words back on the Marianna about destiny and knowing the future, she decided that was enough.

"So this is when I give you Connor's blood, right?" said Grace, looking over at Simona a little wearily.

"Ja. Then I can diagnose him and make the medicine to make him better," said Simona.

"But why don't you just tell us how to make the medicine, or write it down?" asked Evelyn, "Then we can tell you in two years and you can make it and bring it back."

"It's complicated, my dear," said Simona, making no attempt to explain. Marco could see that the children weren't going to just leave it at that.

"Do you know what an ontological paradox is?" he asked.

Adam's hand shot up, but Grace and Evelyn just looked blank.

"Adam?"

"It's a paradox about the creation of objects or ideas." Grace and Evelyn's looks remained blank and Marco could see further explanation would be required.

"OK, a paradox is a something that contradicts itself." Marco scratched his eyebrow and looked around, but he was still getting nothing from the children. He shared a smile with Adam and continued. "OK, so an ancient philosopher called Socrates said 'All I know is that I know nothing'. But if he knows that he knows nothing, then he knows something. But if the only thing he knows is that he knows nothing and he's wrong about that, then he really does know nothing. In which case he knows that he knows nothing. And so on. Do you see?"

"Yeah, I think so," said Evelyn, "So the second thing makes the first thing a lie, but if you correct the first thing it makes the second thing a lie."

"That's right, so the sentence can never be totally correct, it is always half wrong."

"I don't get it," said Max.

"Ah, don't worry about it sweetie," said Simona.

"Stop talking to me like that." The others chuckled but Simona scowled in his direction.

"Max, it's OK," whispered Marco to his great nephew, "I don't think they really get it either." He gave the boy a wink and a smile.

"OK, so what's this got to do with the medicine?" asked Grace.

"Would you agree that everything has to be created? Someone has to make it?"

"Yes."

"Including ideas?"

"Of course."

"Well, if we tell you how to make the medicine now, and then you tell us in two years, and then we come back here and tell you, the idea of how to make the medicine is never actually created, it's a recipe that just goes in a big circle, around and around."

"OK, I understand that," said Grace, "But what's so bad about that? What would happen if we created this 'paradox'?"

"I don't know Grace, and I don't want to find out."

"No, but I still don't understand what's wrong with it?"

"Grace, I have created a working time machine. To our knowledge, the only working time machine in the universe. There's a big responsibility associated with that. I can't afford to do anything wrong so I am being extra cautious, OK. Can we leave it at that?" Grace nodded, aware that she was talking to perhaps the most intelligent man who ever lived and so, if he wanted her to do something, she probably ought to do it. "Excellent," he continued, "I've probably told you too much already."

"What's your baby's name?" asked Evelyn and they all realised they had been overlooking the one member of the crew they didn't previously know existed.

"His name is Leonardo," said Simona.

"We call him Leo," said Marco.

"Can I hold him?" asked Evelyn, reaching out to Simona. Reluctantly the scientist passed the child across and Evelyn delighted in showering him with attention.

"Right, listen, we have a lot of work to do before we go again, but I can answer questions a little longer."

"How long are you staying, Uncle Marco?" asked Max.

"At the moment the ship will only stay in one place for twenty-four hours at a time. But I'm working on it."

"So you're going tomorrow? That's not fair."

"I know, but we'll meet again, I'm sure."

"So how did you get here?" asked Adam, "Did you come in the Dream Genie?"

"Oh, you saw that interview, did you? Yes. We came in the Dream Genie. We left about a year ago and I've been trying to fix it ever since. Well, make it work better anyway."

"Why did you call it the Dream Genie?" asked Evelyn.

"Because it came to me in a dream, out of nowhere, it seemed like magic."

"Connor thought the Dream Genie filmed your dreams," said Grace, chuckling. Marco chuckled too.

"No, no, no. That's called an Auto-Somnolent Heliographic

Recording Device. I invented that too. That's what I recorded my dream of the Dream Genie on. I tell you, you have the best ideas when you're asleep!" He chuckled again.

"So what happened? Everyone thought you were dead," asked Grace.

"I can understand that. You disappear in an explosion for a couple of hundred years, it's a natural assumption to make," he said, laughing again. "No, it just didn't quite work how it was designed to. Still doesn't. But we're getting closer, aren't we honey?"

"Oh, ja," said Simona, sounding thoroughly annoyed with the whole thing.

"Look, don't mind her," said Marco, "I just told her we'd be gone for a week. Two tops. Like a honeymoon."

"A year later, here we are. Our second meeting with humans in all that time, and both times it's been his relatives."

"It's been... difficult. But I'll get it sorted, and we'll get back home."

"But you..." Adam stopped short. Everyone turned to stare at him and for perhaps the first time in his life he thought it might be best not to say what was in his mind. But then Marco and Simona must have already known it too. Grace had already told them that everyone thought they had died in the explosion. They knew they wouldn't be going back to earth, otherwise the children would have known all about it already.

"Anyway," said Marco, breaking the awkward silence, "We're here to help you guys out. That ship of yours up there needs an overhaul. Now Adam, from everything I've heard, you're the man I need to work with. We're going to design a way to make that engine of yours capable of flying you wherever you want to go."

"Can we get back to earth?" asked Max.

"If that's where you want to go," replied Marco.

"Is that where we should go?" asked Grace. It was a much more important question. Where they were, they were stranded;

no humans within light years. Making the right next step was vital.

"Wherever you choose to go, I promise you it's the right decision," said Marco. "I can't tell you more than that."

"So while you and Adam design this engine, what do we do?"

"I need you guys to all go and collect the parts and equipment you'll need to convert this beast. I can start your list now, but we'll be adding to it.

When Marco had finished his initial list of two dozen components for the children to find, he and Adam sat down at a desk, called up the schematics of the Marianna and got to work. Adam was going to be taking charge of the rebuilding process and it was vital he understood how everything was going to work.

"Adam, before I explain how this works, I need to effectively rewrite astrophysics for you," said Marco, a little dauntingly. "My theory isn't quite perfected yet, but it seems to work in principal."

"Are you sure we can do this? You're only here for another 21 hours."

"The basic concept is simple. Here..." Marco pulled a black piece of cloth from his pocket and spread it flat on the desk in front of him. "General theory says that the universe is, in relative terms, flat, like this cloth, and it is spreading outwards. However, we know that the movement of light is influenced by gravity. My theory says that the universe is, effectively, still one plain, but that plain is not uniformly flat."

Marco picked up the cloth and crumpled it into a ball in his hand. "Now, if the universe were like this cloth, points which were incredibly distant on the uniform plain are now considerably closer on the 'crumpled plain', as I am calling it. The issue is that gravity still restricts light and matter to travelling along the uniform plain. The engine we are going to build mirrors elements of the engine in the Dream Genie. It enables the craft to break free of gravity on the uniform plain and take a direct route through the crumpled plain to your destination."

Adam sat open-mouthed in wonder. "But that... How did you...? That doesn't make...? What about the laws of...?"

"Ah yes, the laws of physics. Actually, they all still apply. This theory works in harmony with all the work that has gone before. Dark energy holds the uniform plain together and means that, for the most part, you may as well consider the uniform model to be correct. The crumpled plain model only applies when you wish to cut corners, otherwise it has next to no effect on anything.

"And you came up with this...?"

"That's a story for another time, when we don't have to build an engine."

Marco then launched into a detailed explanation of how the engine worked, how it would increase velocity in the uniform plain as well as allow travel through the crumpled plain, how the map of the crumpled model changed and how to plot a route in the ever changing schematics of the crumpled universe. Navigation was significantly more complex and would require a lot of his attention while they were in flight. Fortunately, flights would be significantly shorter from now on.

Adam would regularly stop him to ask questions and Marco was impressed with their insight. He didn't often come across a student with Adam's skills and knowledge and he was reminded of himself at the same age. Finally Adam got round to asking the one question that Marco was not looking forward to.

"So what do we use as fuel?"

"Now," said Marco, pausing to take a breath. His demeanour changed, his face became more serious and he looked Adam in the eye. "This is the one problem. It runs," he paused again, "on the souls of children. You and your friends will have to choose someone to..."

Adam saw through him right away. "No, seriously Marco,

what does it run on?"

"Oh, you're good. I was sure that would get you."

Adam was offended and not afraid to show it. "Do you really think I'm that stupid? I doubt even Connor would have believed that."

"OK, OK, I'm sorry. It's a good question though. We can't run this engine on the renewable fuels you normally use. In fact, I had to invent a new fuel – a compound I call Moranasthite."

"Moranasthite?"

"Hey – I invented it, I can name it after myself. Anyway, it's incredibly unstable. Let even a small quantity come into contact with oxygen and it will either violently explode or evaporate into nothing."

"Those are very different reactions. Surely it does either one or the other, it can't do both, can it?"

"It can. And there's no way of telling which it will do so you have to be incredibly careful. It was Moranasthite that destroyed my lab back on earth."

"So how do we get some of this Moranasthite?"

"You use a Moranasthiser, of course."

"A Moranasthiser? Couldn't you choose something that was a bit easier to say?"

"Don't you find it fun? Moranasthiser, Moranasthiser, Moranasthiser."

"Marco," said Adam, his voice filled with concern, "I think that year spent in the Dream Genie with just Simona and Leo might have... Well, it might have had an effect on you."

"Tell me about it. There was three months in the middle when Simona didn't even speak to me. It was only when she was giving birth that she finally broke the silence. Anyway, we're getting off topic. Focus, Marco, focus." He stopped speaking and gave himself a slap around the face, shaking his head and blinking before returning to his young student. "Right. Sorry about that. OK, where was I? That's it, Moranasthiser. I have a spare one in the Genie. Consider it yours."

Adam was a little alarmed by the disturbed state of the genius in front of him. For a fleeting moment he considered whether he could truly trust the advice he was being given, but he had to concede that the man's theories, no matter how outlandish, made sense. He also knew from his own recent experiences that an extended period of time in an enclosed space with only a few other people was enough to test anyone.

"Thanks, Marco," the boy said, and then, trying to get the conversation back on track, he asked, "So what do I need to create Moranasthite? What's it made of?"

"Ah!" Marco called out, as though having a eureka moment, "Good question, my boy, good question. Moranasthite is an incredibly complex compound. The Moranasthiser will take in any substance you give it, harvest the elements it needs to create the compound and spit out the rest. Then it'll give you a read out of what else it needs, what is missing. It can turn any trip you make into a bit of a treasure hunt, just to warn you."

The lessons continued. Marco retrieved the spare Moranasthiser from the Genie and demonstrated it for Adam. It was a sleek, black cone-shape, about two feet tall. At the bottom was the submission draw, where substances were inserted for evaluation and harvesting. Marco picked up a handful of dirt from the ground and deposited it, sliding the draw back in. The machine came to life, beeping and whirring. The outside lit up with hypnotically swirling patterns in a variety of shades of green. Adam stared at them for a full thirty seconds before being able to tear his eyes away.

"Why the patterns, Marco?"

"Oh, presentation. I just liked them, really. You can program it to display all sorts of pictures. Whatever you fancy, really. There comes a point where something doing a task is all well and good, but you want it to look good too."

It was then that the Moranasthiser finished its evaluation. It made a chugging sound before spitting out a cloud of dust and smoke from the top, like a miniature volcano.

"And we're done."

"That's it? You made Moranasthite from the earth?"

"No, no, no. It's taken the trace amounts of cobalt and vanadium from the soil and rejected the rest. Now if you look here," he said, pointing to a small readout screen near the base, "you'll see what it's missing. Apparently we need iridium and francium, amongst others. They might be hard to find."

"Might be hard to find?!" said Adam, astonished, "Francium is one of the rarest elements in the natural world."

"Well, exactly. But you can use the synthesised version if you want. You only need about 4 atoms of francium per hundred grams of Moranasthite. Anyway, there's enough fuel in there already to get you back to Earth. Or wherever you decide to go."

"But only enough for one trip," stated Adam, very clearly indicating he wasn't asking a question.

"Well, it depends how far you go, but, most likely, yes. Sorry. But you can refuel it wherever you go. Assuming you can find the required elements."

Before Adam could question him further, Grace came running over to them.

"We've got everything from that first list. What else do you need?" she asked. She was very flushed in the face and had obviously been putting a lot of effort into the scavenging mission.

"Oh, still plenty to go," Marco said, and updated her on the next group of components they would require, before announcing "Right. I need to sleep. I'll wake up in 30 minutes. Adam, study up on what I've been telling you." And with that, he slumped back in his chair and immediately started lightly snoring.

"Is he alright?" Grace asked her brother.

"To tell you the truth, I think he's a bit crazy, but his ideas and theories are amazing. He's rewritten... well... everything."

"Simona has been telling us what he's like. He sounds like

a nightmare."

"Well, you can't expect a genius to be like everyone else," said Adam, and Grace had to agree. She knew Adam was unlike anyone she had ever met but she wouldn't have him any other way. Particularly now. "Anyway, I should get on with studying this. We've only got another nineteen hours with them."

Grace took the hint and went back to hunting down the new items on the list.

*   *   *   *   *

The light was blinding. He shut his eyes but it seemed to burn through regardless so he draped his arm across his face to block it out. For a moment he thought he had died, but then he noticed the cold, wet, sticky clothing he was covered in, drenched with sweat. He took his arm away and tried opening his eyes again. Slowly his retinas adjusted and he could see his surroundings. He appeared to be lying on a couch in the middle of a relatively basic living room. He didn't recognise it at all.

Connor dragged himself into a sitting position and stretched his arms and legs. His muscles felt very weak but his mind was starting to warm up. At first he thought he was back on The Magellan, but slowly the details filtered back through. First the Shark attack, then the failed rescue mission, the crash on Zulfura, the journey to Baldr, but then nothing. He knew they'd been aiming for Speropolis so there was only one deduction he could make. "I must be somewhere in the city," he said to himself.

He felt more and more alert but his body refused to work as fast as his mind. He pushed himself up off the couch but had to sit back down again almost immediately. He gave it a moment, willing energy from his mind to his limbs. He took a deep breath and raised himself again. This time he managed one foot in front of the other and with each step he could feel more energy returning. It was like he was recharging his batteries through his own movement. He slowly walked through to one of the bedrooms where he tracked down a change of clothes. Getting out of the clammy garments he had been wearing and putting on the fresh, light, airy clothes he'd found seemed to provide him with another boost.

He pushed on outside, pausing when the bright daylight from Tau Ceti first hit him and burnt his eyes again. After a few seconds his vision adjusted and he looked around. Speropolis wasn't as he'd imagined it. While the buildings were suitably high-tech inside, the vegetation covering them made them look very rural. It was a look that was reflected in the roads, which were merely dirt tracks cut into the grass. It made for a strange mix of rustic and state-of-the-art. The road to his left led to the gateway back out of the city. He looked to his right and tried to discern where the others had gone. He was a little unnerved by the silence and stillness of the city, if truth be told, and he wanted to find someone to speak to. He started a slow trudge in the opposite direction to the city gates.

"NkghnkghnkghnkghNKGHNKGHNKGH!!!"

At first Connor didn't recognise the noise but as he got closer he realised what it was. "Follow the snoring," he told himself, before growing puzzled. He had shared the Marianna with the other 4 for months and had never heard a peep while they slept, and yet this snoring could probably be heard all over the city it was so loud. So who was it?

He turned the corner and saw Adam sat at a table in the square with a strange white-haired man slumped back in one of the seats, snoring very loudly indeed. Connor didn't recognise him. From his angle, all he could see was the top of his head.

"Hey, Adam!" he called out, picking up some speed, but the boy didn't look up. "ADAM!" he shouted as loud as he could muster, but still no reaction. How rude. The white-haired man jolted a little as though he might be waking, but then fell still and resumed snoring. "Nkghnkghnkgh..."

He made it to the table and sat down, suddenly alerting Adam to his presence. The boy pulled some earplugs from his ears and Connor realised why Adam had ignored him.

"Connor, you're up! We were so worried about you."

"Why, what happened to me?"

He hadn't considered his memory gaps until then but it suddenly dawned on him that he had no recollection of arriving in the city, no idea what had happened to him at all. He tried to force his mind back and through a fog he dimly recalled slashing the lumi-firma knife through the undergrowth at the edge of the forest, but everything from then on was shrouded in darkness.

"You collapsed, you'd..."

"Wait, so this is after we'd let you in the city?"

"No, Grace and I let you in." Adam pointed to the roof above them and Connor saw the gaping hole that had been smashed through.

"So we didn't even..." he said, trailing off. As he brought his eyes down from the roof they came to rest on Marco. "Wait, is that... Uncle Marco?"

"Yeah, him and Simona gave you the antidote to whatever it was that poisoned you."

"Poisoned?" Connor was getting even more confused. What had poisoned him? When had this happened? Clearly it must have been sometime out in the forest but he couldn't put the pieces together. As he tried to put his mind to it he saw Grace walking over towards them carrying some pieces of electrical equipment.

"Hey Grace!" he called, smiling broadly at her.

Grace stopped in her tracks and almost turned away in embarrassment. Connor wasn't sure what to make of her reaction and started to worry about what he may have done. She started to walk towards them again but her step faltered, she was reluctant. Connor got up from his seat and went to meet her.

When he reached her she greeted him meekly. He awkwardly tried to give her a hug but the equipment she was carrying got in the way and prevented her from reciprocating.

"Is everything OK, Grace? You seem a little... weird."

"Yeah, I... Let me give this to Adam and then we can talk." She clearly wasn't comfortable and Connor was terrified he had done something to upset her. Grace, for her part, didn't know how much he remembered. All she could think of was her leaning in to kiss him and him pulling back and throwing up. No matter how much or how little he remembered, she had been dreading having to talk to him again.

She handed the components to Adam and clarified that they were, indeed, what he was after, before taking Connor by the hand and dragging him off to walk the streets as they talked.

She filled him in on the whole story, answering any questions he had. She had prised all the details from Evelyn as they gathered the items on Marco's list, and made sure she recounted them as best she could for Connor. She told him about the fly that had opened up his arm. He pulled back the bandage covering the wound as she told him and saw the long scar that sliced its way along his forearm. She told him about the birds that had taken Max, about the ships that had chased her and Adam, how they had crashed into the roof of Speropolis and then into the forest, inadvertently saving him and his siblings. And then she reached the end. She debated how much she should say. Should she tell him? Would he want to hear? In the end, she decided that either Max or Evelyn were bound to say something so she really should confess all. They stopped walking and she turned to him.

"When you came through the gates, we'd been so worried. I had been so worried. I ran over to you to give you a hug, I was so happy to see you." She looked up at him, their eyes meeting for moment before she turned away in embarrassment. "I gave you a hug and, in the moment, I don't know what came over me, I kissed you. I was just so happy to see you."

"Oh Grace. I'm so sorry. I just don't remember..."

"You really weren't well. You pushed me away and threw up. Then you collapsed and almost died..." Her voice trailed off and tears sprang to her eyes. He put his fingers to her chin and turned her face to look at him. She held his gaze for a second or two before turning away, embarrassed again by her tears.

"Grace," he said, his voice softer than she remembered ever hearing it before, "I'm sorry. Really I am. I ruined your first kiss. You've nothing to be embarrassed about, you didn't do anything wrong. It was my fault."

She laughed through the tears. "Yes, it was," she said, but she still couldn't look at him. He turned her face to him again and leaned in. For a moment Grace's heart skipped a beat. "Here it comes," she thought. He leaned in and kissed her on the cheek. A pang of rejection shot through Grace again. Why had she thought he would be interested in her in the first place? And why was she interested in him?

"Come on, let's go back to the others. I need to be introduced to my uncle."

They walked back, arm in arm. Grace vowed to herself she would never again be lulled in by such foolish thoughts. Connor was oblivious, excited about meeting his long lost great uncle.

Chapter Nineteen
Exit Planet Hope

Their time with Marco, Simona and Leo was all too short. Marco had spent all his time with Adam, planning the reconstruction of the engines of The Marianna; the others hadn't got a look in. Even Connor's excitement had to be tempered. Circumstances were against him, something he reluctantly accepted. Instead, they spent their time collecting the final few components required for the build. Grace had appreciated the distraction, anything to get her mind away from her embarrassment with Connor, but now their visitors were leaving she had a tear in her eye.

Simona stood in the doorway of the Dream Genie, clutching Leo to her chest while Marco gave each of the children a hug and a kiss goodbye, even Connor, and promised them he would spend more time talking with them the next time they met.

"Three minutes, Marco," shouted Simona, and he leapt into action.

"Right, kids, I'm going to get this ship as high as I can before we leave, but I want you stand well back. Inside might be a good idea," he said, giving them a wink and a cheeky grin as he followed his wife inside. And with that, the steps raised back up, reforming the black-mirrored sphere that had arrived a day before.

The kids froze, staring up at the perfection of the craft as it gently raised itself from the ground. They were jolted back to life when they heard Simona's shrill voice boom out of a hidden speaker, "Marco said 'Stand Back!'". They bolted backwards, keeping their eyes fixed on the sphere levitating higher and higher under the cracked dome of Speropolis. The air fizzed and electric bolts shocked their way across the surface of the ball. It had almost left the city's airspace when...

BOOM!!

A ball of flame erupted in the sky, shattering an even bigger hole into the roof. The fire dispersed into a puff of smoke and the Dream Genie was gone. Thousands of glittering particles lit up the sky like fireworks and the kids marvelled at the display, until they realised that, rather than part of some beautiful light show, these particles were getting bigger. Shards of roof were rapidly falling towards them. They turned and ran for the nearest building.

Connor grabbed Max and threw him over his shoulder, making sure he didn't get left behind. They were the first through the door, followed by Isaac, then Evelyn and Grace. Finally Adam, his bag full of plans and calculations trailing from his shoulder, threw himself in as the first chunks of roof debris hit the ground. Far from being the tiny particles they had at first seemed, some of the lumps of rubble were big enough to crush a man. The noise as the debris hit the ground was deafening. Even worse was when it fell directly on the roof of the building they were hiding in. Grace instructed them all to stand in doorways in case the building was damaged and started to fall, and each of them could feel their hearts pounding almost out of their chests. Dust fell from the ceiling and the ground shook. Max's legs were trembling and he clung onto Connor in fear, his eyes firmly squeezed shut.

It wasn't long until the shuddering, juddering, crashing and smashing came to an end and Grace went to the window to take a look outside. She could barely see a thing. The air was thick with dust either churned up by the debris that had hit the ground or still floating down from the roof of the giant dome.

"You can come out from your doorways, but it looks like we might be in here a little while," she said, and the others gathered round her.

"What now?" asked Adam.

"We should start taking things up to The Marianna," said Connor. "No point in hanging around."

"Once the dust has settled, of course," said Grace, "You don't want that dust getting in your lungs and eyes." She shuddered at the thought of the tiny fragments of roof, like glass-dust, getting in her eyes.

"How long will that take?" asked Max, already getting bored now the fear had subsided.

"I don't know," said Grace, "It could be an hour, could be a day."

"Oh drek!" He said it with such exasperation that it caused everyone else to laugh. "What? What's so funny?" he asked, confused, but they could only continue to snicker.

When the laughter had died down, Grace got back to business.

"So we head back to The Marianna, and Adam, Isaac and you, Connor, install the new engines. Then we've got the power to get ourselves back to Earth, right?"

"Grace," said Connor, trying his best to be diplomatic, "While I don't disagree with you necessarily, why would we go back to Earth?"

"What do you mean, Connor? Where else are we going to go?"

"Well, Connor's got a point," ventured Adam. "It's been over 150 years since we last knew what was happening on Earth, and that was when The Magellan left because the planet was ruined. How do we know if there's anything to go back to?"

"OK, but seriously, where else are we going to go?"

"If we go back to Earth and there's nothing there, we won't be able to fire up our engine again and we'll run out of supplies and that will be that."

Grace was becoming infuriated. "Adam, just listen to my

question. Where. Else. Are. We. Going. To. Go? By your rationale we'd be better off staying here because we have plentiful supplies."

"Let me get my Slice and we can check out the star charts," he said. He left the room to grab his bag, calling behind him, "And yes, we would be better off staying here than going to Earth." When he returned, he spread the Slice out on the floor in front of them and called up the galactic plans that Marco had given him, plans which looked utterly different to any previous map of the space they had seen.

Adam explained that, with the amount of fuel they had, they could travel about 14 light years, just a little beyond Earth. However, because of the way Marco's theories re-dimensionalised the universe, that actually meant they could potentially travel to somewhere hundreds of light years away in the flat model, but not to other places only 20 light years or less.

"What?" asked Max, "I don't get it."

"OK, see this," said Adam. He brought a picture of Marco's crumpled model of the universe up on the screen; space as a big ball. "This is the universe, and we are here." He zoomed in on Tau Ceti, the star they were currently orbiting. "And we can go anywhere that is lit up in blue." He pressed a couple of points on the Slice's screen and a bubble appeared around Tau Ceti, encompassing hundreds of stars within the crumpled model.

"And how do you propose we choose a star from all of those?" asked Grace. "Do we even know which ones have planets around them?"

"No idea," said Adam.

"Err, what's that?" asked Connor.

"What's what?"

"That red dot, there."

Adam zoomed in on the blinking red dot near one of the stars around halfway inside the blue bubble and stared at it intently.

"You're not going to believe this," he said. The rest of them looked at him, not knowing what to expect. "But I think that's The Shark."

"What??" exclaimed Grace.

"Let me have a look," said Evelyn, pulling the Slice towards her.

"Well, it's decided then, we have to go there," said Connor.

"How do you know it's The Shark?" asked Grace.

"Yeah Adam. It just looks like a dot. It looks nothing like The Shark," said Evelyn.

"When the ships from The Shark were chasing us I managed to plant a tracking device on one. It went back to The Shark and then The Shark disappeared," Adam explained. "It seems that The Shark has reappeared about six and a half light years away, as the Marianna flies."

"So that's where The Shark is now? Terrorising someone else?"

"We've got to chase it down," said Connor, starting to get excited.

"Well, it's not technically there now, not necessarily," said Adam.

"What do you mean?" asked Connor, his excitement cooling.

"Well, from that position, and with the way the signal from the tracker travels, The Shark would have to have been there something like, ooh, four or five thousand years ago."

"What? But you only put that tracker on it a day ago," said Connor.

"I know."

"So The Shark can travel through time?" asked Grace.

"Like Uncle Marco!" shouted Max.

"It certainly looks that way," said Adam, "Which explains a few things really."

"And it means we'll never be safe from it. It could come get us at any time," said Grace, a slight tremble in her voice.

"So do we chase it or not?" asked Connor. He was starting

to get confused. "I mean, I want to get whoever they are, but are they going to be there when we get there? If they were there four-thousand years ago, are they still there now?"

"Seems unlikely," said Evelyn.

"I'll tell you what I don't understand," said Adam, "They leave here, travel back in time and reappear at a time and a place that means we will get their signal, right here, right now."

"That's a big coincidence," said Grace.

"It seems too much to be a coincidence," said Adam.

"You think they want us to follow them? That makes it sound even worse!"

"But then they must know our technology. I mean the technology we had. Before we met Marco we would never have been able to make it there. It would take a hundred-thousand years in the Pod. Maybe it is just a coincidence," said Adam.

"Yeah, look. They've probably travelled all over the universe and all through time. The chances are that one of those locations would mean the signal would reach us, it doesn't mean that the signal was meant to reach us," said Connor.

"Grace, you know how much I hate to say this," said Adam, "But Connor is probably right. It may not seem like it right now, but it probably is just a coincidence."

"So let's go check it out!" said Connor.

"What?" cried Grace. "But that's just even more arbitrary. We have no idea what's there, and the one thing that we know has been there is the thing that killed our families and destroyed our home."

"Well look, we know that Earth is unlikely to be in a good state, and we know that Speropolis is a good last resort," reasoned Connor. "So we should go somewhere that will use half our fuel or less so we can get back here. That fits the bill perfectly. What have we got to lose?"

"Our lives, Connor. That's what we have to lose."

"Adam. Can we arrive at... Hey, what's this star called?"

asked Connor.

"It doesn't have a name, as such. It's known as HD-143436."

"Catchy. OK, well when we get to HD- errr -123456..."

"143436."

"Whatever. When we get there, we can arrive at whatever point we want, right? I mean, we don't have to stop right by where The Shark was?"

"No. Of course."

"So why don't we show up some distance away from The Shark's location, check things out and, if there are any problems, we just jump back here? No problems, we hang around the check it out."

"Why? Why put ourselves in unnecessary danger and use the only fuel we have doing it?" asked Grace.

"The Shark was there 4000 years ago, not now! Drek!" Connor was starting to get frustrated. It all made sense to him and he didn't understand why it didn't to Grace. "And the fact that it was there suggests there's something worth seeing, some kind of resource or something."

"Not necessarily. What do we know about The Shark? Only that it seems to destroy whatever it comes into contact with."

"Speropolis is still here. In fact, all of Baldr is still here. That's a lot of resources left behind, Grace."

"OK, OK. Adam, what do we know about this star? Do we know anything at all?"

Grace was starting to waver and Connor could sense it. He waited with bated breath to hear what Adam had to say about their proposed destination.

"Not very much," he said. "Just that it's a solar twin and there's some evidence that there may be planetary objects orbiting it, but there's no proof of that yet."

"Solar twin, what's that?" asked Connor, hoping the answer matched his guess.

"It's a star similar to the Sun back in our own solar system," replied Adam, "In fact, it's more similar to the Sun than Tau Ceti is."

"Brilliant! So it's even better placed to have a planet safe to land on than where we are now. And this seems pretty safe," said Connor, hardly able to contain his glee.

"May I remind you that you almost died on this 'pretty safe' planet, Connor," chastised Grace.

"Yeah, but I didn't. And I know what I did wrong here. I won't do that again," he said nonchalantly.

"Look, can you two stop arguing, please." It was a statement, not a request, from Evelyn. "I am fed up with this. You had been doing so well recently and now you're back to bickering again."

"OK," said Connor, "Let's settle this one way or the other. We'll have a vote on it. How about that, Grace?"

"Yeah, but I don't think you understand the danger..."

"If you don't like the result, you can always stay here, but I think a vote between the five of us is the only fair way to decide what we do as a group."

Grace knew she had lost. If she conceded to a vote she was sure that Max and Evelyn would vote with their brother and she wasn't even sure of which way Adam would go. But she couldn't refuse a vote either; how would that look?

"Fine," she said, a note of resignation in her voice that they all detected.

"So," began Connor, "We have two choices. Firstly, we can go to Earth, a planet our families left over 150 years ago because there we no resources. And once we are there, we will have no fuel to go anywhere else. Or we can go to HD-whatever-it-is, check it out, see if it's safe. If it is, we can investigate further, else we can come back here – somewhere we know to be safe and to have the resources we need to live? So, what do you say? Hands up who wants to go to Earth."

"Connor, that's not fair," protested Grace, unhappy with the way Connor had summed up their options.

"Sorry. Grace, do you want to add anything to either of the options?"

"The Shark…"

"Ah yes, The Shark was at HD-blah-blah-blah four thousand years ago." He really drew out the 'thooouuuusssaaannnd' to emphasise just how much time had passed since The Shark was there. "While it was orbiting this particular planet just yesterday. It sounds to me like we'd be safer at HD than we are staying here! Grace?"

"Yeah, fine, whatever…"

"So, all those in favour of HD?"

Evelyn, Max, Connor and Adam all put their hands up and Grace conceded defeat, though she was far from happy about it.

*   *   *   *   *

It took the children eight days to fit the new engine according to Marco and Adam's specifications. Isaac was at his most useful lifting the heavy parts, tightening stiff nuts and bolts and reaching into awkward crevices. The time hadn't been without its tribulations; Connor and Grace had decided that Gordon should really stay behind and Evelyn and Max hadn't been happy. It took a lot of explaining to convince them that it was unfair to take him away from his natural habitat, and they negotiated visitation rights while they were still orbiting Baldr.

Eventually the time came though. Marco had given Adam some instructions to run tests on the engines before they pumped it full of the unstable Moranasthite, and each test went perfectly. Finally he loaded the engine with the compound and headed back to the bridge.

"OK, is everybody ready?" asked Connor.

The others all nodded and murmured various affirmative

noises.

"Come on guys, we're about to travel faster and further than any human in history, except Marco of course. You can be a bit more excited than that!" he said, trying to perk them up. "Are you ready??"

Max and Evelyn called out a resounding "Yeah!", while Adam said "Yes, I'm ready" a little more firmly than the first time. Grace was still wavering but Connor decided to ignore her.

"OK then. Adam, start... the... engine..."

On the command, Adam pushed a button on the screen in front of him to fire them off into the unknown.

Nothing happened.

"What's wrong? Why aren't we there? Why aren't we going anywhere?"

"We are," said Adam. "What did you expect? Flames? A big sonic boom? We're travelling 6.5 light years, even at the speed we're going it'll take almost a month."

"But I thought we'd, like, disappear or something?"

"If you'd been observing outside of the Marianna, when I pushed the button you'd have seen us vanish. But we're inside, travelling with the ship, we're all moving together."

"Well can I see outside on the screens?"

"You won't see anything. We're travelling faster... than... light." He slowed down to let the words sink in, hoping Connor would understand.

"Right then," said Connor. As he sat down, he exhaled. "If we've got a month to go, we should probably think of something to do." He paused, hoping someone would leap in with an idea. When no one did he said the only thing that came to mind.

"I spy, with my little eye, something beginning with S."

THE END...

...OF THE FIRST VOYAGE

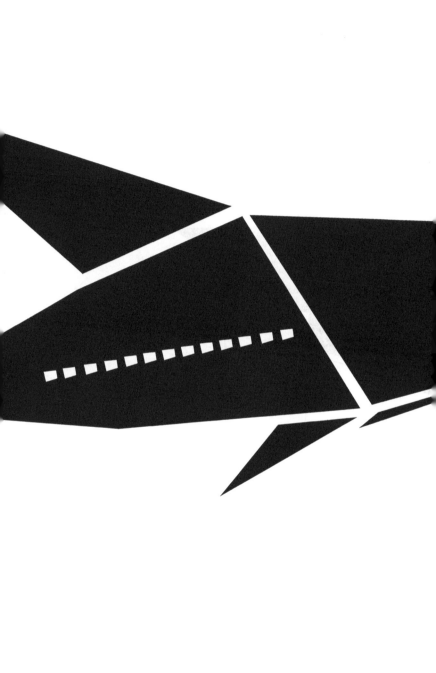

Connor, Grace, Adam, Evelyn, Max and Isaac will return in

THE MARIANNA VOYAGES ii:

THE REVOLUTIONARY KIND

COMING 2012

About The Author

Benjamin Hendy was born and raised in Southampton. Some time after being born and raised he went to live in Canada. He then returned. He worked on numerous writing projects while maintaining both a series of real-world based jobs and his anonymity. Finally he embarked on writing How To Fill A Black Hole, his first novel. Even more finally, he finished it.

He still lives in Southampton* with [FOR CURRENT LIST OF PETS, PLEASE CONSULT WEBSITE]. He would like to travel around 500 years into the future, assuming he could safely return (should he so desire).

He sporadically maintains a website, www.benjaminhendy.com, and invites you to come and take a look. There are some blog elements in which he infrequently writes about whatever he feels like, but he is also happy to answer any questions you may throw his way. If you can keep your questions to fewer than 140 characters, you can also reach him on Twitter, where he is quite sensibly known as @BenjaminHendy.

*Author location subject to change without notice.